RITTER

NO MAN DIES TWICE

RITTER: NO MAN DIES TWICE

Bavaria, 1942. Inspector Peter Ritter of the Rosenheim police is a man on borrowed time. His refusal to toe the Nazi party line has earned him too many enemies; the Gestapo are closing in and his marriage is falling apart. Ritter seeks refuge in the brandy bottle, and in ghostly conversations with his dead father-in-law. Ritter's determination to investigate the murder of an unidentified Jew offers his critics a case in point: he is a man locked in the past, out of step with the priorities of modern Germany. But when a second victim is discovered brutally stabbed in a local hotel, Ritter finds himself at the heart of a deadly plot that could affect the outcome of the war itself. With not just the solving of a double murder but his own life at stake, Ritter needs to find an ally. And he has only two options: the Gestapo or the woman he believes to be a ruthless British spy.

No Man Dies Twice is the first book in a new series starring Ritter. Inspector Peter Ritter will return.

Michael Smith is an award-winning UK journalist and author. He served in British military intelligence before becoming a writer, working for the BBC, the Daily Telegraph and the Sunday Times. Smith uncovered the Downing Street Memos, which exposed the truth about the intelligence used to justify the war in Iraq. He is the author of numerous books on spies and special operations including the UK No 1 bestseller Station X, the US bestseller Killer Elite, and Foley: The Spy Who Saved 10,000 Jews, which led to the recognition of former MI6 officer Frank Foley as Righteous Among Nations, the highest award the Israeli state can award to a non-Jew. He lives in Oxfordshire in England.

Safe House Books is an independent British publisher of spy fiction which is reviving quality espionage for a new audience.

RITTER

NO MAN DIES TWICE

By Michael Smith

SAFE HOUSE BOOKS

www.safehousebooks.co.uk

Safe House Books Ltd
London, England
www.safehousebooks.co.uk

Published by Safe House Books, 2022
First published in the USA by Diversion Books, 2018

RITTER: NO MAN DIES TWICE

Cover design by Trevor Scobie.

A catalogue record for this book is available from the British Library.

ISBN 978-1739754006 (paperback)

For my mother Joyce Marguerite Smith

Chapter One

Monday 9 November 1942

The beams from the patrol car's headlights threw long shadows out over the icy river. The light flickered across a scattering of the fresh, powdery snow that had been falling off and on for a couple of hours. But there was only mud on the dead man's clothes. The body lay sprawled in a shallow ditch beside the Adolf-Hitler-Strasse, several metres in front of the bridge. The heels of the shoes and the turn-ups of the trousers were covered in mud. Whoever he was, he'd been dragged somewhere. Ritter knelt down beside the body and felt the skin on the neck, trying to work out how long it had been there.

'Wherever he was strangled, it definitely wasn't here. The body's stone cold but there's no snow on it at all.'

Ritter turned back the front of the dead man's raincoat and worked his way through his pockets. Nothing. Not even a few coins. A gust of freezing wind blew up from the river, bringing with it the stench of rotting fish. He grimaced, braced his face against the wind, and stood up, staring down at the body, trying to imagine the dead man alive. What sort of man was this? What had he been doing in Rosenheim? And more importantly, what had he been doing to get himself killed? The back of the jacket collar was frayed at the crease. The dark hair was tinged with a few streaks of grey and the face had the tired look of someone for whom life had thrown up one challenge too many. But there was an undeniable toughness there. It was a good case for the new trainee from Munich to cut his teeth on.

'You'd think twice before picking a fight with this one anywhere, wouldn't you, Messel, let alone here by the bridge?' Ritter pivoted his body at the waist as if preparing to throw a punch. Could you have caught this guy out that easily? No. Definitely not. 'He's got too much room to avoid you and come back at you. You'd want a gun in your hand if you were going to take him on, and he certainly wasn't shot. See the bruising around the neck. This one was strangled.'

Ritter turned the lower half of the man's body on its side. Strangulation victims emptied their bowels. But there was no stench, no sign of any stains on the trousers.

'There's something not right here, Messel.'

He carefully lowered the body and placed the jacket and coat back. Gently. As if he was tidying a scruffy child for church.

'Whoever did it took his papers. No wallet. No pass. No workbook. Nothing that might identify him.'

It was easy to suggest a motive for the murder. The dead man's money had gone and the papers had probably already been sold on. There were plenty of buyers for new identities nowadays. Jews. Criminals. Even the odd Party member looking to get out before it all fell apart. And yet…

'I don't see this as robbery. Thieves always go for a certain type of person. Does this one look to you like a natural victim?'

He turned to where the trainee detective had been standing and realized he'd spent the last few minutes talking to himself.

The two *Schupo*, the uniformed police officers who'd called them out, were trying to persuade several passers-by to go home, while Stefan Messel, the latest high-flier attached to him by the idiots in Munich, had moved off to intercept *Obersturmführer* Klaus Kleidorfer, the deputy head of the local Gestapo.

He and Kleidorfer had studied law together in Munich immediately after the last war. He'd disliked the man even then and he saw no reason to change his view now. Kleidorfer was an arrogant fool who insisted on using his SS rank, a ridiculous affectation, even for a Gestapo officer. And what was someone like that doing in Rosenheim?

In Gestapo terms, it was scarcely frontline stuff. Even Ritter wasn't there by choice. When Himmler took over the Munich police and started clearing out anyone who wasn't trusted, he'd slipped back home, out of the way. Why Kleidorfer felt the need to follow him wasn't clear. Sophie always said he was making too much of it, insisted it was a coincidence, nothing more. But it didn't feel that way. Every time he turned out on a job the Gestapo man was there, a few minutes behind him, watching him, an ever-present threat.

And then there was Messel.

Probationary Commissar Stefan Messel, straight out of the Hitler Youth and onto the *Kripo* fast track. Blond and blue-eyed. Aryan beyond the dreams of the most demanding of Goebbels's propaganda merchants. The idiots at the detective training college in Furstenberg had fed him all the Party shit about 'racial criteria in criminality,' and the boy had swallowed it whole.

He turned back to the body, already stiff from rigor mortis. Or was it frozen solid? It was difficult to tell. Rigor mortis. It had to be. It just felt that cold out here on the bridge. He crouched back down and for the first time noticed a small white briar rose tucked into the buttonhole of the man's jacket.

'So perhaps it wasn't the money after all,' he said, louder this time, trying to attract Messel's attention. It didn't work. He looked around.

The boy was talking earnestly to Kleidorfer. He could only hear the occasional fragment of conversation. He caught the words 'genetic criminality.' Ritter closed his eyes, swallowed hard, and called out, 'Hey, Messel. Get your arse over here. You're supposed to be helping me investigate a murder, not pontificating about the state of the world.'

The boy's face betrayed a flush of irritation at being so openly addressed as a junior in front of Kleidorfer. Or maybe he was simply embarrassed. Who cared? Messel was there to learn. The chance to examine the body of a murder victim was rare in a place like Rosenheim. The boy needed to focus on what was important, and convincing Kleidorfer that he was a useful ally for the Gestapo was definitely not on that list.

Ritter stood up, leaned back slightly, and sighed as he watched Messel and Kleidorfer walk towards him. His irritation with the probationer wasn't going to go away anytime soon, but he needed to keep a clear head, to get on with the job.

'Look at that, Messel.'

He pointed at the tiny flower. The two of them crouched down to examine it more closely. Kleidorfer remained standing. Disinterested. Aloof from it all. His long shadow looming over them.

Messel had caught Kleidorfer's mood.

'It's a flower. It looks half dead. Does it matter? He was probably trying to impress some tart.'

'It's a white rose, Messel.' His voice showed no emotion, no reaction to the boy's dismissive response. 'It means something. They say it's the symbol of the resistance.'

Kleidorfer's indifference came to a swift end. The Gestapo officer crouched down, briefly looking over at the two *Schupo* before turning his attention back to Ritter.

'I hope, Inspector, that you're not seriously suggesting that there might be any kind of real opposition to the Führer here in Bavaria.'

It was a thinly disguised warning. Kleidorfer letting him know there were dangers in not being a true convert to the new ways. But he couldn't stop himself.

'Come on, Kleidorfer. Everyone's heard of the White Rose. It's not a state secret.'

The banter between the two *Schupo* officers and the drunken sightseers died away. The Gestapo officer leaned in towards him, puckering his face in an exaggerated act of smelling the alcohol that lingered on his breath before continuing with his lecture.

'The White Rose? Degenerates and delinquents. Nothing more. Inside the Reich…' Kleidorfer paused, stood up, and smoothed down his coat in a curiously prim fashion, playing to his audience. The Gestapo officer looked straight into Ritter's eyes, and began the sentence again as if to ensure that he, and anyone else who might be listening, understood that what he was about to say was not to be challenged.

'Inside the Reich, there is nothing for anyone other than a fool to oppose.' Another pause. 'Do you understand what I'm saying?'

Kleidorfer turned on his heels and walked off towards his Mercedes before he could respond. The performance was so ridiculously theatrical, Ritter struggled not to laugh. And yet, somehow, it had a chilling effect. No one said a word. Halfway to his car, almost as an afterthought, Kleidorfer turned back towards them, gesturing at the body dismissively. 'This man, whoever he was, was murdered for the contents of his wallet. If you want to find your killer, I suggest you look among your collection of usual suspects, the dregs of Rosenheim. I'm sure I really don't need to teach the *Kriminalpolizei* how to do their job.'

Messel watched Kleidorfer get into his car, trying to catch the Gestapo officer's eye, looking for acknowledgment of their newfound friendship. When it didn't come, the boy turned back to him, as if he was to blame for Kleidorfer's stupidity.

'See what you've done? Klaus has a lot of influence in Munich. This won't look good for either of us.'

'Klaus?' He couldn't help but sneer at Messel's overfamiliar use of Kleidorfer's Christian name. 'Klaus fucking Kleidorfer? Do you seriously think that if he had any influence, they'd have sent him to a backwater like this to babysit a suspect detective and his damn fool apprentice?'

Messel's cockiness was replaced by the hurt look of a scolded child. Ritter briefly felt a pang of guilt. The boy wasn't a bad sort. Just eager to please. The nonsense he talked was drummed into all the kids now – at school, in the Hitler Youth, by the idiots at Furstenberg. Messel wasn't alone in believing it and he could scarcely hold up his own stubborn refusal to conform as an example of how to get on. All he'd got from sticking to 'good old-fashioned detective work' and refusing to join the SS, like some of his more compliant colleagues, was no promotion and a Gestapo nursemaid. It only made it worse that his minder was Kleidorfer, Sophie's childhood sweetheart. He heard his wife pleading with him again to hide his hatred of the Nazis and what they represented.

'If you'd only shown willingness, joined the SS, we could have stayed in Munich. We wouldn't have had to come to this boring little place. Klaus doesn't criticize the Party. He's a good man, too. Why do you think it's only you who can save the world?'

Her words of support for Kleidorfer still cut deep into his psyche. He'd never doubted her until then. Until he realized how close she still was to that Gestapo bastard.

'Klaus Kleidorfer is a good man.'

It took him a moment before he realized it wasn't Sophie speaking. It was Messel defending himself, and Kleidorfer, against his criticism. He tried to soften his tone. 'Listen, Messel. You're here to learn. I've only got six months to teach you how to do the job before you move on to higher things. So I'm going to make damn certain you know what you're doing before we're done. There are enough idiots out there telling us what to do, without me adding another one to the pile.'

It was no good. He knew the boy was keen to impress. But he couldn't hide his anger over Messel's attempts to butter up Kleidorfer.

'Let's just concentrate on doing our job. Our body is clearly not local. The label on this jacket is from some Jewish tailor in Berlin. It must be years old. Go through the hotel guest lists. Find out who's missing. We'll never get anywhere until we know who he was.'

Chapter Two

Monday 9 November 1942

It had begun to snow again by the time Ritter decided he'd seen enough, wondered too much about who the dead man was, tried too hard to imagine the circumstances in which he came to be lying lifeless by the bridge over the Inn. The uniformed police officers were showing their impatience. Stamping their feet on the ground. Slapping the sides of their bodies to keep warm. He called over *Oberwachtmeister* Kurt Naumann, the most senior *Schupo* officer still there, and told him to have the mortuary assistants take the body away.

'There's nothing in his pockets. I've looked. I want everything else left as it is for the pathologist Kozlowski. I don't want anyone removing anything they think might be more use to the living. Kozlowski sees it all. Got it?'

Naumann nodded, with half a smile, as if to say: 'It's fine. I understand. Some of us remember the old days.'

It wasn't something Naumann would say. It wasn't something any police officer would think about discussing openly anymore. Only Ritter seemed able, or willing, to suggest there might be merit in the old ways. He looked across at Messel, standing by the BMW, waiting for him, still embarrassed by the dressing-down. Ritter had trodden too carelessly on his sensitivities and he probably needed to ease the situation. Maybe he'd find an opportunity, but right now he was too angry, still seething inside over Kleidorfer's intervention and Messel's eagerness to impress the Gestapo officer.

Ritter turned away, took the silver flask out of his coat pocket and snatched a quick swig, just to ward off the cold. Then he strode over to the car. Back straight. Ever the soldier. He had nothing to prove to these idiots, with their fancy uniforms and constant heel-clicking. He'd served his country on the front. He still served his country, putting criminals away, putting the real criminals away, when the likes of Kleidorfer and the Special Court in Munich let him. Whom did they serve? Other than themselves and the idiots in Berlin?

He got into the passenger seat without a word. Messel was already waiting behind the wheel. The boy started the engine and set off in the direction of the Kufsteiner Strasse. Ritter closed his eyes, trying to work out how and why the dead man might have come to be lying there by the bridge and whether the White Rose resistance was anything more than a bunch of students protesting for the sake of it, the way students had always done, and always would do. He was tired, dead tired. The snow on the road had been compacted by traffic, and frozen solid. Messel was taking great care to drive slowly. With the gentle swaying of the car and the steady noise of the engine, Ritter began to doze off.

He woke as the BMW went into a sudden skid. Messel spun the wheel to regain control over the car. It slid sideways across a sheet of ice. Heading straight for a tree. Dragging Ritter back five years to the accident. He was the driver, with Sophie in the passenger seat. He couldn't control the car. Couldn't prevent it smashing into the tree. Couldn't prevent the devastation of their marriage.

But this time there was no collision. The BMW slid gracefully into a drift, stopping with a slight jolt. For a moment, he stared straight ahead, stuck five years in the past, with Sophie beside him.

There had been no drift to save them back then. He saw the blood dripping slowly onto the floor of the car. Perhaps it would have been better if she'd died back then. The early beauty of their love would have survived.

'Sorry, boss.'

Messel's apology dragged Ritter back. He shook his head, as much to remove the bitterness as to clear his mind.

'You can't help the state of the roads, Messel.'

'A lucky escape.'

The boy was seeking reassurance. Ritter breathed in deeply and motioned to him to drive on.

'Yes, Messel. A lucky escape.'

He kept quiet for the rest of the journey. The tension from the confrontation with Kleidorfer played on his mind. Messel glanced over occasionally, as if waiting for him to initiate a conversation, but he declined to take the hint, until suddenly, as the car came to a halt outside the house in the Kufsteiner Strasse, the frustration and anger boiled over.

'Nothing Kleidorfer is going to tell you is going to be worth a pile of shit. You do know that, don't you?'

'I was just…'

'Just what? Just do your job. You're a detective. You've got one job. One role. To find out who committed the crime. Not to cosy up to the Gestapo. Who killed that boy? That's all that matters right now. All I care about, all you should care about, is who killed him and how he came to be lying there by the bridge.'

Ritter paused, his lips contorted as if trying to remove a nasty taste from his mouth. But he wasn't finished yet.

'Kleidorfer isn't about to help you, or me, work out the answer to how that body came to be lying there. He has one job alone: making sure we all lift our Pavlovian paws to the Führer. Nothing else. That's all he does.'

He turned his eyes to the road and took a moment to control his rage.

'You're lucky, Messel. In a world where truth has lost its meaning, you've landed a job where moral choices actually matter. Someone murdered that man. Your job – my job – is to find out who it was. To stop them doing the same thing to someone else. Understood?'

'Yes, of course.'

It was an instinctive response, almost indignant, and with no great enthusiasm. Messel looked at him with a mix of perplexity, pity, and fear. For a brief moment he thought it might be respect. But no. It was pity and fear. At least the boy was going to do as he was told for the time being.

Messel had stopped the car outside his house. He couldn't have parked with more precision, right outside the gate. But there was absolutely nothing about Messel and the situation they were in that didn't irritate him right now. He knew there was no logic to his mood. That it was Kleidorfer, not the boy, he needed to confront. But he couldn't help it. He was angry even at Messel's attempt to give him the least possible distance to walk to his house. He got out of the car without saying anything more and stood waiting as the BMW drove off. He watched the freezing fog from the river wrapping itself around the taillights until they disappeared. Only then did he look up at the bedroom window for some sign that Sophie might still be awake, waiting for him. He knew the answer already.

They'd met in Munich a few months after the last war. He'd been wounded on the Somme during that final push, the abortive Kaiser's Battle, and had gone to university to read law. Sophie Kuster was the professor's daughter and all the young students were chasing after her. Kleidorfer among them. But none of them could match up to the dashing war hero with his Iron Cross First Class and Bavarian Order of Military Merit. Even old 'Ludo' Kuster, the Ludwig Maximilian Professor of Legal Science, had seemed impressed. Ritter had been young back then. Slim. With a mop of dark hair brushed straight back over his head and the upright bearing of a proud Bavarian officer. Sophie's eyes always seemed to light up whenever she saw him. They were happy. Very happy. Or so he'd thought. Until the accident. Now his hair was receding and peppered with grey, while nothing he did seemed to stop the fat from piling on.

He and Sophie barely said a word to each other. The only reaction he ever got from her was when he criticized Kleidorfer. She seemed to care more about that bastard than she did about her own husband.

Ritter went into the front room, poured himself an Asbach, a good German brandy, and sat in the old leather chair, staring up at the painting of Sophie's father above the fireplace, trying to draw inspiration from his long-dead professor, trying to imagine what had really happened out there by the bridge. Kleidorfer had been dismissive of his mention of a resistance movement, and in truth it was difficult to imagine. But this was definitely not a straightforward killing. Why the white rose? And the jacket, with its old Berlin label? It was too worn for the rest of the man's clothing. The shirt and trousers were in good condition. Why wasn't the jacket?

The pressure from the vipers at the Gestapo offices over on the Adolf-Hitler-Strasse was grinding him down. His response had been to bury himself in the unsolved cases piling up against his office wall, working ever-increasing hours in an attempt to prove to himself that somehow he could make a difference. But his only achievement so far seemed to be to put yet more distance between himself and Sophie. They supposedly shared the same bed, but all too often he was too tired from the constant fights with the Gestapo, or too drunk, to do anything other than slump down in old man Kuster's leather chair and wonder what the professor would have made of the new order ushered in by the Führer and the Kleidorfers of this world.

'It's just politics, Peter. Why should I make anything of it?'

'What are you saying, old man? That you think all this shit is right?'

'It's no different from the last war, Peter. You were a good Wilhelmine. You went off to fight for the Fatherland. Look at the slaughter that happened then. What did you make of that?'

'I thought we were on God's side, Professor. That's what we all thought. We realized pretty quickly it wasn't like that at all. Anyway, it's not the war I'm talking about, it's all this…'

'Every soldier who ever went to war thought he was fighting evil. Do you think this is somehow different? How can you be sure you're on the right side here? What makes you think your squabbles with Kleidorfer are about good and evil?'

'Hold on a minute, Professor. Aren't you the one who used to give every class that little lecture about how working in the legal profession gives you the opportunity to make moral choices?'

'The one you gave young Messel, you mean? Yes, I did. But it wasn't until I heard you parroting it that I realized how vacuous it was.'

'Who asked you, anyway, old man?'

'That's your problem, isn't it, Peter? You're not really interested in what I make of it all. You're not interested in what anyone else makes of it. You're the same arrogant fool who came back from the last war. There's more to life than good versus evil. There's no point in trying to take on Kleidorfer. Whatever you think he's doing. The Gestapo look after their own. And anyway, whoever murdered that guy, it certainly wasn't the Gestapo.'

Chapter Three

Tuesday 10 November 1942

Ritter was delayed on his way to the office next morning by a 'demonstration.' A handful of members of the Nazi Women's Organization, the *NS-Frauenschaft*, were demanding money from passers-by for a relief fund to aid the victims of the British Terror in Munich. The stench of rotting fish drifting up from the river had infiltrated the old town. The *Frauenschaft* fishwives were blocking the Munchener Strasse, where a freezing wind blowing in from the northeast was churning up the snow, reinforcing the heavy drifts. It was early November and it was already clear it was going to be a tough winter. A combination of the snow and the women with their banners warning the citizens of Rosenheim you'll be next was preventing a truck from getting through. The driver was arguing with Gertrud Heissig, the leader of the local *Frauenschaft*, over whether he should be allowed to pass. He wasn't winning the debate.

'We're not letting you pass, you repulsive little man. Who knows what rubbish you're bringing in, contaminating our city?'

The driver didn't seem to know what to say to her. He stuttered an answer. 'I have to get through. I've got to do something for my wife. She's…'

'Your wife? What about the Reich? Why aren't you at the front? Why are you hiding away here while good men die?'

The driver was an elderly, bearded man in dirty olive-green overalls, heavy boots, and an old army camouflage cap. He looked way past the age when he might have been anything other than a hindrance at the front.

'But I'm sixty-two.' He was bent over as if in supplication, begging her to let him through. 'Please. My chemicals are important for the war effort. If you want to win the war.'

'Your chemicals? Your chemicals! They're the Reich's chemicals, you horrible man.' She turned away in anger and saw Ritter. 'Here you are, ladies, Inspector Ritter will help. He's a good citizen. He was at university in Munich with my Oswald. He'll surely put his hand in his pocket. The inspector supports the war effort even if others choose not to. Look at this scoundrel, Inspector. He should be at the front, not driving a truck.'

Ritter stepped in to rescue the old man. 'Frau Heissig, your members are blocking the traffic. This man is simply doing his job. Remember: "The entire nation is at war. Some at the front, others at home."'

The use of one of the Führers' mantras confused Gertrud briefly, but she soon recovered. After all, what was Gertrud Heissig if not a leader of the 'others at home'?

'The inspector's right, ladies. Let this man through. His work is vital for the war effort. You know what the Führer says: "Let the wheels turn for Victory."'

It was remarkable how effective those idiotic Party slogans were. The driver shook Ritter's hand gratefully before getting back into his cab. Now those very same women who only a few minutes earlier had been scowling and baiting the old man were cheering him on in the name of 'Victory.'

Ritter turned away, pulled his coat in around him, and hurried on to the *Mittertor*. The three-story, grey stone medieval building, with its large arch and tall, round watchtower, was right at the heart of the *Altstadt*, the old quarter of Rosenheim. The top floor was occupied by the municipal museum. The entire city police force, eighteen officers, plus a half dozen clerks and secretaries, was crammed into the ground floor and cellar. There were just four detectives in the tiny *Kripo* section. There should have been only three, but his forced exile from Munich had given them one more man than regulations allowed.

By the time he got into his office, hidden away in the cellar, there was a report from Messel waiting on his desk. The boy must have been hitting the phones all night. Perhaps he wasn't so useless after all, although in truth the report said very little. A brief note from the pathologist, Viktor Kozlowski, confirmed what he already knew from his own examination of the body.

> *The extensive bruising to the deceased's neck, which could only have been caused by severe pressure applied to the throat, leads to the inescapable conclusion that he was strangled. I shall be able to tell you more tomorrow.*

But Messel had managed to come up with something new. The dead man had checked into the Schweizerhof claiming to be a Hans Schinkel. He'd given an address in Frankfurt-am-Main. Both the name and the address matched. But that particular Hans Schinkel had been killed two years earlier during the invasion of Norway. God knows who Messel had woken up in Berlin to find that out. Some poor duty clerk in the records office? But perhaps the British bombers were keeping them awake anyway.

He sat back and looked around his office. The former prison cell was sparsely furnished, the antithesis of the plush Gestapo offices on the Adolf-Hitler-Strasse. It was musty, but with no hint of decay. The flagstone floor and the vaulted ceiling had an enduring honesty. The wooden desk and file cupboard were bare and functional, untarnished by the various paraphernalia of the Nazi regime. There were no swastikas in Ritter's cell.

He had the file open on his desk when Messel arrived, acting as if the previous night's tension had never occurred. If the boy expected thanks for all the hard work he'd put in, he could forget it.

'So. Schinkel died in Norway?' Ritter barely looked up as he said it.

'Yes, boss. And then he died here.'

'No man dies twice, Messel. Even Jesus Christ didn't manage that trick.'

'No, boss. I don't know what those *Schupo* pissheads were doing. They're supposed to check all the hotel lists. They should have picked this up.'

'You can't blame them. Schinkel's name will still be on the census. They would have had to contact Frankfurt or Berlin to find out anything different. Let's wait for the post-mortem report. See what it says.'

But Messel seemed to have thought of this already. He smiled, evidently eager to come up with the key piece of information that would close the case. 'I've spoken to the pathologist Kozlowski. The guy was circumcised. That more or less wraps this one up.'

Ritter groaned, resting his elbows on his desk and cupping his hands over his forehead. 'What the fuck are you talking about?'

'Look, boss. You said it yourself. The label in the jacket is from some Jewish tailor. The post-mortem will say he was circumcised. This man was obviously Jewish. Do we really care what happened to him? He's another one we don't have to worry about. Whatever he was doing, even if he was a subversive, he can't do it now.'

'For Christ's sake, Messel. What did they teach you at that detective school? The fact that someone's circumcised doesn't make them Jewish, and most of the tailors in Germany were Jewish when that jacket was made. We keep going. Get on to someone in army security. I want to know precisely how and where the real Schinkel died. We'll close this case when we've found out what happened and not before.'

A few hours later, Messel was back. Schinkel had been a corporal in the 1st Parachute Regiment. He'd died during an airborne assault on British troops at Dombas in Norway in April 1940. He wasn't killed by the British. His parachute failed to open.

More important to the case at hand, Messel had persuaded Viktor Kozlowski to produce the post-mortem report on time. The boy handed it over without a word. Ritter scanned the pages quickly before coming to an abrupt halt.

The circumcision appears to have been performed at a very early age and shows every indication of having been part of the standard Jewish ritual.

He read the sentence several times, hoping there might somehow be another interpretation to put on it. Ten years ago, it would have been immaterial. Now he knew he was going to struggle to keep the case alive. No one upstairs was going to lose any sleep over the death of a Jew.

Messel stood there, clearly unsure whether he should sit down. Ritter ignored him. Let him stand. Make him realize who was in charge. He continued poring over the report, leaving his trainee to glance around at the unsolved case files stacked against the walls. The bruises from the strangulation suggested someone with small hands, possibly a woman. At last there was the first sign of a workable lead.

Messel was impatient to get on.

'I don't think there's any doubt the victim was Jewish, boss.'

He had known what the boy was going to say the minute he read the reference to 'the Jewish ritual.' The more he stared at the sentence, the more the anger welled up inside him. It wasn't Messel's fault. But right now, he didn't care. Messel was there. He didn't need to look up. He could already see the smug satisfaction on the boy's face. Could tell precisely what the boy was thinking. I was right, you were wrong. This is how we do things now, Kleidorfer and I. Your ways, the old ways, they're history.

He closed his eyes. Carefully steeling himself. Mentally rehearsing what he wanted to say. What he needed to say. Ready to make clear to Messel that Kleidorfer wasn't the one investigating this case. It was his case, and in his eyes, if not in Kleidorfer's or Messel's, murder was murder. It made no difference if the victim was a Jew or a Party boss. When it came to deciding what cases to investigate, the religion, the sex, the nationality of the victim didn't matter a damn. He opened his eyes and looked up, ready to blast the smug smirk from the boy's face.

The earnest look that met his eyes completely threw him. Confused and unsure of how to react, Ritter turned back to the relative safety of the report.

At least Kozlowski agreed with his other conclusions. The preliminary examination was, of course, correct. The bruising on the neck left 'little doubt that the victim died of strangulation,' although there were small pieces of cotton in the throat suggesting an unsuccessful attempt to smother him first. More importantly, the pathologist's findings proved that Schinkel could not have been killed by the bridge. Death had taken place at least four hours before the body was found. The *Schupo* foot patrol that spotted it had passed that way only two hours earlier and seen nothing.

'The circumcision isn't the only problem, boss.' Messel flicked through his notebook, looking for the right page. Ritter felt the adrenaline draining slowly away, replaced by an overwhelming feeling of tiredness. 'All right, come on. What is it?'

'Liesl Olbricht? The owner of the Schweizerhof?'

He nodded.

'She says there were only six guests in the hotel that night, including Schinkel. One of them was Marianne Müller… she's a prostitute, boss.'

'Jesus Christ, Messel. I'm a fucking police officer. You think I don't know the names of the local whores?'

The words hadn't come out the way he'd intended. He'd certainly felt genuine anger at Messel treating him like an idiot. But somehow, he couldn't raise his voice above an impotent whisper. He knew he was facing a battle he couldn't win. Müller was the final straw. The woman had only managed to stay out of jail by attaching herself very firmly, and by all accounts very frequently, to Commissar Gerhard Drexler, head of the local Gestapo, and while the boy seemed to have spotted the problem, he either didn't realize the scale of it all or he didn't care. The smirk he'd expected earlier was now spreading all over Messel's face. He had the look of a schoolboy waiting impatiently to tell the dirty joke that everyone already knew.

'She's registered as an informant, boss. But I've heard the guys over on the Adolf-Hitler-Strasse joking about her relationship with Commissar Drexler.' Messel made an obscene gesture. Ritter ignored it. His mind was already racing ahead, trying to work out how he was going to handle that viper Drexler, willing the younger man to tell him something new. Messel got the message, swallowed any disappointment he might have felt at yet another failed attempt at humour, and reverted to a more serious, point-by-point account of his findings at the Schweizerhof.

There had been four other people staying there that night, all of whom appeared, in Messel's considered opinion, to be unlikely killers: Hans and Elsbeth Braml, a couple in their fifties from Bad Ischl in the Ostmark, the old Austria; and Bettina Grob, a middle-aged Swiss woman visiting relatives with her daughter Martyl. The last two had returned to Zurich and the chances of the Swiss police helping to track them down were non-existent. But the local *Kripo* in Bad Ischl had spoken to the Bramls. They seemed genuine enough. Hans Braml was a Party member. He had brought his wife along on a business trip to Rosenheim.

'All right, Messel. We're going to have to go back to Liesl Olbricht, together this time, and talk to her again. At length. Meanwhile, I have the unhappy task of telling that fat toad Drexler that his new lady-friend is caught up in a murder inquiry.'

He went out the back of the *Mittertor* and across the Ludwigsplatz. The Gestapo headquarters was only fifty or so metres down the Adolf-Hitler-Strasse, but its ugly, modern facade was in complete contrast to the beautiful eighteenth-century buildings of the *Altstadt*.

Drexler was in civilian clothes, an expensive-looking woollen suit, and stank of cologne. The Gestapo boss was leaning over his secretary in a casually lecherous way. He glanced up at Ritter and didn't seem either surprised or even intrigued by his arrival. He must already have known that Müller's name had come up in the murder investigation. Who had Messel been talking to, and why? Drexler thumbed him into his office, which – with the exception of a plush red carpet – was utilitarian rather than extravagant: a desk, two chairs, and a wooden cabinet with carved swastikas on each of its two doors. The only other decoration was a Nazi flag draped over a framed photograph of Hitler giving a Nazi salute.

Drexler motioned him to sit down and then did so himself, leaning forward. He was short and fat with a bull-neck and a nose turned red and bulbous from too much Schnapps. But he didn't need to take a prostitute as a mistress. His wife was very attractive, and from a wealthy family. So, he was unlikely to admit that the gossip about Müller was right, and certainly not to him.

'I don't know what muck you're trying to dredge up here, Ritter. I've heard the rumours. But that's all they are. My relationship with Frau Müller is a matter of record. She's a registered informant. I don't want you, or your damn fool apprentice, going anywhere near her. Her usefulness to me depends on the people she knows believing that they can talk to her freely. If I hear that you or any of your clumsy *Kripo* fools over at the museum have been climbing all over her…'

Drexler's train of thought seemed to trail off as if he'd suddenly realized his words might be interpreted with more humour than he'd intended.

'So, she's a whore. That's what makes her useful to us, right? She mixes with criminals and subversives, she picks up information. That's the only reason she's on my books.'

Drexler hesitated again. Ritter waited, saying nothing. Force the Gestapo boss to do the talking. He'd slip up soon enough.

'Listen, Ritter. I'm not trying to impede your investigation. But neither of us saw anything. There's nothing we could tell you that might help.'

Ritter decided to leave it there. Better not to push things with Drexler. After all, if he found out that Schinkel was a Jew, he could probably get the investigation closed down. At least the Gestapo boss had given him one piece of information that Liesl had decided it wasn't in her interests to disclose.

'Neither of us saw anything.'

Drexler had been in the hotel with Müller.

Chapter Four

Wednesday 11 November 1942

'Look, Messel. Your interview with Liesl Olbricht was fine.'

The Schweizerhof was only a hundred metres or so across the Ludwigsplatz from the *Mittertor*. A short walk. But Messel was unhappy at having to go back and Ritter could see why. So far as the boy was concerned, he'd done his job, asked Liesl the right questions.

'The interview was fine. Textbook. Really.' Maybe there was a chance here to make up for being so hard on Messel down by the bridge. 'Your instructor at Furstenberg would have been proud of you. He really would. But you're here to learn and one of the things you have to learn is that if you stick by the book you're bound to miss something.'

'So what did I miss?'

'You mean apart from Liesl covering up the fact that Drexler was in the hotel on the night of the murder?'

Another disappointed look. It was unfair to blame the boy for Liesl's failure to mention Drexler, but he had to learn quickly and, unlike Messel, Ritter was very happy to go back to the hotel. Liesl was a difficult woman. No doubt about it. But the Schweizerhof was full of memories of happier times. The thought of the beautifully ornate stucco front and the solid baroque stone arches on which it sat had sustained him throughout his time in the trenches and the years in Munich. The most comforting image had been the relief of the Virgin Mary cradling the baby Jesus that looked down from the top of the hotel. The blues and whites of the paint had faded but it retained a simple beauty, reflecting the Catholic beliefs of the Olbricht family, who'd owned the Schweizerhof for several centuries.

'Good morning, Inspector. Please. Come in.'

Liesl led them through a door marked private office into a large room, more of a living room than an office. There was a long and ornate glass-covered cabinet in dark wood along one wall. A faded brown and green carpet covered most of the wooden floor. A sofa and several armchairs separated off the rest of the room from a small dining area, with a table and chairs, again in dark wood. She ushered the two of them into armchairs, glanced in a mirror to check that her bun was in place, and then stood watching them, hands clasped together in front of her blue-and-white pinafore dress.

'Perhaps a glass of something, Inspector?'

'That will be very kind, thank you, Liesl.'

Heinrich Olbricht, Liesl's husband, had been his best friend. They'd gone to the same school, served in the same regiment, been hit in the same battle. He'd come back. Heinrich had stayed behind. He remembered watching as his friend's body arched backwards, forced through the air by the momentum of the machine-gun bullets. The body was too far out in no-man's land for them to retrieve. What was the first line of that Stramm poem?

The earth bleeds beneath his helmeted head.

He hadn't wanted to leave Heinrich behind. But he'd been wounded, and by the time he got back to the trench, any chance of retrieving the body had gone. The British pushed them back. Life moved on.

Not for Liesl.

'I've told the young man everything I know about that day.'

Liesl placed her chair directly opposite them, carefully tucking her skirts beneath her legs. The glasses of Asbach were on a small round table between them. She hadn't forgot. Just the two. None for Messel. Each glass sat on a small, light-brown lace doily, the bottle on another, slightly larger one. It took him a moment to realize that they were part of the set of Plauen table lace he'd bought for Heinrich and Liesl's wedding.

His response to Liesl's irritation was gentle and patient.

'I know what you told the probationary commissar, Liesl. But I need to go over it with you again. Who booked in when, and what they said. What they did. What they ate for dinner. What they ate for breakfast. Everything you know about them. Start with the morning. What did you do? What did the maids do? Tell me everything you can remember about what happened that day. I need to know everything. I particularly want to know about anything unusual, anything at all.'

'Well someone died.'

Liesl's response was sharp, but if it was intended to put him on the defensive, it failed. He knew Liesl too well to be put off by a flash of anger. His response was patient but firm, with only a hint of frustration.

'I know, Liesl. I know. That's why we're here.'

Liesl knew more about her guests that night than she'd told Messel, and he wanted to know what she was holding back.

At school, Liesl had always been one of the most popular girls in their class. There was no doubt that Heinrich Olbricht regarded her as a good catch, someone fit to share the family's inheritance. They'd all regarded her as a good catch back then. The best of the bunch. No doubt about it. But she'd never recovered from Heinrich's death. She still had her figure, but there was more grey in her hair now than blonde, and the blue eyes were surrounded by sharp lines. There was a sharpness in her voice too, particularly when she was speaking to him. A bitter resentment. Most likely because he'd gone out of his way to avoid her since the war, embarrassed by the fact that he'd come home and Heinrich hadn't. There were other reasons. He'd gone to Munich, to university, and then into the *Kripo*. By the time he came home for good, he was married to Sophie. Too much water had flowed under the bridge.

'Frau and Herr Braml booked in at three. They went straight up to their room, number 14. I remember Frau Braml said she was tired.'

As Liesl went back over the events of that day, retelling an account that was already beginning to sound over-rehearsed, the resentment in her voice faded away, replaced by a dull, emotionless monotone.

'The Bramls went out to visit friends in the Party at six. For dinner, that was. In the Stockhammer. On the Max-Josefs-Platz. They didn't eat here. They were back by ten. Very polite, they were. The older generation, you understand. No trouble at all.'

As she spoke, Liesl stared at a point about three feet up on the wall behind them; occasionally closing her eyes briefly, as if trying to shut out everything else so she could remember the routine of that day; sometimes turning her head slightly to look at him.

At first, he thought she must be doing this to emphasize something important. Then he realized it was when she was telling the truth. If she could look into his eyes, she was being honest. Whatever it was he was looking for would come when she was staring at the wall.

'Herr Schinkel came alone. Not long after the Bramls. Half three, I think that's what I wrote on the card. He had a limp. I suggested to him that this must be why he wasn't in uniform. He didn't reply. Well, not really. I think he just grunted.'

'Where did he say he was from?'

He asked all the questions in the same way. Going through a routine. Matching the monotone of Liesl's voice. Deliberately not showing which parts of her account he found interesting.

'Frankfurt. He said he was from Frankfurt-am-Main. I gave the young man the address.' She nodded dismissively towards Messel, who looked irritated. Ritter glanced briefly across at the boy before turning back to Liesl.

'It was a false address, Liesl. It left us with some important questions and we need the answers as quickly as possible. So please, go on. What happened after he checked in?'

'I asked him if he wanted dinner. He said, 'No, thank you,' and went up to his room. That was the last I saw of him.'

'You didn't see him leave?'

'I can't be everywhere.' She was still staring rigidly at the wall. Her voice was agitated. 'There's a bell. If someone needs me, they can ring.

He didn't ring. He owes money for his room. And will I get it back? Of course not.'

For a brief moment, she'd definitely been frightened. But she'd manoeuvred the conversation away from the problem area and now the resentment was back in her voice as if to dare him into questioning her further on the most vulnerable point of her testimony – the claim not to know when Schinkel left the hotel, and whether, when he did leave, he was still alive. He let it ride, consulted his notebook, deliberately taking his time, putting Liesl under pressure to say something. But she was too restrained, too scared to say anything without prodding.

'What about the Swiss woman, Bettina Grob, and her daughter, what was her name?'

'Scharf. Martyl Scharf.'

'Was that her married name?'

'No. I queried the different names when they booked the room. Frau Grob said she'd divorced the girl's father and remarried. That's why they had different names.' Liesl shook her head, her evident disapproval reminding him of how deeply Catholic the Olbricht family had always been. Drexler could spend as many nights in her hotel with his mistress as he liked, but a woman who'd been divorced was beyond the pale.

Ritter had a fleeting but vivid memory of the beautiful, young, carefree Liesl laughing with him and Heinrich on a church picnic.

Long blonde hair. A blue pinafore dress. Similar to the one she was wearing now.

'That was the really interesting thing.'

'What, that she was divorced?'

'No. Not that. I told the young man, but he didn't seem bothered.' Suddenly, Liesl was enthusiastic about something that had happened that day. 'The mother, Frau Grob, came first and then her daughter later. With the priest.' Liesl emphasized the last three words before pausing for effect, pulling back slightly and giving a sharp nod of her head, as if to say: What do you think of that?

He raised his eyebrows, shrugged, and shook his head, as if to say that he thought nothing of it at all, then leaned in towards her, urging her on, determined not to let her get away with any break in her story, with any suppositions of her own. For the first time he gave a hint of irritation himself, putting her back under control.

'Please. Stick to the details of what happened. Do not deviate from the details. Just tell me precisely what happened and when, and do so in precisely the right order.'

Liesl looked put out, her lips pursed. But with a slight shake of the head, she resumed telling the story of those two days.

'Frau Grob arrived at eleven and took a room with two beds, one for herself and one for her daughter. She only had one suitcase. She said her daughter was visiting friends and would come later. The daughter arrived about five o'clock. She was dropped off by a priest. I saw him say goodbye to her and drive off in a black car.'

'You didn't recognize him?'

'No.'

'What sort of car?'

'A black car, I told you.'

'Yes, but what make of car?'

'An Opel, I think. But I don't know anything about cars. It was just black.'

He stood up and walked over to the cabinet, peering at a line of decorative porcelain plates, each with a different scene of Munich at Christmas and each marked with an individual year. The last one was 1913.

'These are nice.'

'They were Heinrich's mother's.'

'I know. I remember them.' He turned to look at her. 'What did they look like?'

She was momentarily confused.

'What? Who? What did who look like?'

'Who are we talking about, Liesl? Pay attention. The two Swiss women. The mother and the daughter.'

'Oh. The mother was obviously older and much larger, a very large woman. I thought at the time too much coffee and cake. Not that one can get any decent coffee nowadays. They have it in Munich, you know. They give it to them after the bombing raids. My sister told me. But in Switzerland, no doubt, they drink real coffee all the time. The mother, Frau Grob, had dark hair in a bun.' She instinctively reached up to her own. 'The daughter, Scharf, was slimmer, with long blonde hair, definitely bleached. A bit of a tart. I was surprised to see her with a priest.'

'But did they look like mother and daughter? Did they look alike?'

'Yes. I suppose so. Not identically alike. But they were mother and daughter, weren't they? There were likenesses, of course, and they both had a light brown mark on their necks, here.' Liesl pointed to the left-hand side of her neck.

'How big?'

'Quite large. Several centimetres across. The mother tried to cover it up, but you could see it was there.'

'A birthmark?'

'I suppose so. I mean, I don't know. That's what it said on the passports.'

'You saw both passports?'

'Yes, of course. The daughter didn't want to show me hers. But I insisted.'

He got up and began pacing slowly to and fro across the room, throwing out questions at her. Liesl's eyes followed him, paying attention only to him; her head turned towards him as she talked. No longer able to stare straight ahead at the wall. No longer feeling it was safe to lie.

'They were both Swiss?'

'Yes, both Swiss.'

'And the photographs in the passports? They looked like the two women who booked into the hotel?'

'Yes, of course. Why?'

'You said the daughter – Scharf. Martyl Scharf? – she had bleached hair. Was it blonde in her passport photo?'

'Yes. Martyl. Martyl Scharf.' She paused as she said the name.

Adjusting her bun. Looking away. Giving herself time to think. Dragging back the memory of the passport. 'You're right, Inspector. The hair in the photograph wasn't the same. She had dark hair in her passport. But you could tell it was bleached. Even if you hadn't seen the passport.'

'What about Marianne?'

'Marianne? She came late. She often stays here. It's easier for her, if she's been out with her friends. She lives out near the Simssee, at Riedering. It's not safe for a woman to travel so far on her own at night.'

'And her friends?'

'What do you mean, Inspector?'

'Do they stay here too?'

'Marianne is a very dear friend. I know what people say, but she's not like that and I wouldn't allow such things to go on in this hotel.'

'So, no friends?'

'No.'

Curt. Resentful. The suspicious Liesl was back, looking straight ahead at the wall, deliberately avoiding his eyes. When it came to what Marianne was doing in the hotel that night, and with whom, Liesl had no choice but to lie. He sat down. Looking straight at her. Making it as difficult as he could for her to look anywhere but straight into his eyes.

'If there were any friends, Inspector, there would be a registration card.'

The resentment had returned to her voice. But he kept going. Trying to entice her into saying more.

'So, no one? Not even a special friend who might not need a card?'

Out of the corner of his eye, he could see Messel shifting nervously in his chair. But Liesl must have thought she was heading for safe ground. She probably assumed he wouldn't dare question her too deeply about Marianne's 'special friend.'

'If such a friend existed, you two gentlemen would know more about him than I.'

She stood up suddenly. Clasping her hands in front of her again. Looking at him and Messel in turn. Making it clear that she had finished and was ready to see them out.

'Please Liesl, sit down. I didn't mean to offend you over Frau Müller.'

Stay patient but firm. That was the way to deal with Liesl. Patient but firm.

'I realize she's your friend, Liesl. But I'm afraid this is a murder investigation. I do need to know as much as there is to know, before I go, that is.'

Slowly, reluctantly, Liesl sat back down. And gently, patiently, without a hint of threat in his voice, he took her back to the morning after the murder.

'So, the next morning. When did they all check out? Talk me through it. One by one.'

'All of them left not long after breakfast, around eight. The Bramls were about to check out when Frau Grob came down with some nonsense about her daughter waiting for her at the station. I told her very firmly that the Bramls were there first. But Herr Braml, such a gentleman, he insisted that I allow Frau Grob to pay first. Such men are a rarity these days, Inspector.'

He ignored the obvious implication.

'And Marianne? What time did she check out?'

'She didn't need to check out. She paid up front. She always pays up front, and even if she didn't, she's a friend. I can rely on her.'

'So, when did she leave?'

'I have no idea, Inspector. As I said, I can't be at the reception desk all the time.'

The interview was over. He'd got as much out of Liesl as she was likely to give. She led them back out into the reception area. Kleidorfer was leaning across the desk talking to Liesl's son, Heinrich Jr. Although the word talking didn't do justice to what was going on between them. The Gestapo officer was gripping the lapels of Heinrich's jacket in his right hand and spitting his words out from between his teeth. Drexler must have realized his mistake in talking about the Schweizerhof and sent his deputy in to mop up the mess. Kleidorfer saw them and let Heinrich go.

'Ah, Inspector. I was just asking Heinrich here what he saw on the night your man was killed. Sadly, it seems he saw nothing. Isn't that right, Heinrich?'

'Yes. Nothing. I saw nothing.'

Kleidorfer followed them out onto the street.

'You're wasting your time here.'

Ritter turned back to look at him, not even trying to conceal his distaste.

'Wasting my time? Am I? Really? The Gestapo think investigating murder is a waste of time?'

'You know what I mean, Ritter. I'm told your dead man was a Jew. There's no sense in wasting any more time or money on him. Surely now Sophie's a member of the Party, even you can see where your duty lies.'

Sophie had joined the Party? What the fuck was the Gestapo prick talking about? Ritter had to work hard to hold back his anger, but he was determined not to give Kleidorfer the satisfaction of having provoked a reaction.

'I don't need someone like you to tell me what my duty is, *Herr Obersturmführer*. Come on, Messel. We can't hang around here chatting. We've got a killer to track down.'

He left Kleidorfer smirking and walked off, his mind reeling from what he'd just heard. Sophie? A Party member? It couldn't be true. Just Kleidorfer playing stupid games. Trying to goad a reaction. It was nonsense. Sophie could never join the Party. It would be a betrayal of everything her father had fought for throughout his life.

Chapter Five

Wednesday 11 November 1942

'So, Sophie, we'll hope to see you at the *Frauenschaft*'s next meeting.'

Gertrud Heissig gave Sophie a cheery wave and turned to smile as she passed Ritter on the path to his house. Sophie eyed her husband suspiciously.

'And why are you back so early?'

He'd sent Messel back to the *Mittertor* on his own and hurried home. Hoping Kleidorfer was wrong. But Gertrud's presence, and the invitation to the *Frauenschaft*'s next meeting, were pretty strong indications that the Gestapo officer was right. The daughter of a famous university professor, wife of a senior police officer, Sophie was a real acquisition for Gertrud's group.

'Kleidorfer claims you've joined the Party. Is that true?'

'Yes. Why not?' She said it as if nothing unusual had happened. As if she'd simply gone out and bought some milk.

'Why not? Because it goes against everything we've ever stood for, that's why not. And why do I have to learn about it from that shit Kleidorfer?'

'Don't be ridiculous. Klaus only knows because he proposed me for Party membership. I didn't tell you because I knew you'd react like this.'

'Kleidorfer proposed you?'

'Yes, and Gertrud seconded me.'

'Jesus Christ. The company you keep.'

'If I were you, I'd be more worried about the company you keep. That drunk Kozlowski you spend all your time with is good company?

And I'll thank you not to blaspheme in this house.'

He needed a drink, and Kozlowski was certainly better company than Sophie was right now. He retreated to the front room. Sophie followed, haranguing him, refusing to let it lie.

'And so what if I have joined the Party? Somebody's got to think of our future. The way you keep sneering at anyone in power, it's a wonder they haven't placed us in protective custody already.'

'Protective custody? Are you mad? The camps aren't there to protect people. That's just their bullshit excuse. Where's the brandy?'

'You drank it all last night. The bottle was empty. I threw it away. Klaus says the Jews and socialists are held in protective custody just in case the war starts to go wrong and people try to take it out on them.'

'Klaus says! You're just as bad as Messel. Just in case the war starts to go wrong? The Russians have got thousands of our boys trapped in Stalingrad and the Americans have landed in Africa. It's not a case of just in case the war goes wrong. It's already happened.'

'The Führer knows what he's doing.'

'You really are mad if you believe that. The Kaiser knew what he was doing, too. Look where that got us. In the shit. And now it's happening all over again.'

Sophie hesitated. He'd forced her onto the defensive.

'Everybody was very optimistic at last night's Party meeting. The mayor said we're only days away from a major victory in Stalingrad, and he warned us against listening to those who try to lower morale.'

'Johann Gmelch! He hasn't the faintest idea. He just repeats the latest mantra passed down from Berlin. Your friends in the Party aren't optimistic; they're delusional.'

'That's typical of you, Peter. I defended you when Klaus called you arrogant. But he's right. You are.'

'Me? Kleidorfer called me arrogant?'

'Yes. You. You think it's only you who knows the truth. Only you who does the right thing. The rest of us are just lambs following the Führer to the slaughter.'

'So where exactly do you think joining the Party is going to get you?'

'It's going to keep us both alive.'

'What? You and Kleidorfer?'

'No. Me and you. It will keep us out of the camps. Ensure we get treated better than those who choose not to join the Party. The other idiots like you who think they know better than the Führer. You'll thank me in the end.'

'No. I won't. I won't ever thank you. So far as I'm concerned, it's a betrayal of everything we believed in. Everything your father believed in. What do you think he'd say about it? Membership of the Nazi Party would scarcely have fitted with his socialist principles.'

'My father was a clever man, and clever men know how to stay alive.'

Ritter put his coat back on and picked up his hat.

'Where are you going now?'

'Back to work, to earn some money. That's what'll keep us alive – doing my job, not joining a bunch of idiots who can't see what's obvious to anyone with half a brain.'

The hands-off approach was never going to work with Drexler. Not once he found out that Schinkel was a Jew. When Ritter got back to the *Mittertor*, his boss, Ernst Nagel, called him into his office. The two men had known each other since training, grown up in the job together, solved some good cases, had a few laughs. But Nagel had stopped finding anything funny long ago.

'Peter. I've had that fat viper Drexler on my back. He says you're treading all over one of his best informants in order to track down the killer of some Jew.'

'Sorry, Ernst. But that's nonsense. Drexler's so-called top informant is that tart Marianne Müller he's knocking around with and, so far as I know, no one's spoken to her at all. Quite apart from that, we don't know for sure this man Schinkel was a Jew. And even if he was, it doesn't alter the facts. Someone's been killed. There's a murderer on the loose. The next person to die could be anyone.'

But Nagel was never going to back him against someone as powerful as Drexler. He stubbed his cigarette out in the ashtray, looked at Ritter, and shook his head.

'You still haven't got it, have you, Peter? You can't go rubbing these people up the wrong way. It's too risky. Drexler won't be crossed. Somebody killed a Jew. So what? Close the investigation down. File it away. Not solved. That's an order.'

Nagel paused for breath. He looked tired. He must have known he was wasting his breath. 'Do you understand what I'm telling you?'

'I understand perfectly, Ernst. Whatever you say.' He stood up to leave, but Nagel raised a hand.

'Wait.'

Ritter stopped halfway out of his chair.

'I've got something I want you and Messel to do. Kleidorfer tells me you two seem to have got off to a bad start.'

'Really? So you've got Kleidorfer reporting back on me now, eh? Isn't it enough that he's monitoring everything I do for Drexler? Now he's reporting back to you as well? You'd think he'd have enough back-stabbing to keep him happy in among that nest of vipers on the Adolf-Hitler-Strasse.' He was jabbing his finger at Nagel. 'Kleidorfer should watch his own back with Drexler around, and so should you.'

Nagel held his hands out in front of him, trying to pacify him.

'Calm down, Peter. I don't take any notice of people trying to stab you in the back. Especially not if they're Gestapo. You know that. If I did, you'd have been gone long ago. But there are always tensions between experienced men and these young, thrusting kids they send us from Munich. A bit of bonding won't do you any harm.'

The *Kripo* boss shook another cigarette out of the pack and lit it, exhaling as if what he was about to say had only just occurred to him. 'I tell you what. I've got the perfect job for you. Young Swiss boy, good German stock, volunteered to fight for us, killed in an enemy bombing raid before he even finished training. Ironic, isn't it? Some of his relatives live in Söllhuben. The mayor's very keen that we give him a good send-off. Before he's taken back across the border. I need a couple of officers to go down there tomorrow and make sure there aren't any problems.'

It was impossible to hide his irritation. This was a job for a couple of *Schupo* errand boys, not an experienced detective. 'You can't be serious, Ernst. I've got stacks of casework to write up.'

'I'm very serious. Drexler's on the warpath, and he's got the mayor on his side. This will get you out of the firing line and show you doing your patriotic duty in a way even Drexler can't argue with. Here's the paperwork. There's a priest down there, a Father Josef Steiner. He's setting up the funeral procession and conducting the burial service. Liaise with him.'

Sophie was cleaning when he got home, vigorously polishing the old sideboard that sat in the hall. It was a post-argument ritual. His wife was still furious over his criticism of her joining the Party. She was getting the anger out of her system by cleaning the house. Best to avoid her in this mood. He took the new bottle of Asbach into the front room.

'I hope you're not expecting me to cook anything?'

'No. I've eaten.' Then, as an afterthought, 'Thank you.'

'Good, because I'm going to bed. Gertrud's coming round tomorrow with a couple of friends from the *Frauenschaft*. I've tidied up. Don't make a mess.'

'Wonderful.'

'What was that?'

'Nothing.'

She opened the door as he was uncorking the Asbach. 'You need to rethink your priorities, Peter. You're not the man I married. You've changed, and not for the better.'

She shut the door behind her before he could say anything. He poured a little of the brandy into a glass and swallowed it straight down before pouring another. She was right, of course. He had changed. But hadn't everyone? Sophie certainly wasn't the woman he'd married. That Sophie would never have thought of joining the Nazi Party. She'd been a left-wing activist at university. The sort of student who nowadays would be joining the White Rose. The transition from socialist student to right-wing, middle-class housewife dismayed him as much as it would have done her father.

But if he was honest with himself, Sophie was right. He couldn't claim to be the man she'd married. That man had been bright, enthusiastic, and eager to please. Just like Messel. And just as Ritter had learned the skills of the detective from Konrad Barth, his mentor during those difficult, early days in Munich, so Messel would have to learn from him. There was more to life, more to survival under the current regime than simply doing what the Party would want you to do. You had to make those moral choices. You had to stick to your principles.

'Please don't pretend you've got principles, Peter. all you've got are pompous opinions. That's what's driven Sophie into joining the Party.'

'What? You can't possibly blame me for that.'

'Why not? She told you why she'd joined.'

'And you believe her?'

'Up to a point, yes. You're just irritated because Kleidorfer knew before you did.'

'No. I'm irritated because my wife has gone against everything we ever stood for.'

'Ah. Your precious principles.'

'What's wrong with principles?'

'Nothing. But as I said, you don't have principles. You have opinions. Your wife's just doing your dirty work. You keep your so-called principles. She ditches hers to keep you alive.'

Chapter Six

Thursday 12 November 1942

Ritter flinched as the ice-cold sleet hammered in at them from an angle. He and Messel stood in the small square opposite the tiny village church of Saint Rupert, watching the memorial service. Messel had turned out in full uniform to pay tribute to the young Swiss volunteer. Ritter was irritated by the way his trainee was prepared to play along with the regime, but at the same time felt guilty for not making the effort himself. It seemed disrespectful. Not that the service had lasted long. A few words said by the priest over the coffin, followed by a speech from some local dignitary who sounded as if he'd never been near the front in his life. Appropriate, really, given that the Swiss boy hadn't managed to make it out east. Over to one side, a few elderly women, presumably relatives, huddled together weeping. Four aging pallbearers in Air Defence League uniforms and a couple of Hitler Youth shuffled the coffin towards a hearse, followed by the priest and two nuns.

He clearly wasn't alone in having mixed feelings over the whole affair. Most of those who'd turned out – mainly women and old men – seemed more sullen than respectful. Whatever the papers said, the news from Russia and North Africa wasn't good. The few young men who'd come back from trying to relieve the troops trapped in Stalingrad were angry over the scant support they felt they were getting. The arrogance evident among soldiers returning from the frontline during the early years of the war had drained away. There weren't many men young enough to be soldiers in the square, but there was no evidence of any patriotic pride in the Fatherland. Growing anxiety over the war certainly hadn't stopped most of the people of Söllhuben from turning out to see the dead Swiss boy off. But then, non-attendance was too much of a risk. There were too many people prepared to curry favour with the authorities, too many willing to take retribution for past grievances by reporting a neighbour's absence as a sign of opposition to the regime. Fear was probably the only reason so many people were making such a big deal of this sad little Swiss boy.

Then he saw her, in a gap between the buildings, leaning against the oak frame of an old house, slightly hidden in the shadow, watching the people attending the ceremony. It was Marianne Müller. She hadn't noticed him, even with Messel standing beside him in full uniform. Or if she had seen him, she was ignoring him, keen not to draw attention to herself. He was about to nudge Messel, when suddenly, Müller started, like a child grabbed from behind by a playmate. She smiled and turned, and there right behind her was a young blonde woman.

For a few moments the two women were smiling and chatting. Then the look on the face of the blonde woman changed. Messel had missed the brief cameo completely. He was still scanning the people clustered in the cemetery and around the square, some of whom were drifting off into the neighbouring Gasthof Hirzinger. Ritter touched the boy on the shoulder.

'Look over there.'

Messel followed his gaze. 'What's Müller doing here – and who's the woman with her?'

'I don't know, Messel. I'm going to get a better look.'

He edged his way through the crowd. He didn't want to get too close to Müller in case she spotted him. But the crowd was too thin to give any cover. He didn't dare get close enough to the blonde woman to be sure. He made his way back to Messel.

'There's something going on between Müller and the blonde. I don't know who she is, but her hair looks like it's been bleached. Definitely not a natural blonde. I couldn't get close enough to see her neck.'

Messel looked at him as if he was mad. 'You can't possibly be thinking it's the Swiss girl? It's just a coincidence.'

'I don't believe in coincidences, Messel. Not with two suspects in a murder. They definitely know each other.'

'But neither Müller nor Scharf are clear suspects, are they? There's no evidence that Müller knew the Swiss girl, and Müller could scarcely have been the murderer unless Drexler was involved as well.'

'We can't rule either of them out. Particularly not now, and Drexler was definitely involved, probably not in the murder, but certainly in the coverup. Don't forget, he tried to ensure that no one knew he was in the hotel that night.'

'Yes, but that was embarrassment at being caught sleeping with Müller. That's obvious. He didn't want his wife to know.'

'Is it obvious, Messel? Is it really?' He paused. 'I'm sure he doesn't want his wife to know about Müller. Christ. What the hell's going on there?'

The woman with Müller was looking straight at the priest and he was definitely looking back at her, Ritter was certain of that. The blonde held up three fingers. The priest nodded a brief acknowledgment before turning his gaze back straight ahead to the rear of the coffin.

'Something's going on, Messel. What is it?'

'I don't know. What do the three fingers mean? Three o'clock?'

Messel might be right; a time would explain it. Was something due to happen at three o'clock? By that time, they'd be halfway to the border. If whatever it was involved the priest they'd be perfectly placed to spot it.

'Maybe, Messel. It could be a time. You're right. But then again, it could be anything.'

The two women were gone. The coffin was being loaded into the black hearse, very carefully, gently even. The pallbearers were handling the coffin as if it were full of eggs. Still, at least they were showing respect for the dead boy. Ritter walked over to Steiner. The priest looked fit, very fit. His face had the sharp features and dark skin of an Alpine farmer. He didn't look like a man who spent too much time kneeling in sanctuary.

'So, Father. You're ready to go?'

'Yes. What were you told to do?'

'To escort you to the border and leave you there. Is it just you?'

'The dead soldier, myself, and the two sisters here.' Steiner gestured towards the two nuns. 'The boy's parents will meet us on the other side.'

'All right. We'll follow you.'

The long journey to the Swiss border with Messel driving gave Ritter the opportunity to remind himself why he'd been glad to return to the countryside. It wasn't just escaping from the pressure in Munich that made him feel freer out here. The spare beauty of the Alpine scenery, the untouched perfection of the snow on the mountain slopes, the forests deep with the dark green of spruce, the ridges of snow perched precariously on the branches, and the clean, fresh scent of pine.

The border post with Switzerland where the priest was to cross was on a minor road running close to the Bodensee, just a small wooden hut with a flag pole and a single barrier. There were a couple of guards in the grey-green uniform of the border police standing outside. They stood to attention as the hearse and the police car drew to a halt in front of the barrier. Father Steiner got out and had a brief conversation with one of the guards before turning back towards his police escorts.

Messel parked the BMW by the side of the road and they walked across to say goodbye to the priest. Ritter reached out to shake his hand. 'This is as far as we go, Father. We'll have to leave you to take him on to his village alone.'

'A beautiful journey, wasn't it, Inspector?' The priest's hand took in a grand sweep of the panoramic view of the Alps. 'Full of the bounty of God's hand.'

Ritter nodded, his mind still occupied with the interaction between the priest and the blonde woman. 'Yes. A lot of time to think, Father. Maybe too much. It's odd, isn't it? So many good patriotic Germans doing everything they can to avoid being sent to the Eastern Front. Yet this young Swiss boy who didn't need to do anything is so desperate to take part he gets himself killed before he's even sent out there.'

'He's not alone, Inspector. There are two more apparently coming back from the Eastern Front next week. I've been asked to take them across as well.'

Messel nodded. 'They're brave, these boys, Father. It was a good thing to do.'

The priest smiled but said nothing. He shook hands with them both and got back into his car. The border guards lifted the barrier, saluting the dead boy as the priest drove past. They returned to the BMW and watched the hearse as it disappeared into the distance trundling along the road beside the Bodensee. Messel was unusually quiet. The boy's head dropped down as if he was trying to work out what to say. Then Messel turned to him and blurted it out.

'We owe that boy and the two coming back from the Eastern Front a lot. A friend of mine in Munich's just got back. They only let him come home because he'd lost part of a foot. He says he was in a firing party that had to shoot two deserters. Young boys. He hated it. He understood why they tried to get out. Everyone had thought the same thing at some point or another. Most of them every day. The way he was talking, I wondered if he didn't shoot his own foot so he could come home. And those Swiss boys are volunteering to go there and die.'

'Careful, Messel. You're in danger of getting caught between patriotism and cynicism.'

'Oh, I know you think it's all nonsense. But there's a good reason why we...'

'There's never a good reason, Messel. Never. I've been through what your friend's had to put up with. I was on the Western Front during the Great War. Maybe it wasn't ever as cold, but it was just as bloody. Trust me, there's no reason on earth that could justify it.'

Messel reverted to silence on the way back to Rosenheim. Like a child sulking over a sign of disapproval from his father. So much for the bonding exercise. He tried to think of some way of breaking the tension. Then suddenly, the priest's words came back to him.

'If you've got one dead Swiss boy going across the border and then you have another two, how many do you have, Messel?'

Messel's answer was instinctive, but even as he said it, his eyes revealed a sudden realization and he turned to smile at him. 'Three. You have three. But what does it mean?'

'I don't know, Messel. I really don't. But it's the key to whatever's happening here.'

Chapter Seven

Wednesday 23 December 1942

Kate Stevenson stood on the platform at Bearsted Station. She watched the troop train slow to a near halt. The 'Other Ranks' had their faces pressed against the windows, glad of their luck at the sight of a pretty woman in her twenties waiting for the London train. Where were they going, these boys? And how many would return? It reminded her of Wilfred Owen's 'The Send-Off.' The way they lined the train with faces grimly gay. She offered them the tightest of smiles, buttoned her coat at the collar, and sought the cover of the waiting room. The matte-black locomotive let off a burst of steam, waited for the signal to go to green, and headed for the next siding to make way for the nine-fifteen to London Victoria.

There seemed to be as many soldiers on the Victoria train as there had been on its predecessor. Jim, the elderly station porter, escorted Kate to the sanctuary of the ladies-only compartment and touched his hat, grateful for an overly generous tip. She could have found the compartment herself but that wasn't the point. The only other occupants were two older women. One briefly broke off from her knitting to smile at the new passenger and then resumed her knit one, purl one routine. The other looked at the intruder suspiciously before retreating behind her copy of The Times. Kate's smile, as she sank back in her seat, was courteous, yet perfunctory. No need for anything more.

The train pulled out of the station, sounding its whistle as it built up a head of steam. After a bad start, 1942 had turned into a good year. She felt confident. Her abilities were at last being recognized by her bosses in MI6. They'd finally accepted that she was good enough to be sent on her first mission, and it had been a success. The end of the beginning. The prime minister's cautious verdict on the victory at Alamein had a good deal of resonance. The war was definitely going better, for her as much as anyone else.

She'd just returned from Switzerland, from that first real job of the war. Her boss, Stewart Menzies, 'C,' the head of MI6, had sent her straight home, to spend Christmas with her parents. But that was just a couple of days ago and something had changed his mind. He'd called her back in to brief her on some other mission. That was good. Very good. If C had to brief you in person it was bound to be an interesting job. Something that hadn't seemed at all likely when she'd first come down from Cambridge five years earlier.

'Glorified dogsbodies. That's what we'll be,' said one of the other girls who joined at the same time. After their initial briefing in the Service's Broadway headquarters, Kate thought she'd been absolutely right.

There were far too many people in the Service who believed 'these young girls' weren't up to being spies. They'd been recruited merely to work as clerks in the Passport Control Offices that provided cover for the various MI6 stations across Europe. The Service's efforts to gather intelligence on Nazi Germany had been badly disrupted by the thousands of Jews who were desperately trying to find a way out. The Passport Control Offices in Berlin and Vienna were inundated with requests for visas. As far as Head Office in London was concerned, the role of the new female recruits was to help deal with the flood of would-be refugees, not to spy.

She stared out of the window of the train at the Kent countryside flashing past. *Hop fields and orchards and ever again, in the wink of an eye, painted stations whistle by.* Robert Louis Stevenson's poem 'From a Railway Carriage' had been one of her favourites as a child. The young Kate had liked to imagine he might be some distant Scottish relative. She'd loved the excitement of going to the seaside on the train. Travelling so fast. Faster than fairies, faster than witches, bridges and houses, hedges and ditches. The sheer joy at that first sight of the sea through the train window. Pa leading them down onto the beach, red spade held high above his head as if somehow they might lose sight of him. Her with the bucket, marching barefoot in his footmarks, struggling to match his stride.

Her first posting had been to work for Frank Foley, the head of station in Berlin. The name hadn't been new to her. She'd heard her father mention him before, just as 'Frank in Berlin.' She'd known from the respect in Pa's voice when he'd said the name that to be working with 'Frank in Berlin' would be useful experience.

That first day in Germany had been trying – elbowing her way through the crowds around the old hunting lodge that housed the Passport Control Office. A commissionaire wearing a huge greatcoat and a peaked cap had taken her for another applicant trying to push her way to the front. 'Hold on, young lady. There's a queue here.' The commissionaire pointed to the end of a long line of Jewish would-be emigrants stretching out onto the Tiergartenstrasse.

'No. I work here. I'm the new officer. Kate Stevenson. For heaven's sake, don't tell me they weren't expecting me.'

With that the commissionaire threw back his head and roared with laughter. 'Why's it always me that has to deal with the difficult ones, eh? Come on, missy. Captain Foley warned me to look out for you. He said to take you straight up to see him the minute you arrived.'

The commissionaire took her up the stairs and down a long corridor. At the end of the passageway, behind a desk that was far too big for him, was a short, owlish-looking man. He was talking to a much taller, slimmer man in a suit at least two sizes too big who was leaning against a filing cabinet and polishing his spectacles with his tie. As she neared the office, she could hear their conversation through the open door. They were talking about her.

'I think we'll have to train the new girl up pretty quick, Leslie,' the small man said. 'Forget the visa work. The ordinary clerks can do that. We need her back here. She's Andrew Stevenson's girl, so she should be all right. Ah. Is this her?' He stood up and extended a hand across the desk towards her. 'Hello. Kate, isn't it? Good timing. That augurs well. I'm Frank Foley. I knew your father during the war.'

She didn't know what to say, so she smiled. It always seemed to work.

They'd sent her to Berlin to stamp visas. Her father had warned her it would be mundane stuff. 'Women aren't suited to Secret Service work, Kate. You'd be far better off going into the Foreign Office.'

She'd become used to her father's attitude. Learned to live with his belief that she was overreaching herself by following him into the Service. But he was wrong about the work in Berlin. It was far from mundane. Ironically, because of her father and what he'd done, Frank had her earmarked for real intelligence operations.

She'd spent the next two years emptying dead letter boxes, deciphering secret messages written in invisible ink on the back of seemingly innocuous letters, and meeting people in crowded nightclubs where a lot of the male guests seemed to assume that an attractive young woman would be happier spending time with them than with her elderly, bespectacled companion. The uninhibited Berlin nightlife had made an ideal backdrop for espionage.

It's Berlin, early 1939. she's young and shapely. very shapely, and beautiful. Far too beautiful for him. Maybe he was interesting once. An officer in the Luftwaffe. Quite a catch in his youth. A nice, kind face. He must have been interesting. Once. But now he's old and going to fat. He's just a trick. Nothing more. He clearly doesn't get to do it with someone like her very often. He couldn't restrain himself. Still. At least it was over quickly. There was little work involved. He's still lying next to her. But it's time to get moving. She's promised to deliver the package. He's been snoring for some time. He won't wake up for a while.

Marianne slides out of bed, still watching him carefully, opens his briefcase, and removes a bulky envelope. She puts it into her handbag and looks at him, momentarily considering whether she should replace it with the other envelope Kate gave her. She could keep that money for herself, could put it to far better use than he would. What will he do with it? Go out and pay for another girl? Waste it on Schnapps or Sekt? But Marianne likes Kate. Maybe too much. She wants to work with her again. She puts the package of cash into the briefcase, shuts it, returns it to the dressing table, and gets dressed. The trick's too far gone to notice her leaving. Anyway, what would he care? He's got both the things he came for. All she's done is make sure Kate gets what he promised in return.

She hurries down the stairs and out onto the street. She turns left into Rankestrasse, then doubles back along Eislebenerstrasse, just to make sure that no one's on her tail. One last check, both ways, before she walks into the Femina. It's packed with people standing by the bar or sitting at tables watching the stage acts. She seems to know everyone, stopping to kiss people and talk to them. Virtually the only people she ignores on her way to the ladies' toilets are Kate and her boss, seated at a table with a couple of Germans Marianne doesn't recognize. She checks the cubicles, leans against one of the doors, and folds her arms. She smiles invitingly at the reflection of a woman touching up her lipstick in the mirror. The woman hurriedly puts the lipstick back in her handbag and leaves, passing Kate on the way out. Marianne leans against the door to prevent anyone else coming in and produces the Luftwaffe officer's package with a flourish. She wants to impress. She makes eyes at Kate. She's joking, of course. Playing the vamp. Although…

Kate smiles at her, raising her eyes slightly, just to keep the interest going. She takes the package. Still smiling. Still making eye contact. Then swaps it for one from her own bag, which she hands to Marianne before walking back out. Marianne goes to the mirror and touches up her own makeup. By the time she emerges to resume working the tables, Kate and her boss are already making their excuses to the two Germans and preparing to leave.

Kate closed her eyes and remembered her first official encounter with the chief, her father's best friend. It was shortly before the war. She'd been brought back from Berlin to take up a desk job in London. It bored her to tears. It wasn't about being a woman. Whatever her father might think. There were men doing exactly the same job. It was just that she knew her worth. She knew that for her to be stuck behind a desk was a complete waste of her abilities.

When Menzies took over as chief in November 1939, she had grasped her chance. She'd knocked on his door and told him she was 'bored to death with pen-pushing.' Frank had trusted her with far more interesting work. Menzies sent her to D Section, which ran 'special operations' behind enemy lines. D stood for 'destruction.' The very idea of sending a woman to work with the thugs in D was laughable to many within MI6 – even if she was Andrew Stevenson's daughter. But Menzies had ordered it; she was dispatched to the New Forest for special operations training, to Beaulieu. Inevitably the thought of Beaulieu reminded her of Jonny and their all-too-brief time together, but she swiftly pushed it to the back of her mind, angry at herself for not letting go.

After six months of training she had been sent off on a week's leave. When she reported back to Broadway she discovered D Section no longer existed. It had been taken away from Menzies to form a new rival organization, the Special Operations Executive – the SOE. She was relieved to learn that she would be staying with MI6 as part of a new section that was under the sole control of the chief. The role of M Section was as secret as its very existence: 'the last-resort removal of any obstacle to the war effort.'

That had been more than two years ago. It had taken a while before they had trusted her with her first mission, but it had left her in no doubt that, just as D had stood for destruction, so M stood for murder. It was a silly schoolboy joke, ridiculously obvious, and therefore ridiculously insecure. But the work was interesting and important. Far better than sitting behind a desk.

The train drew into Victoria. Every time she travelled into London she felt like a child again. The busy sound of trains letting off steam, doors banging, the disembodied announcements of trains arriving or departing echoing around the station canopy,

and the porters. 'Mind your backs please, ladies. Excuse me, sir. Just trying to move the bag for this lady 'ere.'

Head Office was a short walk from Victoria Station.

Chapter Eight

Wednesday 23 December 1942

The briefing was scheduled for eleven o'clock in the chief's office on the fourth floor of Broadway Buildings, the grubby, stucco-covered MI6 headquarters opposite St. James's underground station. When she arrived, she found Claude Dansey, newly promoted to Vice-Chief, standing outside the chief's door. Dansey was in charge of all but a few MI6 operations in occupied Europe and notorious for his disapproval of the use of women as spies. He gave her a curt nod and turned his back on her. It was rude and irritating, but she wouldn't have been here if the chief didn't think her capable. Whatever Dansey's views, and they were pretty clear, they couldn't have had any impact on her selection.

The green light went on above the chief's door and his secretary, Miss Pringle, showed them in. Menzies waved Dansey into a brown leather armchair with the back of his hand, leaving her unsure whether she was also meant to sit down.

'I've asked you here because we have another job for you, Stevenson.' The chief smiled at her benignly. 'Please. Sit down.'

He motioned her to a chair. His voice had a clipped, business-like tone to it. 'Claude. Perhaps you could explain.'

'Yes. Of course.' Dansey moved his head around, as if trying to ease the pressure from a collar that was one size too tight. 'You've been selected for this job, Stevenson, largely because of your knowledge of Germany and specifically because it involves the Hunter Network and this priest who I understand you recruited.'

'Steiner?'

'Precisely.'

Dansey seemed to be struggling to hide his distaste. 'The Special Operations Executive, the old D Section, of which I believe you were once part, seems intent on making as much trouble as possible. They're sending one of the Germans they have on their books into Bavaria to try to assassinate Hitler. They've already lost one man. This is their second attempt.'

She looked at Menzies. He nodded, picking up the story. 'Colonel Dansey and I are of the same mind, Stevenson. We cannot allow SOE to succeed. Isn't that right, Claude?'

His deputy nodded vigorously. 'Frankly, these special operations people are damned mad,' he said. 'Hitler's our best general. He intervenes all the time in the German High Command's decisions, won't take advice from his own generals, and makes stupid decisions. If the real generals took over, we would have far more problems.'

He was working himself up into a lather. Dansey was forever bickering with the SOE about the 'amateurish' nature of their operations. It was the one area where she could see Dansey's point. The special operations boys were far too eager to mount operations that were more likely to cause damage to the fragile MI6 agent networks than to the German war effort.

Dansey was in full flow. 'If SOE get their way, and his murder is traced to the Allies, it will turn Hitler into a martyr, a great German hero. It will make the Hun all the more determined to win the war. That's why we have to stop it, Stevenson. That will be your job.'

He looked at Kate quizzically as if to question whether she was up to it. Menzies intervened. 'I'm sure you agree that we have to protect the Hunter Network at all costs, Stevenson.' Menzies sounded almost apologetic. 'But SOE have asked for the Simssee safe house and I'm afraid the PM has backed them. However, if they fail this time, the PM won't sanction another attempt. So we have to ensure they do fail, and you're the obvious person to do that.'

The obvious person. She doubted that Claude Dansey thought

she was the obvious person, but if the chief had decided she should do it…

Dansey wasn't finished. He still wasn't convinced. He'd mentioned her previous membership of D Section. Was he concerned over the potential for divided loyalties?

'We need to stop the assassin by any means possible, Stevenson. Do you understand what I'm saying?'

'Yes, of course, sir.'

Dansey looked doubtful but he handed her a buff-coloured file. 'Here's the target.'

She managed to keep her composure, but only because Dansey had given her the briefing paper to read before naming the target. If she'd been looking at either of them when Dansey mentioned Jonny's real name, she wouldn't have been able to hide her horror.

Dansey's obnoxious attitude was now the least of her problems. Johann Litwak, her Jonny, was the SOE assassin, her target. They wanted her to kill a man she'd loved, still loved, someone she couldn't dismiss from her mind, no matter how hard she tried.

'You and I are going for lunch, Kate. I think we need some clarity around this mission.'

Dansey had gone, looking a touch suspicious that Menzies wanted her to stay.

'I thought it would be easier to discuss this matter away from the office. Pringle has booked us a private dining room in St. Ermin's.'

Away from what, or who? Did he know about her affair with Jonny? Would it be better if someone else took over? They would certainly have fewer qualms about killing Jonny. But how would that be better?

The Admiral, the previous chief, had used the St. Ermin's Hotel as an extension of Broadway Buildings, providing accommodation for visiting intelligence officers from allied services and staff who had to stay close to the office. She'd stayed there herself, even put an agent up there when no safe house was available. Menzies had continued the use of the hotel after he took over. It was now virtually an annex of Head Office.

She stayed quiet on the walk over. Menzies didn't speak either.

It seemed to her later that he'd deliberately left her alone with her thoughts. The memory of that first meeting with Jonny kept playing in her mind like an old film. She'd been relaxing on the lawns during a break in lectures, reading The Magic Mountain, when Jonny strolled over, claimed Thomas Mann was his favourite author, and offered to light her cigarette. An obviously contrived act of gallantry with only one purpose in mind, destined, or so she'd thought, to fail. Along with the lighter. They'd both laughed at his embarrassment. Who would have believed how quickly – and so very unexpectedly – they'd become close? She, the epitome of a pragmatic, intelligent, middle-class English girl; he the impatient, idealistic German Jew, hell-bent on taking revenge on the Nazis over the death of his father.

The oak-panelled dining room on the first floor of the hotel was small but elegant. The plasterwork on the ceiling was more impressive but seemed out of place. A waiter laid out a cold buffet and opened a bottle of 1929 Chateau Bouscaut Sauvignon Blanc for the chief to taste.

'It's the last decent year for French wine, I'm afraid.' Menzies smiled mischievously. 'I wouldn't be able to look your father in the eye if I served you anything more recent.'

He nodded to the waiter, who poured some of the pale yellow liquid into each of their glasses before placing the bottle in an ice bucket on the sideboard, bowing slightly to the chief and discreetly leaving them on their own. Menzies got up and walked over to the buffet.

'There's some ham and cold chicken, and what looks like a decent enough salad, a few boiled eggs and some cheese. Not bad at all, considering. Come on, Kate.'

'I'm not exactly hungry, I'm afraid, sir.'

Menzies took some chicken, a couple of slices of ham, and some salad and sat down. 'That's entirely understandable in the circumstances. But I need to eat, even if you don't, and I need someone to eat with me. I don't want to be drinking such a good wine on my own.'

She gave in and helped herself to a small piece of chicken and some assorted leaves.

'That's better. I imagine Dansey has left you feeling under pressure with all this talk of murder and mayhem. Let me reassure you. You proved yourself on that side of things last time round. This time we need something more subtle.'

'I'm really not bothered by murder, sir.'

'Well, I am. I'm very bothered by it. It's not what we're about. It should only be the very last resort. And I imagine that in this case you are yourself very much against the idea of murder.'

He knew. Of course he did. It was stupid to imagine that they wouldn't have known that two of the students on the Beaulieu course were having an affair. They'd both realized it couldn't last. It was Jonny who'd ended it, insisted his prospects were uncertain, that there was no point in pretending they had a future. She hadn't tried to convince him otherwise, despite her inner turmoil.

'This Litwak fellow. How much do you feel for him?'

'I don't know, sir. I mean, nothing at all. I'm sure I can do the job.'

'I am too, Kate. But to make things clear, Claude was being far too bloodthirsty. I don't want you to kill Litwak. In fact, I think it could turn out very badly indeed if you did.'

'So what do…?'

'I don't want the Hunter Network, or the priest, put at risk. Steiner's done a lot of good work, getting key people out of Germany for us. And his intelligence network is very productive. It's also very well placed, that close to Hitler's Alpine retreat.'

'But another killing would draw attention to the priest and to Hunter.'

'Exactly. So I need you to go in and stop your friend from carrying out his mission with the absolute minimum of fuss. Do whatever you need to do to stop him. But don't kill him. We seem to have got away with removing one mystery man from the game; two might seem too much of a coincidence.'

'So the Germans aren't looking for anyone over the Schinkel death.'

'No. Steiner says that since he was a Jew, nobody cares. But a second murder. Even of another Jew. Well, as I say, it might be seen as too much of a coincidence.' Menzies smiled at her. 'This ham is really rather good. You should try some.'

She smiled back and looked down at her plate. She couldn't manage what she had. Even knowing that she didn't have to kill Jonny, her stomach still felt fragile with anticipation. Menzies interrupted her thoughts.

'Your father can be a difficult man.'

'I think he shares Colonel Dansey's view of women, sir.'

'I'm sure in part. But I know for a fact that your father's views on your ability are far more complex than Claude's. Your father cares about you. He doesn't want you to be disappointed, and he doesn't want you putting yourself at unnecessary risk.'

'We're all at risk, sir. Plenty of people have died in the Blitz without ever trying to put themselves in danger. I could as easily die sat at a typewriter or putting out the washing, or whatever it is he thinks I should be doing.'

Menzies sat looking at her for a few moments, deep in thought, then he smiled.

'I don't know how much you've ever heard about what your father did during the Great War.'

She knew Menzies and her father had run a network of German agents together in Belgium during the Great War, feeding false information down the line to fool the German High Command. She'd occasionally heard snippets of derring-do over dinner when Menzies came down to Kent for the weekend, although he and Pa had always clammed up when they realized the ladies had gone quiet.

'There was an operation in Brussels in 1915. I was back at headquarters, running the op. Your father was inside the city. A blind man.' Menzies laughed lightly. It would have been barely discernible without the smile. 'I wouldn't dare use that cover now – far too obvious. But they were different times. Something went wrong. Your father was arrested. He had to kill three Boche policemen to get out.'

Menzies had been typically spare on the detail, but it was the first time she'd heard the story all the way through. She'd heard Menzies mention the blind man over dinner at home, but her father had always changed the subject.

'There was a woman back then as well. She didn't get out. Got caught in the crossfire. I don't think your father's ever forgiven himself.'

Menzies became less reflective. The clipped tone returned to his voice. 'Colonel Dansey was my boss at the time. When the operation went wrong, he blamed the woman. But it wasn't her fault. It was just bad luck. Every op needs its share of luck.' Menzies smiled another mischievous smile. 'Your father had the luck of the devil. But sooner or later everyone's luck runs out. That's what worries your father. Not whether or not you can do the job.'

Chapter Nine

Monday 18 January 1943

Ritter sat in his usual corner in the Rothenbach. Back to the wall. Perfectly positioned to see anyone coming in. He savoured the fumes from the free brandy, a perk that singled him out as one of old man Manninger's most valued customers. The landlord of the Rothenbach was a cantankerous and notoriously mean sod. But he'd taken a shine to Ritter when the detective first returned from the war. This was a proper war hero, unlike so many other holders of the Iron Cross. For Ritter, the first drink was always to be on the house. Despite his reputation, Manninger was as good as his word. The promise had lasted throughout the economic turmoil of Weimar, whenever Ritter was back home visiting his mother, and continued after he'd been posted back to Rosenheim. But as Manninger never tired of pointing out, a man like Ritter was unlikely to settle for the one drink. So the landlord of the Rothenbach could claim to have made a substantial profit on his investment over the years.

The warm Asbach brandy diffused the tension of a day spent dealing with petty claims of dissent, largely from disgruntled neighbours aiming to settle old scores, or workers trying to get their bosses out of the way so they could take his job. There was no shortage of people like Gertrud Heissig prepared to denounce anyone they didn't like as an 'enemy of the state' and see them hauled off to the Special Court in Munich. Rosenheim's half-dozen Gestapo officers couldn't cope with the deluge and were forever insisting the *Kripo* should step in to help.

With the investigation into Schinkel's murder shelved, he had little choice but to lend a hand.

The complaints weren't all lies. There was no doubt that many people were willing to say things openly that they would never have dared thought a year ago. The bad news from Russia and North Africa had come as a shock to most people, gulled into a false sense of security by the optimistic reports of the summer. It was difficult to see how a supposedly unbeatable position had turned so quickly into disaster and people were beginning to realize that they'd been taken for a very dangerous ride. Invading Russia had been a foolish mistake, and with American troops joining the British in North Africa things were only going to get worse. There were plenty of people in Rosenheim who still believed in the Führer. But those prepared to swap jokes about his state of mind, albeit in private, were increasing in number. Hardly anyone didn't know of some poor kid who'd died in Stalingrad or was still stuck there with no hope of getting out.

'Albrecht was a communist before the war. He claims to be a loyal German, but he's one of those who are brown on the outside and red on the inside. Look. I'll show you.'

Hanna Stolz was undoubtedly the most loathsome informer he'd met in some time. She was a well-turned blonde in her early thirties who'd never shied away from using her feminine charms to improve her social position. Her husband, Albrecht, was a lot older than her. He'd had a profitable business as a bookseller before the war. It had made him an attractive target for Hanna. But books didn't help the war effort, especially not the sort of clever stuff that Albrecht sold. He wasn't fit enough for the forces, so he'd been sent to Munich to oversee French prisoners of war clearing rubble from the bombsites. With the money from the bookshop gone, Hanna Stolz had evidently decided it was time to get rid of him.

'He used to disappear every night. I never knew where. I thought he had another woman, some whore. But when they sent him to Munich, I found this. It's a radio, see? It's tuned to Radio Moscow. While our boys have been dying at the hands of the Russians, Albrecht's been off listening to enemy propaganda. He's a traitor. I won't have him back here.'

Ritter looked at Georg Bauer, the nervous young Gestapo officer who'd come with him to check out Hanna Stolz's complaint. He was salivating over finding the radio and the evidence of a genuine 'enemy of the state,' already thinking of the potential promotion the case might bring.

'Don't worry, Frau Stolz,' Bauer said. 'We'll have him arrested in Munich. It'll save on the cost of transporting him to the Special Court.'

Bauer laughed at his own joke. Hanna smiled at him. The Gestapo officer was keen to keep her happy. He wouldn't want to lose a case like this. He took off his spectacles and polished them with his handkerchief.

'This looks like an open-and-shut case to me. For myself, I'm heartened by your patriotism. It shows the strength of German womanhood that you're prepared to put the needs of the state above your own.'

Scarcely. Bauer clearly hadn't noticed the young SS officer who'd been moving his belongings into the apartment while they were interviewing her. Ritter wondered whether she'd thought the whole thing through.

'You do realize the implications of what you've told us?'

'Yes, of course, Inspector. Albrecht won't be coming back. Not for a long time.'

'No. Albrecht won't be coming back. Ever. There's only one punishment the court's likely to consider for such a crime.'

'Oh.'

He was right. It simply hadn't occurred to her until now. But it didn't seem to concern her for very long. 'Well, I'm sure if the Special Court thinks he deserves it.'

There was only the slightest hint of hesitancy in her voice. But it was enough to make Bauer nervous. The Gestapo officer rushed to reassure her that she was doing the right thing. 'Of course he does, Frau Stolz. Of course he does. We have to remove all enemies of the state if we're going to win the war.'

Even if Bauer had noticed what was actually going on, and Ritter was pretty sure he was too stupid, it wouldn't have made any difference.

The Gestapo officer wasn't alone in being willing to use an obviously malicious complaint to improve his own success rate. And there were enough complaints to boost everyone's careers.

One woman – in the highlight of an otherwise irritating day – had even gone so far as to suggest that her neighbour was putting out her washing at specific times of the day to summon members of the White Rose to protest meetings. Ritter took a small degree of pleasure in telling the informant – on the authority of *Obersturmführer* Klaus Kleidorfer no less – that no such organization existed.

None of these so-called cases of treachery was anywhere near as interesting as the sighting of Marianne Müller and the young Swiss woman in Söllhuben. He had no doubt that it was somehow linked to the Schinkel killing, but it made no difference whatsoever to the status of the case. Nagel was adamant that it was to be written up and put among all the other 'Not Solved' files stacked up against the walls of Ritter's office.

Officially, it was dead, or at the very least in limbo. But neither Nagel nor Drexler could stop him thinking about it, and he and Messel spent their evenings going over it as they sat in the Rothenbach, winding down after work. Messel had been unsure at first. If their bosses wanted the investigation closed down, then surely they shouldn't be talking about it. But Ritter told him it was an exercise in detection. It would be good training for him to think the thing through. Anyway, since the case was no longer active, it was all hypothetical. No possible harm could come of it.

It was a lame excuse that would never have withstood scrutiny from his bosses. But they were the ones who'd given him Messel to train. He was only answering the boy's questions, and even if they did find out that he hadn't really dropped the case, it would be him they blamed, not Messel. They were never going to do anything to damage their blue-eyed boy's inexorable rise through the ranks.

It was more than two months since Schinkel's body had been discovered on the side of the Adolf-Hitler-Strasse. Christmas and the New Year had come and gone with very little to celebrate. The snow by the bridge had melted to slush, frozen, and been covered by another layer of fresh snow half a dozen times since the body was found, and they still hadn't been able to come up with any sensible answers as to how and why it came to be lying there. The case had been closed for more than a month now, and any evidence they might have missed had long since been washed away.

The Rothenbach was noisier than usual. Messel turned up clutching two large glasses of beer. Ritter gestured to him to sit down. 'I was wondering, Messel. Why do you think the Swiss police are so reluctant to cooperate over Frau Grob and her daughter?'

Messel didn't think the lack of cooperation mattered much. He didn't rate Grob – or Matronly Swiss Woman, as he now called her – as a potential suspect.

'I can't see how she could possibly have done it, boss. How could she have got him out of the hotel – the best part of a kilometre along the road – and into the ditch without anyone seeing her? Even if she'd got him into a car, she would have had to drag him out down by the bridge and there would have been tracks in the snow. If she and her daughter threw him, there would be marks on the body, and there was nothing apart from the bruising caused by whoever strangled him.'

Ritter was only half listening to what the boy was saying. He was going back over the service in Söllhuben again in his own mind, reliving the sight of the blonde woman signalling to the priest. Wondering if she really was Grob's daughter and what the raised three fingers might mean.

Over on the far side of the bar, Drexler was holding court with other members of the Gestapo detachment, Kleidorfer among them. Bauer was celebrating his great success and his colleagues were making sure his glass was topped up. The drink was already having an effect. Bauer was becoming noisier by the minute.

Kleidorfer looked over and smiled at Ritter, testing him, looking for a psychological advantage. Ritter declined to play the game, deliberately avoiding the Gestapo officer's eyes, refusing to acknowledge him. Kleidorfer turned back to his colleagues. He must have made some sort of joke, because they all looked over and laughed.

'Of course, there's always Father Steiner.'

He looked at Messel in surprise. It seemed an odd coincidence that the boy should mention the priest now.

'Your friend from Söllhuben. You know. The service for the dead Swiss boy.'

'He's not my friend, Messel, and I know who you mean. I was wondering what the link between him and Matronly Swiss Woman might have been. Is there any evidence he ever met her?'

'Well, he helped her earlier.'

'What do you mean he helped her earlier?'

'The priest brought the daughter to the hotel…'

'That was Steiner?' Ritter was incredulous, but Messel appeared not to notice.

'Yes. Steiner. Matronly Swiss Woman arrived earlier in the day and checked in.'

Ritter was going through the various possibilities thrown up by the confirmation of a link between Martyl Scharf and the priest. Messel continued in a matter-of-fact tone, oblivious to the impact of this revelation on his boss.

'Her daughter Scharf didn't arrive until later. About five o'clock. With the priest. But the priest didn't stay. He had to get back to his parish, to Söllhuben. So even if one of the women did kill Schinkel, the priest couldn't have helped.'

'Steiner was the priest who brought Scharf to the hotel?' Ritter's face contorted with anger. 'You said in the report that Liesl Olbricht didn't know who he was. She told you he was from Söllhuben? For Christ's sake! Why the fuck didn't you mention this before?'

'I didn't think it was relevant.'

'You didn't think it was fucking relevant? Even after the blonde made that hand signal to the priest? Where are the fingerprints we took from the hotel?'

'They're in the file, boss. But they won't be much help. We couldn't find any for Scharf.'

Ritter stopped, closed his eyes, and took a deep breath. So maybe

Matronly Swiss Woman couldn't have killed Schinkel. Perhaps there was another possibility they hadn't considered. Ritter stumbled out of the Rothenbach, still trying to get his arm into the sleeve of his coat. He was followed by Messel, and the laughter of Drexler and his cronies.

'It's your sense of moral superiority that gets up their noses, Peter. That's why they laugh at you.'

'Moral superiority? For Christ's sake, old man. Can't you stop nagging? Leave me alone with my drink. Anyway, I haven't seen any sign of morals in Rosenheim in the past few years.'

'So what about your attitude to the Stolz woman? You were full of moral judgments there.'

'She's no better than a whore. I know Albrecht Stolz. I bought books in his shop. He loved books. It's all he was interested in. He's one of the few people in Rosenheim with clean hands.'

'What? Clean hands on a commie? Don't make me laugh. There's not a cigarette paper of difference between Stalin and Hitler.'

'Albrecht Stolz isn't Stalin. Just because he's a communist, it doesn't mean he's like Stalin.'

'So just because Kleidorfer's a Nazi, it doesn't mean he's like Hitler?'

'That's completely different.'

'It's not different at all. That's always been your problem, Peter. Too much passion. Too little intellectual precision. Anyway, it's not the bookseller's wife you should be worried about. It's your own. Sophie needs a child, someone to carry on the family line. That's where you need to be directing all that passion of yours.'

'She's not interested. Not since the accident. She seems far more interested in that shit Kleidorfer and the rest of her Party cronies.'

'Women need to be loved, Peter. If you don't give them love they'll find someone else to give it to them. That's all Hanna Stolz has done. You need to stop thinking about her and worry more about your own wife.'

'You think I don't worry about her? Her and Kleidorfer? If she really is screwing him, I'll kill the bitch. One way or another I'll do for both of them.'
'Really, Peter? So where's your precious morality gone now?'

Chapter Ten

Tuesday 19 January 1943

'Liesl. I need you to tell me the truth. It was Drexler who moved the body, wasn't it?'

She was flustered, panicky. Clearly terrified of the Gestapo boss. 'I can't. I really can't. And it's not fair of you to ask.'

Ritter had made a detour via the Schweizerhof on his way into work to ask Liesl about Steiner. She didn't know who the priest was. She'd already told his assistant that. Didn't *Kripo* detectives talk to each other? And she was adamant that she didn't know how Schinkel's body had come to be lying in a ditch by the bridge.

'You must know if Drexler left in the middle of the night.'

'He comes and goes as he pleases. He always leaves in the middle of the night. But look, it wasn't Drexler anyway.'

'How can you be so sure, Liesl?'

'Georg Bauer told me.'

'Bauer? When?'

But Liesl had said too much. She clammed up and refused to say any more. 'I told you, Peter. There's nothing else I know.' She was almost in tears, using his Christian name for the first time in years. 'I can't help any more. Can't you see that?'

'Yes, Liesl. I understand. But if there's anything, anything at all, that I can do to help you, you must call me. You understand what I'm saying?'

'Yes. I will. I'll call you if I need to. But there's nothing more I can tell you.' She opened the door of her private office to show him out. Heinrich Jr. was standing outside with a lopsided grin on his face. He must have been listening in to their conversation. Liesl scowled at him and lifted her hand to clout him round the head. 'Haven't you got anything to do? You stupid boy.'

Heinrich swayed back out of Liesl's reach. Her hand hit only thin air.

Ritter walked the short distance back to the *Mittertor*. There was a file containing a report from Berlin lying on his desk. The results of the checks made against the fingerprints found in the Schweizerhof were short and to the point. Only one set matched anything in the records. He barely had time to sit down and absorb its implications before Drexler barged into his office, demanding to know what game he was playing. Ritter placed the report back into the file and closed it before looking up.

'I'm not playing any games. I'm investigating a murder.'

'Yes, a murder you were told to leave well alone. A Jew died. Whoever killed him saved the Reich some money. I'm going to have your arse for this. You've disobeyed a direct order. You were told to close the fucking case.'

'And I did close it. But now I'm reopening it.'

'What on earth makes you think an idiot detective like you can decide to reopen a case when I say it's closed?'

Drexler was red in the face with anger. He was screaming, thrusting his face right into Ritter's. It was so close that the detective could feel tiny drops of saliva hitting his cheeks. But he remained calm. He stared at the Gestapo boss, waiting for him to stop. Then he let him wait for a few seconds more before he spoke. Get the timing right. No expression. Keep it matter-of-fact.

'Because there was a British spy in the hotel.'

'Rubbish. That's complete crap. How would someone like you know that?'

Drexler hadn't missed a beat. But his response was a bit too dismissive. An attempt to cover a growing lack of confidence? Now was the time to hit him with the fingerprints. It was a dangerous tactic.

It could easily backfire. But Ritter knew he had little choice if he was to keep control of the investigation.

'From the fingerprints. We checked all their prints out with Berlin. And one set matched those of a British spy.'

Drexler's face turned from puce to a deathly grey. For a moment he spluttered, physically incapable of responding with anything sensible. Then he realized he'd been handed a way out. He began to recover his composure.

'A British spy, eh? That's very interesting, Ritter. It also makes it one for my boys. We'll take it over. You can drop it again, and this time I do mean drop it. Kleidorfer can take it from here.'

'No. I don't think so.'

'Listen to me, Ritter. You're a no-hope detective hiding out in the cellar of a museum in the back of beyond. What gave you the idea that you were in charge of anything? Why do you imagine that I, or anyone else for that matter, should take any notice of what you think or don't think?'

He showed no emotion in the face of Drexler's abuse. The angrier the Gestapo boss became, the calmer and more patient he grew. He knew Drexler had no choice but to allow him to continue with the case.

'You don't want me to hand the case over to you. Because if I do, I'll have to write up my notes for Inspector Nagel and the mayor so they can rubber-stamp my decision. And as part of my report I'll have to explain how and why the body of a man murdered in a hotel in the middle of Rosenheim found its way to the side of a bridge over the Inn.'

The grey pallor returned to Drexler's face. 'I don't know what that stupid woman Olbricht's been telling you, but she's lying.'

'She didn't tell me anything. At least, she didn't say anything about you and I suppose that since that left out your key role in all this, it was effectively a lie. But I didn't need her to tell me. You've already said you were in the hotel that night with your prostitute friend Müller. And I've got a witness who saw Bauer and one of your other goons dumping Schinkel's body down by the bridge.'

'You're bluffing. What witness? Where's their statement?'

'What? So you can persuade them they didn't see anything? That is not going to happen. But I'll certainly append it to my report to the mayor, and to Munich.' All his instincts, all his experience of interrogating criminals, told him Drexler was close to cracking. It only needed one more twist of the knife. 'I'll also feel bound to reveal the evidence that there was a British spy in the hotel at the time.'

The look of horror returned to Drexler's face.

'So you see, the way it will look to anyone in Munich or Berlin is that either you were too incompetent to notice a British spy asleep in the same hotel as you, or you were busy covering up the fact that the spy was there. They might even wonder why you needed to stay in the Schweizerhof at all, given that you've got a very nice house only a few hundred metres away, unless you were planning to meet up with the British spy.'

Drexler's corpulent frame slumped back in the chair in front of Ritter's desk. His cheeks sagged. The colour drained away. The sweet scent of his cologne mingled with the pungent odour of sweat. 'You know that isn't true.'

'No, of course it's not. You were trying to stop your wife finding out about your floozy. But your friends in Munich might not be so understanding. You do have friends in Munich, don't you? Are they good friends you can rely on? I mean really rely on. After all, they'll need to cover their own backsides. Did you know they executed twenty communist spies in Berlin just before Christmas?'

'I'm no communist.'

'Of course not. You're a good Nazi. But you said it yourself. These are dangerous times. Some people might think it better to get rid of a good Nazi rather than take the risk that he was actually a British spy hidden deep inside the Gestapo just down the road from the Führer's holiday home.'

Drexler sat there, sullen, trying to marshal his thoughts, trying to work out what he should do next. Ritter looked down at the file in front of him and then back at Drexler, hoping the Gestapo boss wouldn't ask to see the report from Berlin. It confirmed that a British spy had been in the Schweizerhof, but it still wasn't clear when. The central records in Berlin had the prints down as those of an unidentified British female spy who'd been in Berlin at some time before the war. Nothing more. There was a cross-reference to another file, but it was missing. No one in Berlin seemed to believe the prints could possibly have been recent. The British spy had long since disappeared. They were trying to track down her file. But how much effort would they put in for a *Kripo* inspector in a Bavarian backwater?

'So, Ritter. What do you suggest we do?'

Drexler seemed to have accepted that his fate lay in Ritter's hands. But for how long? The Gestapo boss wouldn't think twice about having him killed. He had to come up with a deal that tied Drexler's hands.

'We treat it as if it's a straightforward murder. I haven't told you about this report from Berlin. You have no reason to take the case over. But you tell my boss you've had a tip that there's far more to the Schinkel case than meets the eye. Nothing you want to get involved in yet. Your boys are too busy dealing with 'enemies of the state.' But you think that I should reopen the investigation. I'll keep you fully informed of any progress. You didn't murder Schinkel. I know that. You just had the body moved. And I'm only interested in finding the murderer. Everything else can be finessed to make you and me both look good. So you've really got nothing to worry about, so long as I get to investigate the Schinkel murder, and if I do find a spy, I'll make sure you get all the credit.'

Drexler steepled his fingers. He'd been left with little choice.

'All right, on two conditions. Firstly, you forget anything this witness has told you, and bury anything that suggests any involvement by me or my men. Secondly, you let Kleidorfer work alongside you.'

'Fine. I'm after the murderer, not you, and Kleidorfer seems to spend most of his time following me around anyway.'

'Right. We're agreed. But remember, Ritter, you keep me out of it.'

Half an hour later, Nagel called Ritter into his office. 'I don't know what's going on in Drexler's mind. But he wants you back on the Schinkel case. He's had some tip that there's more to the Jew's murder than meets the eye. I asked him why he didn't just pick up the case himself. But he insists he's happy with you working on it. I don't suppose you've had anything to do with this?'

'Not a thing. Did he say what the tip was about?'

Nagel picked up his pack of cigarettes and went to shake one out before thinking better of it and stuffing them back in his pocket. He looked up, embarrassed at his own indecision. 'I'm supposed to be giving up.' He grinned sheepishly at Ritter. 'What were you saying? Drexler? No, he didn't seem to have much idea himself what it was about. Only that it wasn't simply about the death of a Jew.'

'I wouldn't trust that fat prick as far as I could throw him.'

Nagel reacted sharply. 'Look, Peter. I don't want you getting involved in some vendetta with Drexler or any of those other vipers over on the Adolf-Hitler-Strasse. If you get into trouble over this, you're on your own. I'm not putting myself, my job, or my family at risk over the death of a Jew.'

Chapter Eleven

Wednesday 20 January 1943

The files were still strewn across the floor beside Ritter's desk the next morning. He must have hit the bottle a bit too hard the night before. There was a brief moment of panic before he remembered that he'd locked the Schinkel file away in the bottom drawer of the desk. But the desk itself was not completely clear. A single folded sheet of paper lay slightly open on the blotter, revealing a glimpse of a handwritten note.

He stood behind the desk. Looking at it suspiciously. Reluctant to learn its contents. He knew who it was from without reading it. The letterhead was showing through the paper. The silver eagle and swastika of the Gestapo. The note was from Drexler.

He wasn't afraid of what the Gestapo boss might have to say. Although, he was surprised that Drexler was prepared to commit anything to writing. Maybe it was just a summons. Drexler wanted to see him the minute he came in. Wanted a progress report. But that wouldn't explain his own reluctance to read the note. It certainly wasn't out of fear. It was something more basic than that. An instinct that the note was a portent of something far worse than Drexler's anger.

There was a half-finished bottle of Asbach on the floor along with the files. He picked it up and registered exactly how little was left. All the while, watching the note. As though it were an illusion that might disappear at any moment. He placed the bottle back in the drawer, locking it carefully away, as much to keep it out of his own reach as anything else, then put the keys back in his pocket. Only then did he reach out to pick up the note.

> *Peter,*
> *We need to talk about all this. There's something you don't know. Meet me in the Schweizerhof at 7. And whatever you do, don't bring your wastrel assistant.*
> *Gerhard*

What to make of it? It was definitely Drexler's handwriting. But it was extremely odd. The friendly, almost conspiratorial tone made him suspicious. It had to be a trap. Drexler had never used Ritter's first name before. He'd certainly never called the Gestapo boss Gerhard. Why would he? And why would Drexler want to help him?

He phoned Drexler's office and got his secretary.

'Anja. How are you?' Anja Vogel, abrupt to the point of rudeness with anyone, even Drexler at times. She wasn't looking to change that reputation for Ritter's sake. 'If you're after the commissar, he isn't here.'

'I was wondering if you might be able to tell me when he's due in.'

'He's made it very clear that I am not to share any details of his schedule with anyone, particularly the *Kripo*. Particularly you, in fact.'

There was a click as she put the phone down. A few minutes later, Messel arrived, irritatingly cheerful. Ritter locked the note in the drawer and bent down to pick up the papers he'd scattered on the floor the night before.

'What happened, boss? An earthquake?'

'Something like that. What are you doing here, Messel? Didn't you have some more questions for Liesl Olbricht?'

'Yes, boss.'

'Then get on with it.'

He half thought about asking Messel to come back later and tail him to the Schweizerhof. Just to cover his backside. But he wasn't entirely convinced he could trust the boy. Given the choice between loyalty to him or to the Gestapo, a probationary commissar might easily think to the future and choose the Gestapo. Better to know from the start that he was on his own rather than give Drexler another card to play.

Ritter didn't manage to make any headway with the case after the boy left. He spent the afternoon rereading the Schinkel file carefully, looking for anything that might explain Drexler's new attitude, making sure this time that there was nothing he'd missed. But he couldn't see a fresh way forward.

It was dark and already freezing by the time he went up onto the street. He pulled his overcoat around him and tugged his fedora down as far as was possible. It would take ten minutes to get to the Schweizerhof. There was no one out in the old town. The silence was broken only by occasional gusts of wind or the barking of a dog. Even so, the oddly conciliatory tone of Drexler's note made him more careful than usual. He didn't head directly for the hotel. He had to make sure he wasn't being followed. He walked into the Max-Josefs-Platz and turned right into Hermann-Goring-Strasse, giving himself time to confuse and lose any tail before looping around to approach the hotel from the west.

He walked with his hands thrust into his coat pockets, head hunched, elbows tight against his sides. A gust of wind from the river sent the mist scurrying away, carrying with it a vague reminder of the rotting fish down by the bridge where they'd found Schinkel's body. Deep black clouds raced across the dark grey sky, taking it in turns to block out the light from the moon. The damp, dirty backstreets of the old town displayed in monochrome. Layers of shadow. Hiding places for Ritter's demons. He turned onto Fruhlingstrasse and then right again into Steinbokstrasse. Across the other side of the street, the ground floors of the baroque, stucco-covered buildings were shielded by a series of stone arches. The pillars were squat and square, creating an inner pavement with vaulted ceilings. A German version of a Renaissance arcade. Less fancy. More solid. More dependable. The damp air settled on the cold stone pillars, condensing into rivulets of water. Clear, cold water that had fallen as snow before being swept off the Alps into the river Inn. Turned to mist as it reached the city centre. Distilled as pure German water. Running down the pillars like tears.

He sensed the movement in the shadows before he saw it. There was someone behind him. He couldn't see the face. But he caught a brief glimpse of a figure in a long dark coat. Kleidorfer. Drexler had put his deputy on his tail. It was no surprise. He'd anticipated company, and that bastard Kleidorfer followed him everywhere else. Watching him. Minding him. Making sure he wasn't given the slightest opportunity to undermine the new order. Drexler wanted to check that he came on his own. What did it matter? He was used to Kleidorfer's methods. Losing him would be easy.

But it wasn't easy.

He turned left onto Am Salzstadel and ducked into an alleyway across the other side of the street. Hugging the cover of the line of arches that led up to the Kaiserstrasse. There was nothing across the street for Kleidorfer to hide behind. But the Gestapo officer was still there. Somewhere. He heard the light footsteps. Saw him turn his back and loiter in a jeweller's doorway, monitoring the reflection in the shop window. Kleidorfer wouldn't be shaken off easily this time. Frustrated by his failure to lose his tail, Ritter turned first into the Kaiserstrasse, then immediately into another alley that led to the back of some apartments. He hid in the darkest of the shadows. Lying in wait for Kleidorfer. But Kleidorfer never came.

Shit. Why had the Gestapo officer chosen tonight to learn from his past mistakes? He needed to know if Kleidorfer was still there. He took his stubby Sauer 6.35mm pistol out of his coat pocket. Held it with both hands, close to his chest. Pointed slightly forward. Ready to aim.

Edging out of the shadows, he looked out onto the street. He ducked his head out and back. He couldn't see anyone. Had he managed to lose him?

A dark figure stepped out of a shop doorway across the street and ran straight towards him. Christ. He'd missed him. Kleidorfer must have been closer than he thought, must have watched him as he hid in the alleyway. The tiny Sauer was swallowed up in his hands. He wondered briefly if it made him look like a child pretending to hold a gun. He brought it down slowly, pointing it towards the oncoming figure. An image of Sophie and Kleidorfer embracing, half-naked, flashed through his mind and his finger pressed against the trigger, squeezing out the slack, preparing to fire.

'No, Inspector. Don't.'

It wasn't Kleidorfer. Although it was a voice he recognized.

'I'm here to help you.'

If he was there to help, why hide behind the pillars? Why try to surprise him like this? He could just make out the folds of a long black cape as the man came to a halt. Ritter's finger tightened against the trigger. As he prepared to fire, the cape fell aside and the moonlight reflected off the white clerical collar, but it was the pistol aimed at Ritter's chest that drew his attention. A Luger 9mm, from the look of it. Far more powerful than his tiny Sauer.

'You need to back off, Ritter.' It didn't sound like a threat, more like advice from a friend. 'Drexler's trying to draw you into a trap. You've got too much on him. Think about it for a moment. He can't let you live.'

Steiner slipped his pistol back inside his cassock and turned away, leaving Ritter alone in the alleyway still wondering how a priest could know Drexler's plans. How did he know what he had on Drexler? Or that he was going to meet him?

Too many questions. Better to take Steiner's advice and go home. If Drexler was genuine about his desire to talk, it could wait. Better to take the priest's advice and pull out of the meeting at the Schweizerhof.

The house was in darkness when he got home. Sophie was out. The black Loden coat with the red and green trimmings, the one that cost an entire week's wages, was missing from the hooks by the door. Where would she have gone in the dark? The same vision of Sophie lying with Kleidorfer returned, lingering longer until he shook it out of his brain, angry at himself for allowing that Gestapo bastard to get to him.

If they really were screwing each other, he would destroy them both. Kill Sophie and set Kleidorfer up for her murder. That was the answer. Get her into a hotel room and strangle her, then make it look like Kleidorfer had been there with her, as if he was the killer. The dead body in the hotel bed, a woman murdered by her lover. After all, who knew the evidence that would implicate a murderer better than he did?

Ritter poured himself an Asbach, drank it straight down, and poured himself another. He went into the front room and sat in his father-in-law's old leather chair, nursing the brandy, hoping for inspiration from the portrait of old man Kuster above the fire.

None came.

He was dozing when the telephone rang, jolting him awake. He rushed to pick it up, thinking it might be Sophie. It was Liesl. She was crying, almost hysterical.

'Peter. You have to come. I don't know what to do.'

He looked at his watch. Half ten. He'd been home three hours and Sophie still wasn't back.

'Please, Peter. Please come now.'

'Calm down, Liesl. Tell me what's wrong.'

'There's a dead body in one of my rooms.'

A dead body in the hotel? Sophie? Had Kleidorfer beaten him to it?

'What? What are you talking about, Liesl?'

'It's Drexler, Peter. You've got to come. He's dead. In his bed… in the room he and Marianne use. There's blood everywhere.'

Drexler dead?

'It's all right, Liesl. Calm down. Have you spoken to anyone else?'

'No. Who could I have spoken to? The Gestapo?'

'No. It's all right. Just close the door and don't let anyone in there until I get there. Where's Marianne?'

'I don't know. She hasn't been here. I thought he was here to see her. But she's not here.'

'All right. Just lock the room. Go downstairs and wait for me. I'll get there as soon as I can.'

He rang the station and told the duty officer to get Kozlowski over to the Schweizerhof along with as many uniformed police as he could muster. 'Seal off the hotel. Nobody goes in or out. Get Messel over there too. Tell him I'll meet him there.'

Chapter Twelve

Wednesday 20 January 1943

Ritter had seen messy murders, but none as bad as this. The room stank of blood and shit. Drexler was naked on the bed, his mouth and eyes wide open, covered in blood. Everything was covered in blood. It was all up the wall behind the bed and all over the wash bowl and jug that were set out on the chest of drawers. As if the murderer had made a panicky attempt to wash the evidence from his or her hands.

He opened the door of the wardrobe. Drexler's suit was hanging inside. Clean. Neatly pressed. Untouched by the devastation. Why would the Gestapo boss have got undressed when he was here to meet him?

The lower half of Drexler's right arm was hanging off the side of the bed. A line of blood ran down his hand and along the middle finger before dripping slowly onto the carpet.

He shook his head, refusing to allow the memory of the crash to interrupt his investigation.

Viktor entered the room busily. Doctor Viktor Kozlowski, Rosenheim City Pathologist. Short, fat, and bald. Squashed-up face. Well-trimmed beard. Fastidious, for which read: pernickety. Frustrated detective. Often irritating. Always difficult. He stood behind Ritter, gripping a black leather doctor's bag in his right hand, waiting for the detective to give way. Ritter held his ground, not so much making a point as still trying to make sense of the carnage.

'Are you going to get out of the way and let me get on with my job, Ritter?' Viktor, impatient and tetchy as ever, shoved him aside and, after a brief glance at the body, reached down to close Drexler's eyes.

'Ah, Dr. Kozlowski. So pleasant to see you again.' Ritter turned to one side, bowed slightly and swept an arm out towards the body. 'I'm only too happy to find you eager to do your job.'

The pathologist chose to ignore the mocking humour. 'I wish I could say the same, Ritter. But I'm afraid I can't think of anything pleasant about the current situation.'

Was Viktor thinking of the murder, or more generally? 'The current situation' sounded as if he might be talking about the state of the war, or the demonic nature of the regime.

'So what do you think of this?' The pathologist looked at him as if he was a fool and then turned his attention back to the body. 'I think it was a frenzied attack. But if you need me to tell you that, you should probably try a different profession.'

Ritter took the hint and let Viktor get on with it, watching as he examined the body and the bloody bedclothes. The pathologist worked methodically, making frequent notes, sometimes stepping aside to direct the photographer to take a picture of a particular thing that interested him. At least they'd managed to find Viktor sober tonight.

Messel walked in. He opened his mouth to say something to Ritter and the stench hit him. He pulled a handkerchief from his pocket and thrust it in front of his face. Ritter acknowledged him with a grim smile before turning back to the pathologist.

'Man or woman?'

'Hard to say. We're looking at a long and very sharp knife. About twenty centimetres long. Double-edged. It wouldn't need much strength to do this, just a lot of enthusiasm.'

'Give me the daggers…'

Viktor turned towards him and smiled at the Shakespeare.

'Lady Macbeth. You think it's a woman?'

Ritter shrugged. There was something unspoken between the two men. A shared heritage. Both part of Erich Maria Remarque's generation, the young men 'destroyed by the Great War,' they'd worked together in Rosenheim for nearly a decade.

Messel had turned a deathly white. Viktor realized what was about to happen before Ritter did. 'Get out of here, boy. I'm not having you puke all over my evidence.' He watched Messel dart out before turning back to the body. 'They don't make police officers like they used to.'

Ritter could hear a croaking sound from the washroom across the hall. 'We'd seen the trenches, Viktor. It's different for these young kids.'

'Not that much. I think the boys stuck in Stalingrad have probably seen a lot worse than you or I ever did.'

For a moment the thought of the slaughter a couple of thousand kilometres to the east felt more real to Ritter than the surreal scene in front of him. An involuntary shudder shook him. There was something small and white lying in the pool of blood beside Drexler on the bed.

'What's that, Viktor?'

The pathologist picked it up with a pair of tweezers. A small white rose lying on top of the blood. 'A white rose on red. The city coat of arms.'

'This isn't about Rosenheim, Viktor. It's a sign of the resistance.'

'I know. I've heard. But unless you want half the Munich Gestapo descending on Rosenheim, I should ignore it.'

Viktor was probably right. He wouldn't report it. But he wasn't going to ignore it, either. It linked the Drexler murder to the Schinkel killing. Best stick to the simple questions with Viktor. Let's not frighten the horses.

'So the stabbing. Could it be a woman?'

'Are you so determined to find your Lady Macbeth? Yes is your answer. The cuts are regular. It's completely ripped open the gut.' The pathologist leaned forward, squinting at the wounds. 'But the edges of the knife must have been like razors.'

Satisfied that he knew as much as he could without dissecting the body on the slab, Viktor stood back up. 'A woman could easily have done this. I think she'd need to be angry. Very angry. But there's a certain quality to female anger, I always find. It's so much more effective than anything we mere men can manage.'

What woman was the pathologist thinking about? Certainly not

Lady Macbeth. This was someone real. Some long-forgot murderess? The pathologist's own wife? Sophie, even? Did everybody know the ins and outs of their marriage?

Viktor was staring at Drexler's body. Whatever woman he was thinking about, it wasn't a pleasant memory.

'You could be looking for a woman, Ritter. Certainly, a woman could have done it.' The pathologist was messing around in Drexler's mouth, pulling the jaw apart, squinting at something. His voice dropped. 'Not that there weren't plenty of men who'd have been happy to do it. But I think you know that better than most. Don't you, Ritter?'

It was far quieter than anything Viktor had said before. The pathologist looked around to ensure he hadn't been heard. Satisfied no one else was listening, he reached into his bag for a large pair of tweezers and tugged a blood-soaked fragment of cloth from between Drexler's lower teeth. He thrust it up towards Ritter's face. 'Suffocated first. See?'

Viktor picked up one of the pillows, turned it over, and held it up, pointing out the tear in the bloody pillowcase that matched the piece of cloth he'd extracted from Drexler's mouth.

Smothered. Just like Schinkel. So there was a possible link. Although Schinkel wasn't stabbed. There'd been no blood by the bridge over the Inn and none in the room where Schinkel was murdered. There certainly was here. By the time his teeth ripped the pillowcase, Drexler must have known it was close to the end. He would have been struggling frantically. Running short of breath. But he was a big man. How could a woman have held him down? Unless he was asleep or completely relaxed when she put the pillow over his face. Viktor was still holding the pillow. He seemed to be thinking along the same lines.

'It looks like whoever did it held this over his head. That would have taken some strength. Unless he was asleep when they started on him.'

'They started on him?'

The pathologist ignored the question and its implication. But Ritter already had another question. 'Look at the other pillow, Viktor.'

'What about it?'

'There's no pillowcase.'

'So I see.'

'Well? What does it mean?'

'How should I know? I'm a pathologist, not a psychic.'

Viktor stared at Drexler's body. Ritter knew what he was doing. He'd suffered these long silences before. The pathologist was attempting to piece together Drexler's last moments. Trying out each possibility, until he was satisfied he had the right one. He would take his time. He always did. Always savoured the moment. His one chance to shape the direction of the investigation. Finally, he spoke. Slowly, in painfully measured tones. Thinking every point through.

'Yes. That's what happened, Ritter. Whoever it was put a pillow over his face when he was drowsy. They weren't trying to kill him. They wanted to starve him of enough oxygen to knock him out completely. To give them time to kill him. He fought back. Grabbing. Scratching. Biting. Doing anything he could. Once he lost consciousness, they stabbed him to make sure he wouldn't wake up again, but there was more to it than just plain murder. Whoever did this got some sort of release from the way Drexler was killed.'

Viktor picked up Drexler's right hand, turned it over to examine the fingers, and placed it carefully back on the bed.

'Your murderer might well have scratches on their face, arm, or hands. There are a few bits of skin under his nails… They, you say?'

'No, Viktor. You said 'they.' It was you who said it first. Every time you mentioned the murderer until now, you said 'they.''

'Did I? Yes. Well. I don't know who they are, do I? But Drexler was a big, heavy man. Holding a pillow over his head wouldn't be easy for one person on his or her own. You asked if it was a man or woman, Ritter. He's not known for his interest in young men, is he?'

Ritter ignored the question. He wasn't prepared to play Viktor's games, and anyway, he had too many questions of his own. Was Drexler already dead when the priest warned him against going to the hotel? If he'd gone ahead with the meeting, would Drexler be dead now?

'When did he die? What was the time?'

That was the most important question.

'Not long ago. Three hours ago, perhaps, maybe four. He's not cold yet.'

Had Steiner really been trying to protect him out on the Kaiserstrasse? It seemed ages ago now, but it was not much more than a few hours. Deliberately or otherwise, the priest had compromised him. If Steiner was involved, he couldn't question him without the truth coming out. Kleidorfer and his SS friends wouldn't waste any time trying to find the real killer. They wouldn't be able to drag him in front of the Special Court quickly enough. If that happened, the guillotine would probably be the best he could hope for. A quick death. An end to the beating and torture that would precede it.

The boy had returned, his face still white, and wet from where he'd washed away the vomit.

'Where's your friend Kleidorfer? Does he know his boss is dead?'

The boy shook his head. 'They can't get hold of him.'

So Kleidorfer had gone missing too, along with the Loden coat.

Viktor spotted his opportunity. 'So the *Kripo* can't find a key witness. Why does that not surprise me. Kleidorfer might at least have a better idea than either of you two as to who his boss planned to meet.'

Messel was clearly riled. 'Drexler was screwing one of his informants, the whore Marianne Müller. But a woman wouldn't be able to hold Drexler down. This has to have been a man.'

Viktor smiled. Ritter had known better than to take the bait. But the boy was still naive enough to give the pathologist the chance to stamp his authority on the case. And Viktor couldn't wait. He'd clearly rehearsed the speech in his own mind. 'You may be right, Messel. And, of course, I'm not the detective. But if I were, I think I might be asking myself why a man with a comfortable house and a rich, good-looking wife would want to spend the night in a hotel not four hundred metres away from his own home.'

Ritter kept out of the debate. Let them both show off how clever they were. The more possibilities they threw up, the less chance there was of him being implicated in the murder. Predictably, Viktor had decided he'd won the debate. 'I think we all know Drexler's sexual inclinations. He's not one for the boys. Ritter's right. In all probability, he was here to see a woman.'

'That's not what I said, Viktor.'

'No. But it's what you implied. And for what it's worth, I think it's right.'

Ritter knew it wasn't. But he could hardly explain why.

Chapter Thirteen

Wednesday 20 January 1943

A bout of turbulence shook the Halifax, jolting Litwak awake. The noise from the aircraft's engines was unrelenting. In the semi-dark, the interior of the fuselage resembled the ribbed carcass of a whale. He was aware of a sickeningly sweet scent, a heavy mix of aviation fuel, oil, and sweat. As his eyes became accustomed to the murky light, he saw the RAF dispatcher checking various pieces of equipment fitted to the ribs that lined the sides of the fuselage. The airman moved from point to point in what looked to be a well-practiced routine, his body swaying easily in reaction to the way the aircraft was thrown about. He was talking into the intercom. Litwak couldn't understand a word he was saying. It sounded like it might be Polish? The dispatcher must be one of the Polish aircrew who'd joined the RAF. The area around Litwak's tiny canvas seat was cramped. With little choice but to lean back against the inside of the fuselage and wait, he closed his eyes. Conserving energy. Sleep came surprisingly easily.

He's asleep in his bed in the family's apartment. There's a lot of shouting, and screams. It wakes him up. In the distance, he can hear cries of 'Juden heraus' *and the sound of breaking glass. A truck screeches to a halt outside the apartment block. There's a clatter of boots on cobbles as the SA Brownshirts jump out. Fists hammer on doors. He's struggling to work out what's going on when his mother rushes into the room, screaming at him to get up.*

The fear on her face shocks him into action. He falls from his bed, scrambling for his clothes. She pushes him out onto the staircase that runs up the middle of the block, connecting the apartments to the laundry room in the basement below.

'Go up to the Haffners. They're expecting you. They'll keep you safe.'

As he turns to run up the stairs, still buttoning his shirt, a pickaxe helve goes through the window of the front door. The sound of shattering glass fills the apartment. He turns back. He can't leave his mother to face this alone. His father's gone. He's the man of the family now. He has to defend his mother.

'No. Go. I'll be safer if it's just me.' Her voice is quiet but very firm. Too firm to brook dissent. 'I'll be fine. It's the men they're after. They took your father. I'm not letting them take you.'

The Halifax bucked again and Litwak opened his eyes. They must be close now, surely? The drone from the engines was so loud he couldn't hear what the dispatcher was saying, even though they were only a few feet apart. They'd dropped into the shadows of the Alps. The turbulence repeatedly jerked the aircraft upward and back down. The dispatcher was struggling to set up the parachute rigging and get the equipment box up above the hatch in the floor through which Litwak would jump. He motioned to Litwak, cupped his hand to one side of his mouth and shouted: 'Hook up.'

As the dispatcher spoke, another sudden movement of the plane sent him lurching towards Litwak, who instinctively put his hand up to prevent the Pole from falling on top of him. They helped each other over to where the parachute rigging and equipment box were hanging from the steel cable above the hatch, fighting the turbulence to get it all hitched up to the harness.

The dispatcher grinned at him, one finger pointed up at the rigging. 'Widow Maker.'

The black humour didn't help. Litwak was well aware of the A-rig's reputation. Three agents dead, one with half his head ripped off as he jumped. He nodded, forcing a half smile, as if sharing the joke. His stomach tumbled over itself. He crouched on the floor to one side of the hatch, watching as the dispatcher struggled to get it open. There was a string of incomprehensible Polish words. Most of them no doubt obscene. The hatch came free and a blast of freezing air hit Litwak in the face, throwing him off-balance. He could feel the pressure in the back of the aircraft drop as the cold air rushed in. He could see nothing but pitch black through the space below.

The despatcher signalled to get into position. Litwak shuffled forward on his backside until he was sitting almost on his hands on the edge of the hatch, his feet dangling out of the aircraft, pressing his legs hard against the sides of the hatch to stop himself falling through. He sat staring out into the darkness for what seemed forever, listening to the steady drone of the aircraft's engines, trying to remember every detail of how he should jump, what might go wrong, and how he could avoid it. He caught a glimpse of movement to his right and felt a hand clasp his shoulder. The dispatcher held up five fingers.

Five minutes to the drop zone.

The tone of the aircraft's engines changed as it slowed to ready for the jump. The pilot had kept the Halifax at around eight hundred feet ever since they crossed the coast. Now he was bringing it down still further at the start of his drop run, heading east from the Bodensee along the northern edge of the Austrian Alps until he saw the Simssee. The drop zone was a sparsely inhabited valley between two forests five kilometres southeast of the lake, the whole area covered in snow. Litwak was effectively jumping blind. His only guide would be a single lantern several kilometres northeast of the village of Söllhuben. It would be difficult to see. But anything more would be too dangerous. The priest wasn't even sure he was coming. Could he be trusted to get it right? What would a priest know of parachutes and drop zones?

The pilot had brought the aircraft down to six hundred feet. A low jump. A very low jump. No time to correct if it went wrong. The engine noise dropped as the aircraft reduced speed. The dispatcher was talking to the pilot on the intercom – again, in Polish. Litwak couldn't understand a word. Was it deliberate? Did they not expect him to survive the jump? The Pole turned towards him, holding up his hand with his fingers extended. Blowing on the hand and forcing it towards him three times. The wind speed was fifteen knots. Far from perfect jumping conditions. There was a clunking noise as the pilot applied the flaps, bringing down the airspeed to as low as possible without stalling. The dispatcher was nodding as he talked into the intercom, looking towards the front of the aircraft, as if somehow the pilot could see him. He turned back to Litwak, his hand held up again, this time with only two fingers extended.

Litwak braced himself, leaning forward to look at what was below. The fear that had gripped him throughout the flight faded away as the adrenaline took over and he concentrated on the jump. The dispatcher grabbed him by the shoulder, pointing up to the red light that had come on up to his right, shouting 'Red on' above the noise of the engines and air rushing past below. Litwak barely had time to absorb what the man was saying before the red light went out and a green one came on in its place, accompanied by the dispatcher's final terse order.

'Green on. Go.'

He pushed himself off, helped by what felt like a boot in the back, and went rigid, following the training manual to the letter. The cold air hacked at the back of his throat. It felt as if he was plunging down a never-ending slide. There was a sudden jerk as the parachute opened. His legs went upward. He caught a brief glimpse of the aircraft above him. The equipment box swung one way and he the other, as if the line to the box were a giant pendulum. Litwak looked up, trying to spot any tears in the chute or twisted rigging lines. It was no longer pitch black. He could see the peaks of the Alps off to the south. Below him was a sea of whiteness broken only by occasional dark shadows. Patches of forest.

Litwak was surrounded by a swirling mass of white. Snow or sleet was beating into his face. Stinging his cheeks. He could see a light down to his right. A tiny diamond glittering in the snow. He seemed to be heading straight towards it. Then it disappeared, leaving him disoriented. The wind was forcing him towards a dark mass on one side of the valley. A forest. He had to avoid it. He kicked his legs out to his left as hard as he could to try to stop the drift towards the danger of the trees, desperate to avoid becoming another of the widow maker's victims. He heard a thump as the equipment box hit the ground. It had missed the trees. Please God, he would too. He brought his feet and knees tight together. Head bent down. Chin on chest. For the first time, he could see individual flakes of snow. Large and soft, like curled white feathers. Stretching out into the distance. An infinite sea of white. The whiteness of the ground rushed towards him. He was down. Buckling his legs beneath him. Falling to the right. Thanking God he was still alive.

Litwak lay there for a moment, checking that nothing was broken. He was only a few metres away from the forest, but he could barely see it. The wind whipped up the snow into a swirling mass of white. A gust of wind filled the canopy, threatening to drag him away, reminding him that the dangers were far from over. Litwak rolled over onto his front and tugged as hard as he could on one of the cords to deflate the chute. He smacked the quick-release box with the flat of a fist, slid out of the rig, and dragged in the canopy, bundling it into a ball. The equipment box was a few metres away. He crawled over to it, brushed away the snow that had already covered the top, and forced it open with his knife. The radio was in a suitcase, protected by rubber padding. It seemed fine. But he would only know for sure once he tried to switch it on. The sniper rifle, protected by an expensive Holland & Holland case, had survived. The telescopic sight was still in its padded box in the rucksack. No point in checking it now. He needed to break up the equipment box and bury it along with the parachute and his jumpsuit. Litwak unstrapped the collapsible spade, extended it fully, and began to dig.

'There's no time for that.'

The priest appeared out of the blizzard, a tall, slim man in Alpine mountain gear and a dark felt-brimmed mountain hat. His face carried the heavy lines of a man used to the open air. The skin under the sides of his jaw was puffed out with age. But he had the stance of a much younger man. A fit mountain man.

'Josef Steiner,' the priest said. 'Don't bother burying it all. Just put it in the box and we'll drag it over to the trees. Someone will sort it out before morning. We've got to go.'

Litwak took off his jumpsuit and shoved it into the box alongside the bundled-up parachute. The priest helped him carry it over to the tree line, hiding it behind a lone beech. Steiner marked the trunk of the tree with a yellow chalk cross. While Litwak struggled with the rucksack, Steiner slung the rifle over his shoulder, picked up the radio, and marched off towards the west. He had a rapid, determined stride, leaning into the wind. Litwak struggled to keep up. His ears were already numb from the cold. The wind whipped up the snow ahead. Litwak could see nothing in front of them other than the swirling mass of white. The shadowy forest perimeter to their right was their only guide.

'How far do we have to go?' The wind snatched the words from Litwak's mouth and flung them back at him. There was no response from the priest. Was he ignoring him or had he just not heard what he said? Litwak had to break into a run occasionally to keep up with the pace of the man's strides. Suddenly, Steiner turned towards him. 'You have to keep up. We can't stay out too long. It's far too dangerous.'

'What about the tracks? What if someone sees them?'

'They won't.' Steiner was shouting at him, squinting against the force of the wind and the driving snow. 'In this storm, all trace of you will be gone in minutes. Just thank the gods for the snow and the wind. By morning, no one will know you or I were ever here.'

They skirted around several patches of forest. Eventually they came to the edge of a village and a small church with a tall thin spire. It was overshadowed by a large house, the presbytery. Steiner took him up some steps to a back door and into the kitchen, where a glass of milk and a plate of black rye bread and cold meat were on the table covered by a damp cloth. The priest motioned him to sit down and eat. Litwak took the cloth off the food and realized how hungry he was.

He heard Steiner speaking to someone upstairs. There was a woman's voice, too quiet to make out what she was saying, although whatever it was, she was annoyed. There was something about the voice. Whatever the priest said in response, it was very firm, clearly authoritative. It was as if he was chastising her for talking out of turn. The voices stopped and Litwak heard footsteps and a door closing somewhere in the distance. He was finishing off the last piece of black bread when there was the sound of someone coming down the stairs and the priest reappeared, motioning Litwak to follow him.

They went up two flights of stairs and down a long corridor. A small oil lamp sat on a rough wooden chair beside the bed; the yellow flame flickered in the draft, throwing shadows across the room. There was a wardrobe with some drawers and a writing desk with another chair tucked under it. Placed to one side on the top of the desk was a white china bowl, a jug full of water, some soap, and a small white towel. For a priest's house, it seemed curiously soulless. The blankets had been turned down to reveal heavy linen sheets. Litwak put down his gear and turned to Steiner. For the first time since they had met in the field four hours earlier, the priest smiled briefly. Then he nodded, mouthed a silent 'good night,' and went out, closing the door behind him.

Litwak washed his face and hands, lay back on the bed, exhausted from the forced march and the adrenaline rush of the jump, and swiftly fell asleep.

He's back in the kitchen. The priest is furious. His face contorted with rage. He's shouting at Jonny. Ranting. His voice fills the room. He seems to be speaking German, but Jonny can't understand a word he's saying. A woman walks into the room and stands behind the priest. Smiling. Nodding. Agreeing with everything he says. Jonny can't see her clearly, but he has the distinct impression he knows her. Slowly the contours of her face come into focus and he realizes that the woman is Kate.

Chapter Fourteen

Wednesday 20 January 1943

At least he knew who the priest had been talking to now. It was odd that he hadn't recognized her voice the previous night, and yet somewhere in the back of his mind it must have registered that the woman arguing with the priest was Kate. That explained the dream. He'd barely thought about her in the past few months. Why on earth would he? It was over. And he'd had far too much else to think about just training for the mission.

He'd been shaving when Kate walked in. He'd assumed the knock was Father Josef. It was a shock to see Kate standing in the doorway. Was this a part of the plan they hadn't told him about? Had they sent her to make sure he did the job properly? And why her? Why Kate? Did they know about the affair? Had the whole thing been a setup from the very beginning? A test?

'What are you doing here?'

'I'm here to make sure nothing goes wrong.'

He was instinctively irritated. Did someone in London think he needed babysitting?

'Goes wrong with what?'

'Goes wrong with your mission. Or rather, goes wrong with our operations as a result of your mission.'

'My mission? What the fuck do you know about my mission?' Op Steeple was highly secret, on very close hold, even within SOE. How on earth would she know anything about it? She sat on the bed and watched him shave. That irritating habit of ignoring anything he said that didn't fit with what she wanted. Like the end of the affair. She'd wanted to keep it going when they left Beaulieu. Was that why she was here? 'Did you wangle this job because of me?'

'What…? God, no!' It was a very firm response. No anger. More dismay. For a moment, he thought he saw tears. 'I was sent out to make sure nothing happens to the priest, to protect the safe house and the work the priest is doing here.'

'What work?'

'Helping people like you, Jonny.' She said his name oddly. Tenderly. As if it were separate from everything else she was saying. 'My bosses in London were ordered to help you. They think this is a mistake, the SOE stirring up trouble, making things difficult for our spies on the ground. But they've been ordered to help you, so they have. I'm here to make sure nothing goes wrong.'

'Goes wrong with what?'

'With everything. Our safe house. Our networks. The priest.'

'Forget your fucking networks.' He wasn't going to hide his irritation. He needed to put her under pressure, make her realize who was in charge. 'You still haven't told me what you think my mission is.'

'To kill Hitler.'

How did she know? He had to keep his head. He mustn't react. Just put the pressure on her to talk.

'I'm not here to help you with your mission. As I said, my bosses think it's a bad idea. They won't be disappointed if it fails.'

Still, he didn't respond. He rinsed the remaining soap from his face and towelled himself dry, giving himself time to think before turning towards her. 'Why? How could killing Hitler be wrong? Whose side are those fucking idiots on?'

'They think killing him will only prolong the war. Hitler's an inept general. That's what they say. If it were left to the real generals, the Germans would have more of a chance. Killing Hitler will be counterproductive.'

'Not so far as I'm concerned.' He was angry, unsure of how to deal with her. First, she'd appeared from nowhere, now she was claiming that her bosses didn't want him to succeed. The idea that anyone in London wanted to protect Hitler was obscene. He sat down beside her on the bed, his mind scrambling to comprehend the situation and work out a way forward.

'This is ridiculous. You were in Berlin. You saw the way we were treated. Your bosses must realize that Hitler's the one ordering the murders of the Jews. If he's dead, that will all stop. They must be able to see that.'

'I don't think they do see that, Jonny. And even if they do, I don't think they care.' She sounded frustrated rather than angry. As if she'd argued long and hard in favour of killing Hitler. 'But it's irrelevant. Churchill's told them to help you so they have no choice. They have to help you. I'm just here to make sure you don't succeed.'

'Really? And how precisely do you propose to do that?'

'It's complicated. But my role's very clear. I have to protect our agents. I have to protect our networks.' She paused, as if she was trying to work it out in her own mind. 'But I can't see how I can do that without at least making sure you don't get detected. So as far as I can see, I am going to have to help you.'

'But your bosses won't like that.'

'No, they won't, but if they want me to protect the networks, they haven't got much choice. I need to cover your backside.'

'I don't need you to cover my backside.'

'Why not? It's quite a nice backside.'

She was the first woman he'd slept with. Beaulieu had been good. He'd needed an experienced woman to show him the ropes.

But it was never going to last. It had been time to move on. Anyway, he knew they were bound to send him back into Germany. He had to concentrate on the job, on learning how to stay alive once he was there.

He'd forgot how pretty she was. She'd bleached her dark hair blonde and pinned it back. But she still had what the English called the look of the girl next door. She returned his smile, but as he moved his lips towards her, she pulled back.

'So how precisely do you plan to kill Hitler?'

'I'll show you.'

'They surely didn't let you bring the plans with you?'

'I had to. If my main plan doesn't work, I'll need an alternative.'

He shouldn't have brought them. It was a risk, a breach of the rules. But he couldn't have done the job without the detailed maps of the security zone surrounding Hitler's home on the Obersalzberg, and the path to the *Teehaus* that the Führer walked every day.

'Let me see them.'

Litwak unfolded the smaller blade on his jack knife, picked open the stitching under his jacket collar, and extracted several folded sheets of paper. He placed them on the desk, smoothed out the creases, and handed them to her, watching her face to see the shock as she read them.

He wasn't disappointed.

She looked up at him immediately, her eyes round with surprise. 'Both of them.'

He shrugged.

'That's what it says.'

Kate reached the last paragraph and burst out laughing. She turned the pages over as if she was trying to find something that was missing.

'What are you looking for?'

'The schematic diagram of how you're supposed to seduce the French cleaning lady on the Führer's train.'

'It was a diagram of the train. Not of the seduction. I didn't bring it with me. I've brought a sniper rifle, with telescopic sights.

'I'll pick them both off as they walk to the *Teehaus*. Seducing a French cleaning lady was always a stupid plan.'

Kate laughed at him, the same way she'd laughed at him at Beaulieu. 'Oh, I don't know. They probably picked the right man.'

She laughed again, then leaned towards him, looking into his eyes; unpinning her hair so it brushed against his face. She lay back on the bed, watching him, teasing him. He bent down to kiss her.

They made love slowly. There was none of the rushed passion of Beaulieu. He felt no need to force himself on her. She was a willing, eager partner. But he refused to let himself go. Even when her soft moans became more frequent, almost frantic, he maintained a steady pace. Afterward, huddled together on the bed, they felt the cold of the room. They crawled under the blankets. He lay on his back, holding her in one arm, her head against his chest. She kissed him on the cheek and smiled.

'Both of them together, eh?' She lifted her head up and looked at him. He nodded. 'Yes. Both of them together. Too good an opportunity to miss.'

'I'm impressed. It might even make my bosses change their minds.' She leaned across and kissed him. Just a peck on the lips. 'I missed you,' she said. 'I didn't want to. But I did.'

She was still in love with him. It didn't really surprise him. What did surprise him was that he still had feelings for her. But he had to be professional, had to keep his mind on the job, and there was still the matter of her row with the priest. If there were problems one way or another with the priest, he had to know.

'So why were you arguing with Steiner?'

'Me? Arguing with Father Josef? When?'

'Last night. That was you arguing with him, wasn't it?'

'Oh, I see. I didn't realize you could hear.'

'I didn't hear what you were saying; I just heard the row.'

Again that laugh. Did she think he was a fool, that he didn't know what she was doing?

'We were arguing because I wanted to come to see you. Father Josef wouldn't let me. Perhaps he didn't think it appropriate for a young woman to go to a young man's room in the middle of the night, particularly not in his presbytery.'

'But now you are here.'

'Father Josef 's out, ministering to his flock. God knows what he'd say if he could see us here, alone in your room.'

Litwak thought of the priest, then back to his bedroom in the old Erfurt apartment. His mother running in as the Brownshirts beat down the door.

Kate slid out of bed and began to get dressed. As she buttoned her blouse, she turned towards him. 'None of those plans have any chance of success. You do realize that, don't you, Jonny? They're right to think the sniper attack is the best hope, but you're never going to get anywhere near the Berghof. Mussolini and Hitler together. The place will be crawling with guards.'

He got out of bed and opened the rucksack, taking out the trousers and jacket of a German uniform. 'It's the uniform of a corporal in the mountain troops. Apparently, everyone wears a variant of this uniform around here, even the guards at the Berghof.'

She laughed. 'Everyone? Do you really think that's likely? And you as a corporal in the mountain troops? You wouldn't last beyond your first encounter with an SS patrol. Dansey was right. Your lot haven't got a clue. Sorry, Jonny. But this is real amateur stuff.'

Litwak wanted to grab her, to slap her, to wipe the smirk off of her face. Who was she to tell the SOE planners – or him – how to mount an operation? So she'd done the Beaulieu course. So what? All she'd done since was sit behind a desk in London living off the risks taken by her agents. 'I think the people who planned this operation have a pretty good idea of what will work and what won't. It wasn't just thrown together. Unless you can think of a better way of getting through the security cordon, I'll take my chances with the uniform.'

'What chances? There isn't a chance of that story ringing true. Your corporal can't have any real reason for being anywhere near the Berghof in uniform. You'd be shown up as an imposter the minute they made a phone call.'

'Why do you care? Isn't that what your bosses want?'

'I'm not sure anymore. They didn't know you were going to liquidate Hitler and Mussolini together. That changes everything.'

'Liquidate?' The word sounded contrived. Did she think he'd be impressed with the easy way it slipped off her tongue, as if this were something MI6 did all the time? But if she'd detected the ridicule in his voice, she ignored it.

'You'd be much better off in civilian clothes, Jonny. A soldier on leave from the front, hiking with his sister, a bit of skiing. That's much more believable. The papers have us both as the priest's nephew and niece. What would be more natural?'

Litwak was instantly suspicious. 'Why do your papers make me your brother?'

'It was the simplest thing. It made sense. It's a cover I created when I was in Berlin before the war, for a man and a woman working together to help the priest: his nephew and his niece. One or the other could be used on their own or together without arousing suspicion. We were asked to provide you with help, so we had to let you use a decent cover.'

She was right. A walking and skiing holiday was a far more plausible reason for being there, and if they were stopped he'd feel more comfortable in civilian clothes.

Chapter Fifteen

Thursday 21 January 1943

Ritter didn't consider himself to be a jealous man. He was by nature a loner. He didn't need a woman in his life. He could live more easily on his own than with anyone else, even Sophie. Right now, especially Sophie.

The more he obsessed about the idea that she was having an affair with Kleidorfer, the more convinced he became. He was beginning to detect signs of betrayal in almost everything she did, so much so that he doubted her far more often than he doubted his own judgment. Sophie's absence combined with Kleidorfer's failure to turn up at the Schweizerhof only reinforced his concerns. The notion of infidelity was bad enough; that the object of her affection was Kleidorfer seemed intolerable. So intolerable that he began to formulate a detailed plan in his mind to kill the bitch and fit Kleidorfer up for her murder. The hotel was a bad idea. Getting them there would be too difficult. Better to wait for her to invite Kleidorfer in when he dropped her off at home. That would give him complete control of the situation, allow him to plant the evidence he needed to pin her murder on that prick.

The examination of Drexler's body took some time and it was around two in the morning by the time Ritter got back from the Schweizerhof. By the time he got up, Sophie was already on her way out. 'Going shopping.' She didn't say where, or for what, and he didn't ask, although he noted that she was wearing her fur coat, unusual for a routine visit to the shops. The next time he saw her, he was walking to work. He'd cut through the Munchener Strasse on his way up to the Max-Josefs-Platz. Sophie was standing outside the department store looking up into Kleidorfer's face, seemingly oblivious to the biting cold wind. Ritter ducked into a shop doorway when he saw them. They were both smiling, chatting comfortably. For a moment, he felt guilty for spying on her. Then she rubbed Kleidorfer's arm and the Gestapo officer bent down to kiss her cheek. Sophie moved her lips to meet his. When he lifted his head, her face was left exposed still mouthing her own kiss, before breaking into another smile. The kind of smile a woman reserves for the man she loves. That line from Stramm. What was it?

The smile that rends my heart.

There were two files lying on Ritter's desk when he got into the office. One was very thin. It looked new. Drexler – Murder Investigation was scrawled across it in Messel's handwriting. The file contained photographs of Drexler's body and the bloody hotel room, plus a note from Viktor Kozlowski putting the time of death at around seven o'clock the previous evening, shortly after Ritter's confrontation with Steiner up on the Kaiserstrasse. The pathologist's note promised more detail after he'd had time to carry out a full post-mortem.

The other file was thicker. It wasn't a *Kripo* file. It had Gestapo in large gothic script on the front above the eagle and swastika emblem and was labelled KK Various. KK. Klaus Kleidorfer. How had one of Kleidorfer's files come to be lying on his desk?

Had Kleidorfer left it there? If he'd been in the office on his own he would surely have been trying to find out what was in the Schinkel file, looking for the name of the witness who saw the body being dumped down by the bridge. Ritter scanned his drawers for any sign of a break-in. He pulled on the top two. Both opened easily. He'd definitely locked them, but there was nothing he was worried about in either of them. The lock on the bottom drawer, where the Schinkel file lay hidden, had some fresh scratches, as if someone had tried to force it open with a knife. But it was still locked. He opened it. The scrap of paper was still on top of the file precisely where he'd left it. Kleidorfer had brought a gift but hadn't taken anything in return. Nothing but Sophie.

So what was in the KK file? He began to flick through the pages. There was little of any interest. Mainly minor offenses, breaches of war regulations. Standard small-time fare for the Gestapo in a quiet Bavarian town. A note on a Polish woman caught in flagrante with a French prisoner of war. A railway worker convicted of sabotage, although the statement from his boss indicated that the damage to equipment was a result of the railway company's incompetence. A farmer arrested for selling black market butter and eggs. The evidence was substantial but he'd been let off with a caution – no doubt having pledged to ensure that Kleidorfer never ran short of food.

There were a number of reports from various *V-Personen*, informants. Mostly uninteresting and unsubstantiated allegations against neighbours who had variously told jokes against the Führer, obtained more food than they were entitled to, or supposedly listened into enemy radio broadcasts, albeit without even the rather insubstantial evidence that Hanna Stolz had produced of Albrecht's 'treason.' It was all typical of the stuff in the 'unsolved' case files stacked against Ritter's walls. He became bored, flicking through the papers too quickly, not paying enough attention. Then a line in one of the reports caught his eye.

The target spent a long time in the company of the prostitute Müller.

He was several pages further on before the name registered. He turned them back. The report was an account of 'the target' spending a Friday night with Müller in room 17 in the Schweizerhof. It was exactly a week after the Schinkel murder. The informant was identified solely as HO. It had to be Heinrich Olbricht, Liesl's son. So Heinrich was a *V-Person*. There was not much doubt who 'the target' was. Room 17 was Drexler's room. The room where his body had been discovered. He and Müller had a weekly date. Drexler's payoff for keeping the prostitute out of jail. But why was the Gestapo boss a target for an investigation by his own deputy?

There were a number of other reports from Heinrich on activity in the Schweizerhof. Several recording Drexler's liaisons with Müller, others the arrival and behaviour of the various occupants of the hotel on the night that Schinkel was killed. Heinrich seemed to have got the arrival times of the two Swiss women mixed up. But nothing in the reports of the events leading up to the two murders told Ritter anything that Liesl hadn't disclosed.

Heinrich's report of the actual night of Schinkel's murder was more revealing. He described 'the target' as having been with Müller in room 17 that night. This wasn't new; Drexler had admitted as much. But Heinrich's report also recorded Drexler's furious reaction to the murder. He'd screamed at Liesl, blaming her for what had happened, and called Bauer and Paul Eckart, the most brutal of his Gestapo thugs, to dress the body and dump it somewhere. Anywhere. They'd taken it out of the Schweizerhof at the back, dragging it into a car and driving off. Once the body had been removed, Drexler had simply gone back to room 17 and spent the rest of the night receiving his payoff.

Ritter was searching through the rest of the file for more reports by Heinrich when Kleidorfer walked in.

'Why didn't you call me last night, Ritter? My boss gets himself murdered and you don't think to call me. I'm disappointed.'

Kleidorfer stayed by the door. The matter-of-fact way in which he'd asked the question was odd. Ritter would have expected anger. There was none. He wondered if he might ask Kleidorfer in a similarly matter-of-fact way whether he'd been with Sophie when his boss was murdered and whether he would really have wanted to be interrupted.

Ritter suddenly felt very tired. He'd assumed the Gestapo had been told. Or had he been afraid of who might answer Kleidorfer's phone? 'Did no one ring you? I thought the desk would have done it. Anyway, weren't you under orders from Drexler to follow me every minute of the day? Where were you?'

Despite Kleidorfer's disappearance on the night of the murder, Ritter hadn't really seen him as a suspect, although the file on Drexler suggested that he might need to adopt a more open mind.

'Nobody rang. Nobody at all. But it doesn't matter now.' The Gestapo boss had ignored the question as to where he'd been that night. But that didn't mean he was the killer. He was scarcely likely to have admitted he was with Sophie. 'I see you've read the file?'

Ritter looked at Kleidorfer, wondering why he'd been so keen to let him see Heinrich's reports from the Schweizerhof. 'Yes. It's extremely interesting. Shouldn't you have handed this stuff over earlier?'

'What? And have you tried to arrest Drexler on the basis of an internal Gestapo surveillance operation set up by me? You must think I'm mad. No. I've been watching him for a while, collecting dirt on him, with Müller's assistance.'

So Kleidorfer had been after his boss's job. Looking to find a way to discredit him, or worse. Well, he didn't need to do that anymore. The job was as good as his. Müller was Kleidorfer's informant, not Drexler's. What a wonderful bunch they all were.

'So why pass this on to me now? I'd have thought that now Drexler's been murdered you'd want to take the case over yourself.'

'No. Why? You're the murder detective, not me. Drexler's just a piece of shit that's been cleared away. Someone's done us a favour. Just like they did with the Jew. I've spoken to Munich and Berlin. I'm to take charge of the Gestapo post.' Kleidorfer said it with obvious pleasure, another notch on his career plan. He didn't have any qualms about stepping into a dead man's shoes. 'But they're insistent that Drexler's murder is to be left to you.'

'To me?'

'Yes. You. For some reason, they want you to do it. Whatever their reasons, they're right. None of our people have got time to go looking for a simple murderer. Munich is too busy trying to deal with your White Rose delinquents and Berlin isn't interested. You're the detective. You're supposed to be the expert on murder. You tidy it up.'

Kleidorfer looked around the room at the various files stacked against the walls, then at Ritter. 'I assume we can trust you to tidy something up?'

The new Gestapo boss wasn't able to resist the joke. He'd have that prick laughing on the other side of his face before long. Munich didn't trust Kleidorfer. That was probably the only reason they'd kept him off the Drexler case. So he was vulnerable and he couldn't know about the spy in the Schweizerhof. If he did know, he'd have used it against Drexler before now and he'd be demanding that Ritter hand the case over to the Gestapo, shortage of staff or not. They had to get as much as possible out of the Schweizerhof reports while they had them. There had to be something there that would help hang Kleidorfer out to dry.

'How long do I have this file?'

Kleidorfer shrugged. 'Munich said to let you see it. So you've seen it. Take copies of any documents you need and send it back to me when you've finished with it. There's nothing else in there that matters right now.'

Messel pushed his way past the Gestapo officer into the office carrying some paperwork. Kleidorfer looked surprised by the boy's lack of respect. But his smile soon returned. 'Anything interesting on Commissar Drexler's murder, Messel?'

'No. Nothing. This is about an old case. Nothing for the Gestapo.'

The boy's reaction was in stark contrast to his previous cultivation of Kleidorfer. An almost studied indifference. If the new Gestapo boss was looking for acknowledgment that he still had an ally in Messel, he was disappointed. Only once the door had closed behind the new Gestapo boss did Ritter feel able to relax.

'What's all that about, boss?' Messel asked.

'I don't know. But whatever it is, it'll be in his interest, not ours.'

'Something's certainly cheered him up. Maybe Drexler's death.'

Ritter looked up. Maybe not Drexler's death. Maybe something else. Quite possibly both. Drexler's death and Sophie. Ritter handed Kleidorfer's file to Messel and told him to go through it, copying all the reports where the informant was given as HO. 'They're Heinrich Jr.'s reports on the Schweizerhof. There's lots of stuff there on both the Schinkel case and Drexler.'

'Why on earth has Kleidorfer suddenly decided to hand this over?'

'No idea, Messel. He says he's been gathering dirt on Drexler. Perhaps he's trying to stop anyone in Munich or Berlin from getting concerned enough to block his promotion.'

'You don't think…?'

Messel let the question hang in the air. But if Munich saw Kleidorfer as a suspect, it would explain why they'd been so insistent that he should investigate Drexler's killing.

'I don't know, Messel. It's clear from the file that he was trying to get rid of Drexler. But murder? Too dangerous. If he'd got it wrong, he'd be a dead man. No. Kozlowski thought it was a crime of passion. The killer got "some sort of release." Marianne Müller's the obvious suspect, and if she didn't do it, she'll have a good idea who did. We need to find her before they do.'

'Are we sure she was there with him last night?'

'He'd taken off his suit and shirt and he certainly wasn't there to sleep. It's their regular night. Looking at Heinrich's reports, they meet there, met there, every Friday.'

'Just after confession?'

Ritter laughed. The idea of Drexler confessing his sins was difficult to imagine. 'Not his style, Messel. You go and talk to Drexler's wife and the secretary Anja Vogel. Charm her. She won't talk to me. Maybe your Party poster-boy good looks will work for her. I'll go to the Schweizerhof and talk to Liesl. Oh, and if you find any indication in the file that Müller was working for Kleidorfer, copy that too.'

'Müller was what…?'

'Yes, Messel.'

'But.'

'Yes. I know. But Kleidorfer admitted it to me. Müller was providing him with reports on Drexler. I doubt he's so stupid as to have left any clues in the file that she was his source. But check carefully. Just in case.'

Liesl proved difficult. She was fussing around the reception desk, still badly shaken by the events of the previous night. She insisted she had no idea where Müller was. Ritter took her into her office. She poured them both a brandy. Her hand still trembled.

'I can't help you, Peter. I haven't seen her. She definitely wasn't here last night.'

'It's all right, Liesl. Drexler can't hurt you now, can he? But if Marianne didn't kill him, she probably knows who did. She's going to be next. You owe it to her to tell me where she is. It might save her life.'

Liesl looked as tired as he'd felt during his conversation with Kleidorfer. She didn't have the strength to resist anymore. She wrote down an address and handed it to him. 'But Marianne didn't do it.'

He looked at the piece of paper, folded it over, and put it in his pocket. 'Then she's got nothing to worry about. Has she?'

Chapter Sixteen

Friday 22 January 1943

The road to Riedering was deep in snow. To the south, the Bavarian Alps cut a jagged edge in a clear blue sky, but Rosenheim seemed permanently swathed in heavy grey clouds. Sporadic falls of snow swirled hypnotically in front of Ritter. The ruts in the snow from earlier traffic were all that kept the BMW on the road. The spruce trees in the forest to his right loomed towards him – dark green shadows sprinkled with white, closing in.

Marianne Müller had to be the main suspect in the Drexler killing, bar himself and the priest, of course, and he knew he hadn't done it. The prostitute would need to have a pretty good story to convince him she wasn't involved. With the murder of any man, the mistress and the wife were bound to be the main suspects.

His suspicions of Müller were increased by the fact that she'd gone to ground since the murder. Liesl said it was natural: Marianne was grieving. But then, Liesl said a lot of things. She'd said Müller wasn't in the hotel on the night Drexler died. She'd also said she wouldn't be seen dead with Heinrich. Ritter remembered all too clearly how that one turned out. He was pretty certain Müller was involved in some way, or at the very least had been there when Drexler was killed. The Gestapo boss would scarcely have stripped off for a meeting with him, and, since Müller was Kleidorfer's agent, any involvement by her in Drexler's demise might be seen as raising questions over what role he might have played. That would be one way of getting rid of him for good.

The house Liesl claimed Müller was staying in was on the other side of Riedering. Ritter found it easily enough from the description. He steered the BMW cautiously into a snowdrift rather than risk skidding on the smooth, tightly packed snow.

It was a remarkably imposing building for a small village, three stories at least from the windows, maybe more, and covered in off-white stucco. The dark wooden beams were left bare and there were two rows of plain windows high up with wooden shutters, some open, some closed. Müller didn't own this house. It was far too big for a small-town prostitute. Maybe she rented a room. There were two arches to the left and a metre-high crucifix bearing the body of Christ above the door. This couldn't be the right place.

Ritter knocked on the heavy oak door. He could hear movement inside, but it was a few minutes before a grille slid open and a nun wearing the white wimple and black veil of a Benedictine nun peered out. She released a series of noisy locks and opened the door. Ritter instinctively removed his hat. 'Oh, I'm sorry. I must have come to the wrong house. I'm looking for Frau Marianne Müller.'

'No, you've come to the right house. I believe she's expecting you.'

Ritter was at first surprised and then irritated that his arrival was anticipated. Liesl must have ignored his insistence that she was not to warn Müller. The nun ushered him into a large, dark entrance hall, off-white like the exterior, apart from the dark wooden beams. The ceiling was very high. The nun indicated a seat on a bare wooden bench. Ritter remained standing, watching as she left through one of the doors. When he turned to sit down, Müller was standing immediately behind him. Looking at him. Waiting for him to speak.

'Frau Müller. I'm Inspector Peter Ritter from the Rosenheim.'

Müller glanced at his proffered hand and ignored it. 'I know who you are and I can guess why you're here. Ask me your questions and go.'

'Is there somewhere more private where we can talk?'

She silently turned towards the first door and took him into a room with a number of bare wooden chairs arranged in a circle. Like the hall, it was a frugal room with off-white walls split by wooden beams. There was another large crucifix on one wall and a very long painting on wood of the Last Supper on another. The wall at one end of the room was entirely covered in a painting of a female saint, a nun. She was ascending to heaven on a golden cloud from the Fraueninsel, the island on the Chiemsee, fifteen kilometres to the east, where the nuns had their abbey.

The room smelled of an incongruous mix of disinfectant and beeswax. The bare wooden floors were scrubbed clean, the chairs dark and highly polished. The windows were all high up on the walls, making it impossible to look in or out of the room. Square beams of intense golden light thrust their way down onto the bleached floorboards, forming a V-shaped frame supporting the nun's ascent. Thousands of tiny particles of dust floated in the light. But still it seemed clean. Pure as the white of the snow-covered mountains to the south.

Another woman sat in one of the hard, wooden chairs. Ritter recognized her immediately as the blonde woman in Söllhuben on the day they'd waved off the dead Swiss boy. Was this really the Swiss woman Martyl Scharf? She was a good-looking woman, but with the bright light behind her he couldn't see if she had a birthmark on her neck. Whoever she was, she seemed confident and unfazed by his arrival, as if she was expecting to see him, even looking forward to it. Müller stood behind her, hands on her shoulders. Scharf, if that was who she was, reached up to clasp the prostitute's hand. A show of support.

'This is my friend, Frau Inge Schultz. She's been sitting with me. It's been a difficult time since Gert's murder. She's been a good friend.'

Ritter nodded towards the woman Müller had called Schultz. The prostitute sat down next to her and motioned the detective into another chair facing them. Ritter was happy to let Müller think she was in control. He wanted her to be sufficiently overconfident, so that she'd make a mistake. She might be worried about whoever killed Drexler, but she certainly wasn't scared of Ritter. Drexler had gone but she probably still thought Kleidorfer was there to protect her. It gave her an arrogance that might encourage her to think she had the upper hand.

But he had to challenge the Schultz woman. It would look odd if he accepted Müller's word, and anyway, he needed to check her papers for any hint of who she really was.

'Good afternoon, Frau Schultz. Can I see your pass and work-book, please?'

'Of course, Inspector.' She leaned across to hand them over. Ritter studied them carefully, ostentatiously holding up the photograph on the identity card to match it against her face. There was no doubt that this was Scharf. The pass and workbook confirmed the name Inge Schultz, with the pass giving a single distinguishing feature, a light brown birthmark on the left of her neck. So the woman who'd booked into the Schweizerhof on the night that Schinkel died was the same woman who'd signalled to the priest at the service in Söllhuben. The birthmark and description were too much of a coincidence for it to be otherwise. One or the other of Müller or Schultz was a British spy, possibly both of them. That much was clear from the fingerprints. And at least one of them was a killer. Ritter was sure of that. He just wasn't sure which one. He needed to split them up, test their stories against each other. It was a shame he hadn't brought Messel with him. Still, he could at least try to talk to each of them separately.

'Thank you, Frau Schultz. That's fine. Now, if you don't mind, I need to talk to your friend alone.'

Ritter stood up, handed the papers back to Schultz, and looked at each woman in turn, waiting for a response. They seemed uncertain as to what to do next. They looked at each other. Then Müller took charge. 'I'm sorry, Inspector. Inge stays. There's nothing that I would want to hide from her.'

Back at the station, he'd have called the shots. They would have done what they were told. But not here. Not on his own. There was no way Ritter could force them to do what he said. He could scarcely manhandle them in a Benedictine refuge. There was little point in arguing. He sat back down.

'As you wish. So what exactly are you doing here, Frau Müller?'

Ritter gestured to the crucifix hanging on the wall. 'I don't mean to be rude, but it's not exactly the kind of place I'd expect to find you.'

'Really, Inspector? The nuns look after me. It's what they do, look after…'

'They know what you do? Do they? When you come to Rosenheim?'

'You mean, do they know I'm a whore?'

Ritter ignored the ridicule in her voice and on her face. Schultz reached across, gently rubbing Müller's arm, as if she was trying to calm her down.

'They know why I'm here, Inspector. This is a refuge for fallen women run by the nuns from the Fraueninsel. The nuns understand life is difficult for women, especially during wartime. Inge understands that. Liesl understands that. I'm not surprised you don't.'

Ritter made a great play of opening his notebook and taking his pen out of his inside jacket pocket, acting the dull, bureaucratic official, determined to take everything down in writing. 'Tell me, Frau Müller. I must ask you about yesterday, the day that Commissar Drexler was killed. Where were you? Please account for your movements at all times of the day. What did you do first thing in the morning?'

Müller's response was sullen. 'I did nothing. I was here most of the day. The nuns will confirm that.'

'Most of the day?'

'I spent yesterday evening with Inge at her uncle's house. He's a priest. Is a priest's word a good enough alibi for you?'

Ritter laughed. 'The priest and the tart. Sounds like an old joke. What time did you arrive at the priest's house?'

Müller looked at Schultz, who answered for her. 'About four o'clock. We ate around half five. Uncle Josef went out for an hour or so. I think he said he had to see a parishioner. He was back by half seven. He could confirm we were there.'

Ritter already knew who the priest must be, but he asked anyway. 'So where can I find him? Your priest?'

Again, it was 'Schultz' who answered. Confident. Not at all concerned by Ritter's questioning. There was something odd about her. This wasn't the type of woman to bleach her hair.

'In Söllhuben. You can't miss the presbytery. It's next to the church of Saint Rupert. Uncle Josef – I mean, Father Josef will be happy to tell you that Marianne was with us all evening.'

Ritter carefully noted down the name, continuing to play the bureaucrat. It certainly wasn't a good enough alibi. Given the confrontation the previous night out on the Kaiserstrasse, when the priest was supposedly 'visiting a parishioner,' and the various links between Steiner and Schultz, or Scharf, they were clearly part of a conspiracy that almost certainly embraced both murders.

'Thank you. I've met Father Steiner. But I'll check the story with him.' He looked at Schultz, giving her the opportunity to say more.

'It's true, Inspector. We played Schafkopf. Marianne's a natural. It's remarkable. She knows instinctively when to play every card in her hand.'

'So, Frau Müller. You were playing cards at a priest's house? You never went to the Schweizerhof?'

'No. But Liesl must have told you that.' Müller was growing ever more confident, increasingly dismissive of Ritter. 'You're a very distrustful person, Inspector. If you won't accept alibis given by nuns and priests, who will you accept them from?'

'I haven't spoken to the nuns or the priest yet. So right now, I've only got your word for it.'

Müller didn't react. Ritter nodded towards both women. 'You two know each other well, then?'

Schultz slid her hand from Müller's arm onto the prostitute's thigh and then moved it towards her crotch, only a few centimetres, but enough to give him the idea. She kept looking at Ritter, smiling, maintaining eye contact.

'Yes, Inspector. We do know each other very well. Very well indeed.'

Ritter got up to leave. He was wasting his time here. Müller stood up and led him out through the hall. It was getting dark. Once inside the BMW, he started the engine and waited for it to warm, lighting a cigarette. The lesbian double act wouldn't have fooled the most desperate of Müller's tricks. But their close relationship suggested that there wasn't just one British spy. So there probably wasn't just one killer, either. Better slip the Sauer into his coat pocket when he went to meet the priest.

Chapter Seventeen

Friday 22 January 1943

It was snowing when Ritter left Riedering, although it was nowhere near as heavy as the blizzards that seemed to have blown in from the Alps on any given day that winter. Tiny flakes danced around the car in the wind without ever threatening to tax the BMW's windscreen wipers or to obscure Ritter's vision.

He'd hoped for a clear run back into Rosenheim but reached the main road a minute or so too late. A long convoy of Wehrmacht lorries was trundling towards him. It was too risky to pull out in front of them. Much of the snow that had collected on the road over the winter had melted. But there was still a ridge of compacted snow and ice running along either side. If the first lorry braked too hard it would have been bound to skid, causing chaos all the way back down the convoy.

A dozen olive-green lorries passed Ritter at a tedious pace. He pulled out behind the last one only to see another half a dozen bearing down on him in his rear-view mirror. He was trapped between two slow-moving heavy lorries. Probably all the way back to Rosenheim. It was at least undemanding driving. But the snow was becoming heavier, the flakes more persistent. There was a hypnotic monotony to the wipers' steady swish from one side to the other set against the convoy's slow, steady progress.

A strip of forest ran along the southern side of the road over to Ritter's left. A small group of deer were clustered at the edge of the forest: a couple of does and several fawns led by a young stag. The stag stood proud and erect, displaying no deference to the lorries, intent only on leading the small herd across to the other side. An old black Bussing truck was coming in the other direction. The stag seemed confused. It first went to run out, hesitated, and then made a dash for the other side. The driver of the old Bussing could do nothing to avoid it.

The army driver in front of Ritter must have stamped his foot right down on the brakes to avoid the collision. Ritter braked hard, only just managing to keep control of the BMW by letting it run onto the verge. In front of him, the brake lights of the army lorry glowed bright red through the snow as the driver struggled to keep it on the icy road. It slithered from side to side, the taillights and brake lights fusing through the snow into a mass of red, the blood red that had dominated Ritter's nightmares for more than five years.

It is always the same. It's dark. the snow is heavy. too heavy. The BMW's headlights are reflecting off the swirling white shroud, confusing his eyes. He looks across at Sophie asleep beside him. Her hands lie on her lap either side of her swollen belly. Holding it. Shielding it. Finally, after fifteen years of trying. Fifteen years of failure. Sophie is pregnant. She's nearly forty. It's their last chance. This will be their only child. Ritter smiles at the effect it will have on their marriage, binding them together. He looks back at the road.

But he can't see the road. It's disappeared. All he can see is white. He's not even sure they're still on the road. There should be woods off to the left. But he can't see them. Can't see anything through the white morass. Dark shadows loom up in front of them. He brakes. The car goes into a skid. Ritter sees the tree too late. But he doesn't feel the jolt. Doesn't see Sophie's body thrown forward towards the dashboard, before the impact tosses her back onto her seat.

Ritter wakes slowly. He struggles to open his eyes. They're drawn to Sophie slumped on the seat next to him, to the small patch of red on Sophie's skirt that he's never noticed before. His brain wants to shut down. To blot out the scene in front of him. He can't resist the compulsion to close his eyes. But reality takes over. Adrenaline pumps

*through his body, forcing him awake. His eyes open wide. Drawn
back to the patch of red that is spreading rapidly across Sophie's skirt.
She is sitting with her legs curled up on the seat. Has she been knocked
unconscious? Or is she simply still asleep? He looks down. A small
pool of blood is collecting on the floorboard in front of Sophie's seat.
He traces it back. There's a line of blood running out from under her
skirt and down her knee before dripping slowly to the floor.*

'Are you all right?'

'What?'

Someone was knocking on the window, dragging Ritter back to
reality. Back from that moment when any hope that they might have
a child came to an end.

Ritter looked around. The convoy had gone. The lorries behind
him must have overtaken him. The black truck was still there. Ritter
wound down his window. It was a woman, wearing scruffy trousers,
a dark, heavy woollen jacket, and a ski cap.

'What is it?'

'I just hit a deer. I need some help getting it up onto my truck.'

Ritter got out of his car. They walked over to where the stag was
lying. The rest of the herd had melted back into the forest. The old
black Bussing seemed to have suffered only minor damage. Given
its condition, it wasn't even clear to Ritter that the dents hadn't been
there before. The stag was still twitching, still fighting, but it was only
a matter of time. It would have been easier just to drag it off the road,
but there was a lot of unrationed meat there, plenty to last a family a
couple of months. It was easy to see why the woman didn't want to
leave it for someone else to find.

'Turn your lorry round, so the back's as close as possible to the deer.'

The woman wasted little time in positioning the back of the truck
over the stag. The two of them tried to grab it by the legs, but it wasn't
quite ready to give up. It kicked out. The woman looked around. She
picked up a rock that was lying by the side of the road and smashed
it against the stag's head, finishing it off. They managed to lift it high

enough to push it onto the truck. The woman jumped up to drag it further in. For a few brief moments the stag's head hung over the backboard, the blood dripping slowly onto the soft, fresh snow.

By the time Ritter set off again, the snowfall had become a blizzard. For long stretches of road, he drove slower than a man could walk. The snow swirled around his car. Soft, featherlike flakes fell onto the windscreen, one after another, gaining strength in numbers until they fused in large, heavy clusters. The wipers struggled to keep up. With the delay caused by the dead deer it took him close on an hour to travel the six kilometres to Rosenheim.

As he pulled into the Kufsteiner Strasse, a black Mercedes slowed to a halt a hundred metres or so in front of him. It stopped right outside his house, the brake lights glowing through the falling snow. Colouring each individual flake deep red. The snowflakes fell slowly to the ground. Ritter stared mesmerized. Detached from everything else but the red light glinting behind the snow.

He watched through the sluggish arcs of the wipers as they struggled to clear his windscreen. A woman got out of the passenger seat of the Mercedes and leaned into the car towards the driver, kissing him. She was huddled in her coat. But Ritter recognized her instantly. He knew every inch of that body. It was only then that it registered with him. The Mercedes was Kleidorfer's car. The woman stood back, still talking to the driver. Smiling. The smile he'd barely seen since the accident. The anger grew inside him. His hand tightened on the wheel. Sophie couldn't have seen him. Couldn't have recognized his car. Perhaps she was blinded by the headlights. Or too engrossed in her own world. Their world, not his. Invite him in now, you bitch. Let's get it over with. But Sophie waved the Mercedes off, before hurrying into the house and shutting the door behind her.

Ritter switched off the engine and the lights. The evidence was overwhelming. The kiss outside Senft. That smile. And now this. All of it circumstantial evidence. None of it proof. He knew that. But if this were a real case, you'd be pretty much certain by now. You'd just be looking for the final piece of evidence that nailed it all down.

Probing. Waiting. Watching. That last piece of the jigsaw that, if it were a murder, would convince a judge. The final evidence of the affair had to be there, and it would turn up soon enough. But there was no longer any doubt in Ritter's mind.

He sat for a while in the BMW, oblivious to the cold. If he went in there now there was no telling what he might do. He imagined his hands around her neck, squeezing the life out of her. But unless it was carefully planned to implicate Kleidorfer, it would only lead to the guillotine. The bitter impossibility of his situation closed in around Ritter. He slammed his fist into the dashboard, so hard that he cut the skin. A thin stream of blood appeared. He put his hand to his mouth to clean it away. He sat a while longer until, realizing how cold it had become, he forced himself to go indoors. There was no sense in freezing to death outside his own home.

'What on earth have you been doing out there all this time? You could have caught your death of cold.' Sophie was still up, cradling a cup of warm milk in her hands. She must have seen him after all. Was that why she hadn't invited the Gestapo boss in?

'What the fuck were you doing with Kleidorfer?'

She laughed, tossing her head back to shake her hair from her face. 'Is that it? You were outside working yourself into a rage over that? Klaus gave me a lift home from the Party meeting. Would you rather I'd walked, in this weather?'

She'd had plenty of time to prepare her excuse.

'I'm not stupid. You're giving him what he wanted back in Munich.'

'What?' She looked at him as if he was mad.

'You're screwing him, aren't you?'

She shook her head and laughed. He leaned towards her, the anger rising.

'I saw you this morning.'

'Of course you saw me. I live here. I saw you too. I told you I was going shopping.'

It was derisive. It only increased the anger inside him. 'I saw you this morning, kissing that prick Kleidorfer. In front of the whole city.'

'Don't be ridiculous.'

'Outside Senft.'

'You were spying on me while I went shopping? I met Klaus in the street. I was talking to him. Nothing important. He kissed me on the cheek to say goodbye.' She laughed, a brief moment of irony. 'If I'd realized the whole city was watching, I'd have made more of it.'

His anger boiled over and he raised his hand to hit her but she backed away.

'Don't you dare touch me.'

There was hatred on her face, and on his. She turned away, shaking her head, and started upstairs. On the landing, she turned to look down at him, her face full of disdain. 'Really? A man I've known since I was ten kisses me on the cheek and you think we're having an affair? Can't you see how ridiculous that is?'

She turned her back on him. Ritter heard the bedroom door shut firmly behind her. He stood there for a moment. The bitch. Did she really think he was so stupid as to believe her excuses and lies? It hadn't just been Kleidorfer kissing her. She'd kissed him, enthusiastically, outside Senft that morning and just now, outside their own house. And it wasn't on the cheek. Ritter retreated to the front room, unnerved by how close he'd come to hitting her, maybe even killing her. He sought refuge in a glass of Asbach.

'Kleidorfer. For Christ's sake. How could she? With that prick Kleidorfer, of all people?'

'It's come as a shock to you. Hasn't it, Peter? You can't say I didn't warn you. Her mother was the same. I told you. They need to feel loved.'

'Shut up, old man. You're just taking your daughter's side. As far as I can see, it isn't her mother she takes after. She's always been her father's daughter. And as for needing to feel loved, I've never stopped loving her. Never. But since the accident, it's been impossible. She's been impossible. It's obvious she blames me. For the loss of the child.'

'Well, it was you. You were driving.'

'How many more times? It was black ice. I couldn't have done anything about it. Anyone would have crashed.'

'Maybe that's true, but it wasn't anyone, was it, Peter? It was you.'

Chapter Eighteen

Friday 22 January 1943

Litwak crouched down a metre or so inside the tree line, holding up his hand. Kate had followed him through the brush and undergrowth to the northern edge of the woodland. The thin, dark strip of spruce and beech curved east to west around the snow-covered mountainside like the gaping grin of a clown. Litwak took off his poncho and spread it on the ground. He waved his right hand downward several times, fingers splayed. They were deep inside the security zone, very close to the Berghof. They needed to stay out of sight of the patrols. Kate moved slowly forward, keeping low, easing herself down beside him.

'We're going to lie here and watch, timing the patrols.'

It wasn't an order, but Litwak's tone made clear that he didn't want a discussion. Kate had offered to help. He hadn't asked her to, hadn't asked her to be here at all, and he wasn't about to enter into a debate with her every five minutes over what they should do. It was his decision. He'd been through it a thousand times at the SOE's Scottish training area, simulating the conditions he would come up against on the Obersalzberg.

The snow was deeper here on the mountainside than at Arisaig. Along the tree line, deep drifts leaned against the lines of spruce. They provided good cover for Litwak's surveillance up the slope towards Hitler's Alpine retreat. This was the perfect location to take a shot at the Führer as he walked along the path to the *Teehaus*. There were clouds stacked up over the Alps but above them the sky was blue. A pale sun flickered on the snow, but the wind was too strong, too sharp, to allow it any impact on the intense cold.

'We need to time the intervals between each patrol and work out how many guards there are.' Litwak didn't look at Kate as he spoke. He maintained his surveillance of the mountainside for any sign of a patrol. She hadn't taken part in the Arisaig training, but they'd discussed the plans at length back at the presbytery. He'd talked her through every moment of the time they would spend together on the mountainside. Kate didn't query anything. She'd done all right on special operations training. Nothing special. But she knew the drill. She nodded, looked at her watch, and wrote the time down in a small notebook.

They lay there scanning the mountainside. The brilliant white of the snow was interrupted by the occasional patch of dark green, spruce and beech woven together with thick undergrowth now beaten down by the snow. Kate laid one hand on his back. It felt awkward at first. Uncomfortable. Unprofessional. He thought of shaking it off. But he let it lie there. She was wearing gloves and he had several layers of clothes on, but still her hand felt warm to him. It was somehow reassuring. A reminder he wasn't alone.

It was twenty minutes before the first patrol came by. The path from the Berghof curled around the slope, across a narrow valley and then up a small hill, the Mooslahnerkopf, on which sat the *Teehaus*. The path had been cleared. A wall of compacted snow about thirty centimetres high marked the edge of each side, concealing the soldiers' boots and lower legs from view. Looking through the binoculars, Litwak counted five men. An Alsatian dog was out ahead of them. Only its head and upright tail were visible behind the snow. It was leaning into the sharp wind like a pointer, tugging at its lead, dragging its handler up a steep section of path towards the *Teehaus*. The soldiers had SS badges on mountain troop uniforms. They were disciplined. No one ambling, everyone doing his job. The Alsatian slowed, relaxing the tension on the lead. Litwak wondered if it was tiring of the pretence that there was some hidden threat out there ahead of them. Something they had to hunt down. But then he realized the dog was sniffing the air. It couldn't possibly have picked up their scent from that distance. But it had sensed something. It turned its head towards the edge of the woodland where Litwak and Kate were lying and started to bark.

The corporal in charge of the patrol stopped, holding up his hand. His men crouched down, rifles at the ready. Some looked towards the tree line while others scanned the slope above. The last man stared back behind them all, watching their tail. Litwak was confident they couldn't be seen, but the dog was dragging its handler in their direction. There were shouts. One man pointed towards where they lay.

'Don't move.' Litwak was absolutely determined they should remain where they were. After all, Hitler wasn't at the Berghof right now, so there was no reason for the guards to panic. And there was no reason for them to panic, either. It was just a nervous dog. If they stayed still, they had nothing to worry about. If they moved, they'd be spotted. He felt her slap his back with her hand. 'No, Jonny. We have to go. Now. Right now.'

He'd briefed her on the backup plan, but she was ignoring it. Slowly at first, and then very rapidly, it began to occur to Litwak that she might be right. Claiming they were only interested in trying to meet the Führer might have worked before they hid in the woods. It wouldn't work now. If they were caught, they were in real trouble. SS interrogation techniques being what they were, eventually one of them would talk. They'd both end up dead.

Kate got up and started to run back through the undergrowth, leaping the brambles, leaving Litwak with no choice but to follow her. The SS guards plunged into the deep snow, chasing them down the hill, the snow hampering their efforts so that, despite Litwak's hesitation, he and Kate reached the southern edge of the forest well ahead of them. Litwak wasn't sure which way to go. His own plan and his instinct were to head straight down to the road, but Kate dragged him back.

'Along the tree line. It'll be easier to run. If you go out into the snow it'll slow you down and make you an easy target. If we're quick we can double back.'

As she spoke, a gust of wind brought a flurry of snowflakes. They heard more shouts and saw the patrol come out of the trees. One of the guards spotted them and lifted his rifle. The corporal shouted, 'No.' But the soldier had already let off a shot. The bullet pinged past Litwak's ears and sent splinters flying as it embedded itself in the trunk of a tree just in front of him. They ducked back into the cover of the trees. Running hard. Leaping over the undergrowth. Kate tripped and fell, clasping her ankle. Litwak dragged her up with one hand and they kept running.

The strip of woodland was getting thinner, providing no cover at all. They plunged into the snow, struggling with every step. Their boots broke through the frozen surface and were swallowed up by the powdery whiteness below. It was snowing more heavily now, the wind whipping up loose snow from the surface, flinging it into Litwak's face. It stung his bare cheeks, melted, and ran down his face. Two guards who had kept to the tree line were gaining ground on them. The dog was barking excitedly. Litwak realized he was scared, terrified of what might happen next. He'd messed up. Tried too hard to get it right. To prove to himself – and to her – that he was in control.

The rush of the wind sounded like the cry of a wild animal, summoning another blizzard. The noise of the storm grew so loud that it obliterated the voices of the chasing guards. Within seconds, Litwak was lost in a white fog of falling snow. Kate was only a few steps in front of him but he could no longer see her. The slope was suddenly much steeper. A feeling of panic gripped him. Then he felt her hand grasp his wrist and pull him into the white expanse. He shouted above the storm. 'Where are we going?'

'The road.' She spoke with utter certainty and what seemed in the circumstances to be an unnatural calm. Somehow more convinced than he that they could survive. 'If we can make the road we'll be safe.'

Litwak couldn't see any way they had a chance of being safe. Not now. He doubted she knew where she was going. But he had no idea at all where they were, no idea whether the SS guards had lost them or were still on their trail. Kate seemed to sense a way out. He followed her down the mountainside.

The patrol was still searching for them. He could hear the shouts of the guards and the barking of the Alsatian intermittently borne on the wind – sometimes reassuringly distant, as if they might yet escape, leaving their pursuers floundering around in the deep snow, at other times frighteningly close, threatening imminent capture. The freezing wind blasted against his face. He had to squint to see anything ahead in the swirling white mass.

They crossed a frozen stream and then hit a flat patch of ground and Litwak realized it must be the road. The shouts of the guards were suddenly very close. They seemed to be on the road a few hundred metres to the west of them. Kate pointed towards the east and they began running. Then through the driving snow Litwak made out the blurred image of a vehicle. He paused, thinking it was more guards. That they must be caught between the two sets of troops with no way out. But Kate grabbed his hand and dragged him with her to the car, a black Opel. The priest sat in the driver's seat. Kate shoved Litwak into the front and got in the back. Steiner put his foot on the accelerator, sending the car skidding forward until he gained control and drove through the blizzard, away from the dangers on the mountain.

They had travelled four or five kilometres when they came to the roadblock. Kate and Litwak had stripped off their jackets, the only identifying features the guards could have seen. An army officer stepped out into the road and held up his hand. The priest wound down the window and looked impassively up at the officer, a major in a local Bavarian reserve regiment. Very young. Barely old enough to be the most junior soldier, let alone a major.

'Father Josef?'

The priest looked momentarily puzzled and then realized that the officer was the son of one of his parishioners. 'Kurt. Sorry. I wasn't expecting – how are you? I was speaking to your mother only this morning.'

'I'm fine, thank you, Father. I'm afraid there's been a security scare. A couple have somehow got inside the security zone. They ran away when they were challenged. It may be nothing, but we have to check.'

The officer looked from Litwak to Kate with a degree of suspicion. The priest realized what he was thinking and laughed. 'Sorry, Kurt. I didn't think. A couple, you say? This is my sister's son and daughter. Johann and Inge Schultz. Not a couple. Not a security threat. Brother and sister, and very well-behaved.'

The major smiled. 'I'm sure they are, Father. But I will have to check their papers.'

'Of course.'

The reservist officer read them through carefully. He looked at Litwak. 'On leave? From where?'

'The East.' Litwak's response was subdued, in keeping with the concern felt by many Germans over the fighting in Russia. It persuaded the young reservist that Litwak was genuine. He turned his attention to Kate. 'It says here there's a brown birthmark on your neck, Frau Schultz. Can I see it, please?'

Kate turned her head and pulled the neck of her jumper down so that he could check the birthmark. He nodded and handed their papers back, waving to the soldier manning the checkpoint to lift the barrier. 'That's fine. Thank you very much. You can go. Drive carefully, Father.'

'Thank you, Kurt. I certainly will.'

The journey back to Söllhuben was spent mainly in silence. Litwak spent the entire ride speculating how Father Josef came to be there at precisely the right time.

Chapter Nineteen

Saturday 23 January 1943

Ritter barely slept that night and left home early next morning before Sophie got up, unsure whether he wanted to avoid a row or provoke one. The way he felt right now, he'd probably kill her without any plan and damn the consequences. He didn't have to go looking for trouble. A small group of women from the *Frauenschaft* were out in the old town noisily collecting for victims of the Munich air raids. For once the women's anger wasn't being orchestrated by Ritter's neighbour Gertrud Heissig. He stopped Dagmar Kahn, a short, plump, middle-aged woman who saw herself as Heissig's deputy, to ask where Gertrud was.

'You haven't heard, then, Inspector?'

There was no cloud cover and the bitter January air froze the back of his throat. It was far too cold to stop and chat, and Ritter wasn't even sure he wanted to know whatever it was about Gertrud that he hadn't heard. But Kahn's question forced him to ask. 'Haven't heard what?'

'Gertrud's husband Oswald was killed in a British terror attack on Munich. The bombing there's getting worse. She's gone to have his body brought back for burial.'

Ritter remembered the banners Gertrud and the *Frauenschaft* had been waving during their previous protest over the bombing. 'you'll be next.' He didn't like Gertrud or her husband. He certainly wouldn't be shedding a tear for a man who'd profited from the war. But reluctantly or not, he'd shared a drink with Oswald Heissig. He didn't want him dead and he didn't wish the loss of her husband on Gertrud. She wasn't alone, of course. There were plenty of wives and mothers losing husbands and sons. Nor were men the only victims. The bombing had extended the killing to women and children. Far too many people to grieve for them all.

As Ritter walked up the Max-Josefs-Platz towards the *Mittertor*, the chemical truck drove down the square in the opposite direction. No doubt mindful of Ritter's previous intervention, Kahn and her cronies waved it through. The driver smiled and raised a hand to Ritter, who nodded, shielding his eyes from the bright sunlight reflected off the snow-covered square. Something about the man's expression triggered questions in Ritter's mind. It seemed forced. More of a fixed grin than a genuine smile. As if it were born out of angst rather than gratitude. What did the man have to be nervous about?

Ritter watched the drab green truck clatter past. French POWs had cleared a channel through the snow, exposing the surface of the street. The truck's tyres were wrapped in snow chains and the drums of chemicals in the back bounced up and down as it rumbled across the cobbles. Those drums should have been tied down. They didn't look safe. Surely there were rules about securing dangerous chemicals. Why did they have to come through Rosenheim, anyway? And why didn't the truck have the name of the chemical company on its side? The name was on the drums. Ritter made a mental note to get Messel to ring the company and find out precisely what the truck was doing that was so important to the war effort.

After the blinding white of the fresh snow, the dingy half-light of the *Mittertor* lobby brought relief for Ritter's eyes. Kurt Naumann was on duty on the front desk. Ritter nodded to him but didn't stop to chat. The stench of body odour and stale vomit from a couple of drunks arrested overnight hurried him through to the stairs that led down to his office in the cellar. But Naumann hauled him back. 'Inspector. Wait. I've got something for you. It's a report on suspicious activity in the Berchtesgaden area. Inspector Nagel said I should make sure you saw it.'

'Did he? Then I suppose I'd better look at it. Thanks.'

Ritter turned back to collect the report, then read the scribbled note from Nagel as he walked down the stairs. A man and a woman had managed to get through the security protecting Hitler's Alpine home at Berchtesgaden. An SS patrol had chased them off the mountain but hadn't tracked them down. They'd asked for various *Kripo* stations across Upper Bavaria to investigate a number of possible suspects. The incident had only happened the previous day but the report was long and detailed, written by someone trying to cover his own backside. The local *Kripo* were in all probability only being called in to ensure there was someone else to blame if things went wrong. Nagel could have had one of the junior detectives look at it. Even if he didn't think Schinkel's murder needed investigation, he certainly knew Ritter had his hands full with the Drexler murder. The killing of a Jew might be easily swept under the carpet but, busy or not, Munich would want to know someone was being held to account for Drexler's death.

Messel was waiting in the office. He had his feet up on Ritter's desk. A mistake. He stood up when Ritter walked in, but not quickly enough.

'Nothing to do, Messel?' Ritter ignored Messel's clumsy attempts at denial. 'Here you are. Get a number for the chemical works in Wasserburg am Inn. One of their lorries keeps driving through Rosenheim. Why?'

'You think something illegal's going on?'

'I don't know. It's just odd. The driver looked guilty.'

'Most people do these days?'

Ritter gave a hollow laugh.

'Everyone bar Kleidorfer and the rest of the cretins over on the Adolf-Hitler-Strasse. Those who are truly guilty never look guilty at all. Find out why the truck comes through Rosenheim. Tell them it's been through here several times and the drums of chemicals on the back don't look safe. Demand to know why the chemicals need to come through Rosenheim at all.'

'Yes, of course.'

'Oh and have a look at this report. Inspector Nagel wants me to read it to make sure there's nothing in it we need to follow up on.'

'Inspector Nagel wants you to read it?'

'Yes, that's right, Messel. But look at the size of it. I've got to go out. I don't have the time. You do. It's from the SS guard detachment up at the Berghof. The note from Inspector Nagel explains what it's about. Berchtesgaden's a hundred kilometres from here. I can't see why the SS need to implicate us in their shit. If they've messed up, they should sort it out themselves.'

Ritter went up onto the street. He'd lied to Messel. He'd no particular reason to go out, other than to get some fresh air, and to justify leaving Messel to read the SS report. He walked up to the Schweizerhof where Liesl was still moaning about the loss of trade caused by her hotel's growing reputation as a homicide black spot.

'It's about time you solved the killings. Two people murdered in their beds in my hotel. People are afraid to stay here. If the Gestapo can't protect themselves, who can?'

'It's difficult, Liesl. We'll find whoever's responsible. But there are a few more questions, I'm afraid.'

'What questions? Haven't you asked enough?'

'Do you know someone called Inge Schultz?'

'No. Should I?'

'Maybe not. She's Marianne's new best friend.'

Liesl raised her eyebrows at the suggestion that someone other than her might be Müller's best friend.

'Aren't you worried about Marianne?'

'She's fine, Peter. The nuns will keep her safe.'

Messel was waiting for Ritter when he got back to the station. He had the SS report in his hand and yet again was looking very pleased with himself.

'You should read the section of this report they wanted our help on, boss. It's very interesting.'

'Really, Messel? Why exactly is it of any interest to us?'

'The SS spotted a young man and a woman up on the Obersalzberg, apparently watching what the guards were doing. They lost them in a snowstorm. But the army put out a series of roadblocks. One of the vehicles the roadblocks picked up was a black Opel driven by your friend Steiner. The priest from Söllhuben. The army officer at the roadblock comes from Söllhuben. He knows Steiner and didn't think him suspect. But the priest had a young couple in his car. He claimed they were his niece and nephew, that they were on holiday and staying with him.'

'And you don't believe him, Messel.'

'The papers for the nephew seemed fine. He was on leave from the Eastern Front. But there was something interesting about the woman. She had a birthmark on her neck, like Scharf. In fact, she fits Scharf's description perfectly. But that wasn't the name on her papers.'

'Let me guess, Messel. The name on the papers was Inge Schultz.' Messel looked puzzled.

'Yes. How did you know?'

'Schultz is the woman we saw with Müller in Söllhuben. The one exchanging hand signals with the priest. She was with Müller when I went to interview her at the women's refuge in Riedering. There was something odd going on between them. We should go and talk to that army officer who was on the roadblock, and to Father Steiner.'

Messel drove on the journey out to Söllhuben. The snow that had smothered the road from Riedering to Söllhuben the previous day had been flattened by a series of military convoys. The surface was frozen solid.

'Who arrives first at the hotel, Messel?'

'The Bramls arrive first, boss. They're straightforward. They're Party members.'

Despite his anger over the growing evidence that Sophie was having an affair, Ritter managed a smile at the idea that being a Party member might indicate that someone was 'straightforward.'

'Does Party membership mean we can write them off as possible murderers, then, Messel?'

Either Messel didn't get the irony or he ignored it.

'I think so, boss. I don't see them as anything other than tourists caught up in it all by accident.' The boy was probably right. 'They're nobodies, boss. They arrive. No one notices them. They leave. No one notices them. When the *Kripo* post in Bad Ischl spoke to them, they didn't even know there'd been a murder.'

'You may be right, Messel. It's entirely plausible that the Bramls were not involved in any of this. But the next person to arrive definitely was.'

'The next person is Schinkel.'

'Correct. And he's walking with a limp. Is it genuine, the limp, do we think?'

'I don't think so, boss. Liesl Olbricht thinks he's been wounded in the war and that's why he isn't in uniform. She asks him if he wants dinner. He says no. He goes straight up to his room. She never sees him again. Not alive, at any rate. If you think we can believe her.'

'Oh, I think we can believe Liesl when she says that was the last time she saw him alive.'

Whether it was Liesl or Heinrich who'd discovered Schinkel's body, it would have been Liesl who told Drexler or Müller. She would have wanted to check that Schinkel was dead before risking interrupting the Gestapo boss.

'Liesl either saw his body when it was first discovered or she saw it being taken away, Messel. But whenever it was that she saw Schinkel again, he was definitely dead.'

Chapter Twenty

Saturday 23 January 1943

Ritter ordered two glasses of dark wheat beer and took them to a table in the corner. A couple of locals in traditional grey-and-green hunting jackets and lederhosen were drinking beer and playing cards on the *Stammtisch*, the table reserved for regulars. But otherwise the *Wirtsstube*, the Gasthof Hirzinger's main bar, was empty. A dark oak bench ran around the walls. There were long wooden tables, the surfaces much lighter than the high back of the bench after years of being scrubbed clean each morning. There was the smell of roasting pork. The place was Bavaria through and through. Comfortable. Reassuring. Particularly with a glass of Rosenheimer Dunkel Weisse in your hand.

'Useful having a Gasthof opposite the church, isn't it, Messel? Very civilized. Gives you the choice. Beer or God?'

They'd tracked down Major Kurt Schäffer, the commander of the roadblock that had stopped Steiner's car. His mother organized the flowers in Saint Rupert's church. He seemed to regard the priest as above suspicion. He'd been very defensive of Steiner.

'The SS got a bit agitated about Father Josef's niece and nephew,' Schäffer said. 'I'm sure it's just overreaction. It's understandable, so close to the Führers security zone, but Father Josef wouldn't hide anyone subversive. He's no risk to anyone.'

Ritter left Messel to ask the questions. Schäffer looked far too young to be a major. Barely out of his teens. Although his bright, round, boyish face and golden locks probably made him look younger than he actually was. He was excited. Overexcited. He couldn't stop smiling. He'd just been told he was to be sent to the Eastern Front to help in the relief of the troops trapped in Stalingrad. He seemed to think this demonstrated that senior officers believed he was an outstanding commander. An inexperienced reservist, in all probability being sent to an early grave. Unless the boy was very lucky, it was only a matter of time before the priest was dealing with yet another grieving mother. Things must be desperate if they thought someone of his age mature enough to command a company fighting the Russians. It had the feel of the trenches. But they'd been permanently desperate back then.

Ritter and Messel were saying their goodbyes when Schäffer suddenly remembered something. 'There was one thing that was slightly odd about them. It didn't occur to me until I'd waved them through the barrier. Father Josef's niece and nephew. They were out in the middle of a blizzard. It was freezing cold. But neither of them was wearing a coat.'

Messel had been handling the glass of dark wheat beer as if it were nitro-glycerine, and grimaced as he took his first sip. He put it back down, still eyeing the cloudy, dark-brown potion suspiciously. After a few moments he turned to Ritter. 'What do you think about Schäffer, boss? The stuff about the coats?'

'I think it's an important piece of the jigsaw.'

'Yes. But without coats, they couldn't have been out on the mountain, could they? Not in that weather.'

'But they weren't out on the mountain, were they, Messel? They were in a car.'

Messel frowned and took a longer, more confident drink from his glass.

'Think about it, Messel. You've read the SS report. What's the description of the man and the woman?'

'Pretty basic…'

'Very basic. Aside from the fact that one of them is a woman and the other a man, the only description the SS can give is the colour of their coats. It's the only way they can be recognized. So to avoid that happening if they get stopped, what do they do?'

'They take off their coats?'

'Precisely.'

Ritter and Messel had had no luck in trying to track down the priest. Frau Gundelach, the housekeeper at the presbytery, had been unforthcoming. Ritter had to do all the talking. Gundelach spoke mostly in *Alpenbayerisch* and Messel couldn't understand a word she said. The woman didn't know where Father Josef was, and when they asked her about Steiner's niece and nephew, she simply shrugged her shoulders and claimed to have no idea. Her face said she couldn't care less. There was disapproval in her voice. Was it aimed at Steiner's niece and nephew or at Ritter and Messel? Ritter couldn't be sure. You had only to go a dozen kilometres outside Rosenheim to find women like this. Wary of the people from the city. Suspicious of their motives. Protective of the village priest, the only man they thought capable of sharing their deepest secrets. In a battle against the Catholic Church, even the Führer would struggle to win the support of such good and faithful servants.

Ritter had always believed that being a good detective was two-thirds hard grind. Checking every little point of everybody's story. Making sure no question was ever left unanswered. Talking to anybody who might know anything. Anything at all that might be relevant. Getting Viktor to part company with the results of his post-mortems. Even now, the pathologist still hadn't provided them with a full post-mortem report on the Drexler killing. The final third of the investigation was pure luck. But you'd never get anywhere near that final third unless you put in the hard grind.

The door of the *Wirtsstube* swung open and Steiner walked in. The same black cloak that had fooled Ritter up on the Kaiserstrasse and a black wide-brimmed soup-bowl hat. He removed both with a single, overly theatrical movement. Beneath the cloak the priest was wearing a white clerical collar above a long black cassock that was belted at the waist. He looked across at Ritter and Messel and smiled.

'Inspector. What a pleasant surprise. How are you?'

Maybe this was the bit of luck their hard work merited.

'I'm fine, Father, and very glad to see you. Please. Come and join us. Let me buy you a glass of something?'

'That's very kind, Inspector. What are you drinking? Ah. Rosenheimer. I'll have one of those too.'

Ritter nodded encouragingly to Messel, who got up and went to the bar.

'Just the two, Messel. I don't want to force you into drinking it.'

'What brings you here, Inspector?'

'You promised to help me.'

Steiner looked puzzled. 'I did? When?'

'The night Gerhard Drexler was murdered. You stopped me up on the Kaiserstrasse. I nearly shot you. You said you were there to help. The next thing I know, the head of the city's Gestapo post's been murdered.'

'Yes. Well, I'm always happy to help the police, Inspector. But that was nothing to do with me.' Steiner smiled. 'Murder is a mortal sin. It's something we priests try to avoid.'

Ritter smiled back. 'Don't worry, Father. I'd be hardly likely to arrest you. Even if I did think you did it. You know I was due to meet Drexler at the hotel. That implicates me. But if you know anything that might help me find the real killer, you should tell me. You're a priest. You can't condone murder.'

'I don't. As I say, it's a mortal sin. Although there are those in the church who argue that there can be justification for killing someone. In his epistle to the Christians of Rome, Saint Paul said a true servant of God could use a weapon in good cause: 'For he is an avenger who carries out God's wrath on the wrongdoer.' Of course, the weapon Paul was talking about was a sword, not that tiny little, what was it, a Sauer you pointed at me up on the Kaiserstrasse?'

Ritter nodded. Even here, in his clerical habit and just a few metres from his church, there was something deeply unsettling about Steiner. A man who could identify a small, specialized weapon like Ritter's Sauer in the dark had a far wider experience behind him than the normal incumbent of a tiny Bavarian Catholic church.

'I hope you weren't God's avenger yourself, Inspector? The way you were holding that gun up there, I had the distinct impression you might be contemplating murder.'

Ritter didn't see any need to respond. If he was going to murder someone, there were a couple of people higher up the list than Drexler. He and Steiner stared at each other for a few moments. It was the priest who broke the silence.

'Is that it, Inspector?'

'No. Ah, thank you, Messel.'

Messel handed them their beers. Ritter took a long swig from his glass. The priest just placed his down in front of him.

'No. It's not it, I'm afraid, Father. We've been asked to check out an SS report of a couple in the security zone around the Führers home on the Obersalzberg. Apparently, you were seen in the area at about that time, with a young man and woman in your car?'

Steiner stiffened. Only slightly. Then he smiled. Confident. Maybe a touch too confident.

'Oh. The couple in my car? They're my niece and nephew.'

'That's what Major Schäffer said. Johann and Inge Schultz. Is that right?'

'You've spoken to Kurt?'

Ritter picked up a slight wariness. Steiner had a certain steel about him. It would probably take a lot to make him nervous.

'It's routine, Father. I didn't want to bother you. I'm sure you've got more important things on your plate. I certainly have more urgent cases to deal with.'

'The murder in the Schweizerhof.'

'Murders, in fact.' Steiner tensed again, but Ritter continued as if he hadn't noticed it. 'There was more than one murder in the hotel and they're probably linked. So I'd rather get rid of this little chore. It's really just administrative stuff. This couple the SS chased off the mountain don't seem to have done anything. It's probably only a coincidence that your niece and nephew were there around the same time.'

The more bonhomie Ritter exuded, the more guarded Steiner became.

'Well, I've no idea. As I say, Inspector, it wasn't my niece and nephew up there on the Obersalzberg. The three of us had just been visiting an old parishioner of mine.'

'Then that's absolutely fine. All cleared up. Easy. I can get back to solving my murders.'

'Indeed. I wish you luck, Inspector.'

'One other thing though, Father.'

'Yes?'

'Marianne Müller. I need to speak to her.'

'I haven't seen her. Not for a couple of weeks. She came to the presbytery to play cards with my niece and nephew, and I think you've seen her since then. Inge mentioned some meeting at the nuns' refuge? She wasn't very impressed, I'm afraid. But I'm sure she got the wrong end of the stick.'

'Really? The feeling, I'm afraid, was mutual, and I'm sure I didn't get the wrong end of the stick. How does Müller come to know your niece?'

'Inge went to visit the Fraueninsel. The holy sisters introduced her to Marianne. They told Inge the poor woman was in trouble and needed a good friend.'

Ritter raised an eyebrow; the priest gave a tight smile. 'My niece has a good heart, Inspector. But in some things, she is – shall we say – naive. Of course, the work of Müller and her kind is a mystery to Inge. She only knows that someone she respects says the woman needs help. So she does what she can.'

Ritter thought back to Schultz's performance at the Riedering hostel. Naive was not the word that came most immediately to mind. 'I see. Well if you do see Müller, tell her I need to speak to her urgently. Her life may be in danger.'

Steiner showed no surprise at the suggestion that Müller was at risk. He simply nodded and got up to leave, his beer untouched. But Ritter wasn't going to let him go just yet. The priest could still provide another piece of the jigsaw.

'Thank you, Father. There's just one more thing I need from you.'

'What's that, Inspector?'

Steiner knocked the dust off his hat with the back of his hand. Was it a nervous gesture or a sign of irritation?

'It's an administrative thing. It's tedious but it's an essential detail. The name and address of this old parishioner. Just to tidy things up, you understand. If I haven't asked, the SS detachment up at Berchtesgaden will complain and make my life hell.'

Steiner paused, staring at Ritter, and then smiled drily.

'Well, we certainly can't leave you to the mercies of the SS, can we? Give me your notebook. I'll write it down for you.'

Once the priest had left, Ritter dropped the bogus bonhomie and returned to his beer. Reflecting. Thoughts of Sophie's betrayal swamped all else. Where did he go from here?

But Messel was anxious to return to the case.

'We were talking about the people in the Schweizerhof that night, boss. It's the women who interest me.'

Ritter turned towards Messel and smiled. The boy was on the right track, at least. The women. Always the women.

'The women are the only ones who are interesting here, Messel. It's their names that keep coming up. We know Müller is a spy, and since they're all linked to each other, that has to raise questions about them all. Tell me about Swiss Matronly Woman again. We know – whatever the good Father says – that Schultz and Müller are more than acquaintances. What about the mother?'

Messel took a notebook out of his pocket and started flicking back through the pages.

'Matronly Swiss Woman. Bettina Grob. She's the one who books the rooms.'

'How, Messel?'

'What do you mean "how," boss?'

'How? How does she book the rooms?'

'By telephone, the day before they arrive.'

'By telephone. So we can't be sure it's her. It could be anybody. What does she say when she arrives at the hotel?'

'She says her daughter won't be getting there until later.'

'And then?'

'She goes upstairs to lie down. She tells Liesl Olbricht she's had a tiring journey.'

'So when does Liesl say she saw her next?'

'She doesn't. Not until she checks out.'

'Okay, so what about the daughter? The woman we now know as Inge Schultz? What does she call herself back then? Martyl Scharf? She's dropped off by Steiner. When's that?'

Messel looked back at his notes.

'Liesl Olbricht thinks it was about four o'clock in the afternoon.'

There were five women in the hotel that night. Liesl; the Braml woman; Müller; Scharf, aka Schultz; and her 'mother,' Bettina Grob. Liesl's and Braml's fingerprints were accounted for. That left three women and only two sets of fingerprints. Either one of them had done a very good job in wiping her prints from everything she touched or there were only two women.

'Does anyone see Matronly Swiss Woman and Schultz together, Messel? At any time? What about when they check out?'

'Liesl Olbricht says Grob checked out. She didn't mention her daughter being with her.'

'They're supposedly mother and daughter. But no one ever sees them together. Why would that be?'

'Liesl Olbricht sees them all. We have her testimony. And Grob and Scharf even look alike right down to the birthmarks on their necks.'

'Exactly, Messel. Right down to the birthmarks on their necks. I've spoken to Viktor Kozlowski. The chances of even a mother and daughter having a birthmark in exactly the same place are virtually zero.'

'So Grob and Scharf are the same woman.'

'Grob, Scharf, and Schultz, Messel. Don't forget Schultz.'

'So whatever her name is, she's a British spy.'

'It would seem that way, wouldn't it? And if she's a spy then her brother must be one too. If he really is her brother. You'd better get back onto Berlin and find out if they've uncovered any more detail on that British spy.'

'Shouldn't we warn the SS up at Berchtesgaden?'

'What? And have the Gestapo send in a battalion of Kleidorfers all demanding to know why we didn't think to call them in earlier? No, Messel. We've got two murders to solve. That's our priority. We need to find Schultz and Müller. One or the other of them is our killer.'

Chapter Twenty-One

Monday 25 January 1943

Kleidorfer didn't bother knocking. He pushed the door of Ritter's office back on its hinges and marched in, waving the SS report back and forth as if he'd discovered something important that Ritter had failed to spot.

'Nagel says you've been looking into the two characters who were up on the Obersalzberg, Ritter. The SS think they're from Söllhuben. That's our area. What have you done about it?'

'They aren't from Söllhuben. They're staying there. In the presbytery. They're the niece and nephew of the priest there. That's all we know so far.'

'That's not what the SS think.'

Kleidorfer flicked through the report, trying to find the page. The SS had, in fact, been far less suspicious of the pair than Ritter was. They only wanted the priest and his niece and nephew checked out. They were just covering their backsides. But had they expressed more concern, Ritter would have seen their point. He very much doubted that Schultz and her so-called brother were related to the priest, whatever the census might say. If Berlin was right about the fingerprints, there was good reason to suspect they were British spies. And what did that say about the priest? But he wasn't about to share this information with Kleidorfer.

Ritter sat staring down at his desk. The presence of British spies on his patch seemed a relatively minor problem to him right now.

Being in the same room as Kleidorfer made him sick to the pit of his stomach. He could barely look at the man. How long could he let this go on? How long should he let it go on? He needed to do something about it. Needed to act. Needed to try to grab back control of his life; to grab back control of his marriage. If there was any kind of marriage still there.

But what should he do? Confront Kleidorfer? Demand to know what was going on between him and Sophie? The Gestapo boss was unlikely to tell him. Surely better to bide his time. He should talk to Sophie. Not Kleidorfer. If he took on the Gestapo boss it would be bound to spill over into the case. Worse, it was likely to descend into pathetic posturing. Children fighting over a toy. No. Say nothing to Kleidorfer. Talk to Sophie. Force her to tell him the truth. Find out the facts before he acted. That was the sensible thing to do.

'What the fuck do you think you're doing with my wife?'

The vehemence of his question surprised Ritter as much as it did Kleidorfer. Quite why he'd so swiftly discarded the carefully considered approach, he couldn't say. Part of him knew it was a mistake. But the other part didn't give a shit.

Kleidorfer had stopped searching through the report. For a moment he didn't seem to know what to say. How to respond. Then he smiled.

'We're just friends, Ritter. Nothing more. Sophie and I were at school together, and at university. You know that. You were at Ludwig Maximilian with us. We were all friends back then.'

Kleidorfer seemed to have a completely different memory of their time as students than Ritter's. Whatever Kleidorfer was back then, it certainly wasn't a friend. Ritter remembered him as a minor irritant. Forever hanging around Sophie. A gnat that might occasionally need to be swatted away. Nothing like the threat he'd become since he turned up in Rosenheim. Now his malign influence menaced everything that mattered to Ritter – his work, his marriage, even the principles by which he lived his life.

'She's worried about you, Ritter. That's all. She's asked my advice. She thinks you don't believe in the Führer. That you've got dangerous, radical ideas. She's not the only one who thinks that. You need to sort things out in your own mind. Remind yourself of your real responsibilities. Perhaps then she won't feel the need to come crying on my shoulder.'

There was a distinct uncertainty in Kleidorfer's voice as he finished the sentence. Ritter pushed his desk to one side and flung himself at the Gestapo officer. Sophie was telling Kleidorfer he had 'dangerous ideas'? Crying on his shoulder? The colour drained from the Gestapo officer's face along with the smug self-assurance. He looked genuinely scared. He tried to recover the initiative.

'Careful, Ritter. One word from me to Munich and…'

Whatever that word was, Kleidorfer was no longer capable of uttering it. Ritter's right hand was firmly wrapped around the Gestapo officer's cheeks and chin, squeezing them together, crushing the cheekbones in towards the jaw. The rage on Ritter's face had been replaced by a steely determination. Kleidorfer tried to twist his way out but Ritter only tightened his grip.

He was forcing Kleidorfer back, the Gestapo officer's boots scattering the files stacked against the wall. Ritter knew he'd gone too far. That word to Munich was inevitable now, and an assault on a member of the Gestapo was an assault on the regime. There was no point in holding back. Might as well be hanged for a sheep as a lamb.

'You were such a weakling at university, Kleidorfer. What changed things, eh? Is it that black SS uniform you waltz around in? Is that what makes you feel so hard?'

Ritter was so angry that he was twisting Kleidorfer's head to and fro, tightening his grip with each yank. 'How hard do you think you are, you prick? As hard as this wall? Are you that fucking hard? Are you?' Ritter was screaming, spraying Kleidorfer with tiny drops of spittle. A look of sheer terror came across the Gestapo officer's face as he realized what was coming. Ritter pulled Kleidorfer's head forward before slamming it into the wall and letting it go. The back of the Gestapo officer's skull rebounded off the stone wall and his body slid slowly down to slump among the scattered files, followed by a trail of blood.

'No. I didn't think you were that hard.'

The cellar wall had been there long before Kleidorfer and his pals appeared on the scene and it would still be there long after they were gone.

There was a clattering of boots on the cellar stairs. Ritter moved his desk back in place and sat down, looking at the cellar wall. There was quite a bit of blood where Kleidorfer's head had hit the wall. It was collecting as a large globule between two of the stones and trickling down the wall like some miracle of the blood of Christ. What was it the priest said? Ritter laughed at the idea of himself as 'God's avenger.'

He was still laughing when Kurt Naumann appeared at the door. The *Schupo* officer looked at Kleidorfer and then at Ritter. 'Jesus, Ritter. Why can't you sort out your files?'

Naumann yelled up the stairs for someone to get a doctor as quickly as possible. Ritter's laughter was replaced by confusion. 'Sort out my files?'

'Your unsolved case files. If you'd put them away, Kleidorfer would never have slipped.'

'He slipped?'

Was it him or Naumann who was being stupid?

'Yes. He slipped. He slipped on the files and banged his head against the wall. I was here. I saw it happen.'

Ritter's brow furrowed. The confusion refused to go away. Naumann repeated it slowly, deliberately, very quietly.

'I – saw – him – slip.'

Slowly, as if waking from a deep sleep, Ritter finally grasped what Naumann was saying.

'You're right, of course.' Ritter looked around the room at the various files stacked against the walls. 'I need to order more filing cabinets.' He looked over at Kleidorfer, who was groaning as he began to come around. 'Is that doctor on his way? Kleidorfer doesn't look too good.'

* * *

'Christ, Ritter. You were lucky Naumann was there to see it. How would it have looked otherwise? What with Sophie…'

Nagel broke off, suddenly aware that he was treading on dangerous ground. He'd clearly bought into Naumann's story, but then, he had an interest in believing it. If Munich heard that one of his detectives had beaten up a Gestapo officer they'd be down on him like a ton of bricks. It wouldn't be just Ritter who'd be in trouble. Nagel would lose his job as well. The problem would come when Kleidorfer told his side of the story.

'Kleidorfer's come round completely now and he's fine. They're keeping him in hospital overnight but they're letting him out tomorrow. He can't remember a thing, so it's bloody lucky Naumann was there. I've ordered some more filing cabinets so you can tidy those files away. I don't want this happening again.

'Now, this report from the SS guards up at Berchtesgaden. I've had Riedel on the phone. There's an important meeting at the Berghof. He wants action now.'

'Shit.'

'Yes, precisely, Ritter.'

Hubert Riedel, one of his old *Kripo* colleagues back in Munich. Riedel had been a mere *Kriminaloberassistant* back then. Efficient enough. But unlikely to make inspector in the *Kripo*. So he'd switched sides. Joined the Gestapo. Made it to *Kriminaldirektor*, an SS *Sturmbannführer* to boot. Not someone it was wise to argue with. For all sorts of reasons.

Nagel was flicking through the report. Ritter had the distinct feeling of deja vu.

'It says here that a young couple and a priest were stopped at an army checkpoint. The priest was from Söllhuben. Our patch. Your patch, I should say. He claimed they were his niece and nephew. Have you checked them out?'

'We're in the process of doing that. Messel and I have spoken to the officer in charge of the roadblock. He knows the priest and insists he's telling the truth. We've spoken to the priest as well. He's adamant the kids are his niece and nephew. I haven't spoken to them yet. But I fully intend to.'

'Maybe you should get them in and sweat them a little?'

'I will talk to them, Ernst. But I'm trying to solve two murders. Drexler's murder has to take priority. I thought you said Munich wanted answers on that.'

Nagel grimaced.

'They do. And now they want answers on the priest and his so-called niece and nephew as well. So you'd better get cracking. You know what that shit Riedel's like. If things go wrong and he can pin it on us, he will. An important meeting at the Berghof means the Führer is coming. We have to protect him at all costs. I'll talk to the editor of the *Anzeiger* and get him to write an article warning people that dangerous subversives have been spotted in the area and that two of them were seen near the Führer's home at the Berghof. I'll give him their descriptions. Someone might read the article and recognize them. That might help.'

What descriptions? All the report gave was the colour of their coats and the fact that they were a man and a woman. The only thing it was likely to do was to bring out the nutters and informants wanting to get one over an unpopular neighbour, or a rival at work. Ritter could see himself and Messel being overwhelmed by the response, but he nodded.

'Good idea.'

He turned and walked out of the office. Somehow, he'd managed to beat up Kleidorfer and get away with it. It made him feel better. But given that Kleidorfer didn't remember why it had happened, it was scarcely likely to stop the prick going near Sophie.

Messel came in at around two o'clock holding a thin file very tight under his arm. He shut the door carefully, making an exaggerated attempt to prevent any sound, and stood looking at the bloodstain on the wall.

'Is that where he hit his head?'

Ritter looked at the wall, savouring the amount of dried blood still clinging to it.

'Yes.'

'They say he's recovered, more's the pity.'

'Apparently so, Messel. We've not got rid of him quite yet.'

'Well, this might help.'

Messel pulled a chair over to Ritter's desk. He placed the file down on the blotter, so it was facing Ritter, and opened it. It contained two pieces of paper. One was a faxed photograph. The other was from *Kripo* headquarters in Berlin. The strips of telex message pasted onto the proforma sheet contrasted oddly with the grand gothic lettering of the Rosenheim *Kreispolizeiamt* at the top. The telex operator had registered it at 09:31 that morning. It had been around for a while.

'The telex from Berlin, boss.'

'So I see, Messel. What does it say?'

'It says that Müller's a British spy.'

'What?'

Ritter picked it up and began to read. Normally the telexes from Berlin were routine. New regulations seemingly designed for no other purpose than to create more paperwork. Requests for data to back up the latest idiotic ideas stemming from the Criminological Technical Institute. Demands for more officers to put themselves forward for membership of the Party or the SS. In a word, garbage. But this message was different. It posed a clear threat, and not just to Ritter's attempts to keep control of the Schinkel and Drexler investigations.

The message itself was terse. Berlin had retrieved the file on the British spy whose fingerprints had been found in the Schweizerhof. They belonged to a Berlin prostitute, last known using the name Marianne Kohl. The fax was a photograph of the spy. There was no doubt about it. The prints were Müller's. The telex repeated Berlin's doubts that the prints were recent but nevertheless suggested that Ritter should involve the Gestapo.

Ritter put the telex down and looked at his assistant.

'Shit. What do we do now, Messel? We can hardly bring the Gestapo in. Müller was Drexler's mistress and she's Kleidorfer's agent. He can't be trusted to deal with this honestly.'

Messel smiled. 'Look on the bright side: at least it gives us a possible motive for the Drexler killing. If Drexler found out Müller was a British spy, that would explain why he was murdered.'

'It's more likely he found out that she was Kleidorfer's spy, Messel.'

'Yes. But remember what Kozlowski said about the killer getting "some sort of release" from stabbing Drexler? That would fit more with Müller than with Kleidorfer.'

The boy had a point. He was developing into a good detective, and he'd completely lost his fascination with Kleidorfer.

'And what about Schultz and her so-called brother? If Müller was working for the British, they must be too. And if Kleidorfer knew she was a British spy, we've got him.'

Messel was building up a head of steam.

'I don't think Kleidorfer could have known she was a British spy, Messel. But you're right. Drexler might have found out. Confronted her. It's the best motive we've seen yet for his murder.'

'But what if Kleidorfer finds out?'

'If he does, Müller's in serious trouble. He'll be after her.'

Kleidorfer would have to keep it quiet at all costs. Did he know already? Was that the real reason he'd been so keen to keep Munich out of the investigation of Drexler's murder, the reason it had been passed back to Ritter? Someone Kleidorfer could keep an eye on?

Ritter couldn't risk showing the telex to Nagel. He'd already made clear he wouldn't support Ritter in a straight fight with the Gestapo. Ritter wondered briefly if he could use Kleidorfer's link to a British spy to bring the Gestapo boss down. It might salvage his relationship with Sophie. But it was risky. The Gestapo would send in a mob of heavies to investigate, and Ritter's own failure to report the presence of a British spy would be discovered. There was no way out. Worse. If Kleidorfer learned about the telex and the photograph of Müller, anyone who'd seen them would be at risk. Kleidorfer would have no choice but to get rid of them.

'Who knows about this, Messel?'

'No one, boss. No one but you and me.'

'And the telex operator.'

Ritter looked at the name of the operator. 'Juliana Kraus.' He didn't know her. Was that the new, young one?

'She's not going to say anything, boss. I think she's a bit sweet on me. I swore her to secrecy. I told her it was a secret assignment to track down a British spy. I had to keep it from everyone. Even you.'

'And she believed you?'

Ritter was slightly offended by the idea that the woman might have thought it possible for Messel to withhold such information from him.

'Are you sure you can trust her not to talk to anyone about it?'

Maybe Messel was right. She was sweet on him. Easy to take in. But she was obviously naive. There still had to be a risk she might say something, or that someone might have seen the telex before Messel did.

'Don't worry, boss. I'm sure Juliana can be trusted. I think she quite liked the idea of being involved. She likes the secrecy of it all.'

'This isn't some sort of game, Messel. Müller was Kleidorfer's informant. If it gets out that he's linked to a known British agent, he'll be in the shit up to his neck. That bump on his head will be the least of his problems. He'll be facing the Special Court. He won't hesitate to get rid of anyone who knows about Müller. You, me, or your sweet little girlfriend. He'll have no choice.'

It was two thirty in the afternoon and Viktor Kozlowski had already drunk more than was good for him or the accuracy of his reports. He stood up as Ritter walked into his office, then fell back into his seat.

'Ritter. Let me guess what you've come for. I've written the Drexler post-mortem. But my secretary hasn't typed it yet. I promise to get it to you tomorrow.'

'I need it now, Viktor.'

Kozlowski looked uncomfortable. Had he really written it?

'Well, look, Ritter. What I can say is that it doesn't tell you anything you don't know. He died around seven that evening. I can't be more precise than that. He was smothered first with a pillow and, once unconscious, stabbed repeatedly. Seventeen times, in fact. It was quite possibly fuelled by passion. A few of the wounds were very close to the groin. You wanted it to be a woman, didn't you?'

Ritter raised his eyes, silently admonishing the pathologist. They'd worked together often enough for Viktor to know that all he wanted was the truth.

'All I'm saying, Ritter, is that it could well have been a woman. I can't be certain. But I can tell you that whoever did it hated Drexler with a vengeance. Very sharp knife. About twenty centimetres long. Double-edged. Neither edge serrated. Very sharp indeed.'

* * *

Ritter sat in the old man's leather chair, warming a glass of Asbach in his hands, struggling to work out a way of getting Sophie to treat his questions about Kleidorfer seriously. He'd tried when he got home that evening but she'd ignored him and gone to bed. She'd left a plate of rye bread, cold meat, and pickles on the table. Ritter wondered if she'd heard about her lover's accident but with Sophie avoiding him it was impossible to tell. It was impossible to find any way of sorting things out, of saving their marriage. The brandy was as close as he could get to comfort.

'You're not handling this very well, Peter. slamming Kleidorfer's head against the wall. Now that wasn't clever.'

'How precisely am I supposed to handle it? The prick's screwing my wife.'

'He's doing far more than that, Peter. Taking Sophie was never going to be enough for Kleidorfer. He wants revenge for the humiliation you inflicted on him in Munich.'

'For Christ's sake, Professor. Why must you always find a way to blame me for anything that goes wrong? I didn't humiliate him in Munich. I barely knew him.'

'That's not the way he sees it, Peter. You won the girl. The girl everyone wanted. The girl he wanted. You humiliated him. He won't be happy until he's ground you into the dirt. You'd better hope he doesn't get his memory back, because if he does you're really in the shit.'

Chapter Twenty-Two

Tuesday 2 February 1943

Litwak moved the dial on the suitcase radio slowly across that day's frequency. The whistle on either side of the carrier wave dipped to a low hum and then returned. He stopped and turned it back slightly until the whistle faded away. London was already up and waiting. Litwak tapped out a simple radio check in Morse code and received a swift reply. Just five characters: QSA5 K – brevity code for 'I hear you fine, over.' They needed to keep as low a profile as possible to evade the German direction-finding units, always scanning the airwaves, homing in on illegal radio stations to pinpoint their location. Litwak's response was even shorter than London's: QRV K – 'Go ahead, over.' London began tapping out its enciphered message. Kate watched over Litwak's shoulder as he took down the stream of figures. There was no danger of discovery while the control station was on the air. It was only while he was transmitting that the intercept units might trap them. As soon as London finished its message, Litwak tapped out a quick five letters: QSL AR – 'Message received, out' – and switched off the radio. He was safe. There was no way the intercept operators could have got anywhere near tracking him down with such a short time spent on the air.

'How's it encrypted?'

Litwak picked up the Latin bible that sat on the bedside cabinet.

'Book code. London decided this would be the safest one to use given that I was going to be staying in the home of a Catholic priest.'

Kate snorted. Still less than impressed with the SOE tradecraft.

'If they ever got so close as to be searching the house I think they'd find the radio soon enough.'

Litwak ignored her and set to work decoding the message. He wasn't going to get involved in these stupid games that MI6 and SOE played. It was unprofessional. Particularly given what was at stake.

It didn't take him long to realize that London wasn't happy.

Newspaper reports suggest recce of target area carried out by man and woman spotted by guards. Concern this end re presence of woman. Essential you liquidate. No sign of target arrival as yet. Lie low. Watch skeds.

Liquidate. That word again. Even his own people used it. Litwak looked at Kate, who'd been reading the message over his shoulder as he deciphered it.

'They think I've picked up some tart. A security risk. They want me to get rid of her. I should probably tell them. Explain who you are. What we're doing.'

Kate laughed. But not like before. This time there was no affection.

'Are you mad, Jonny? Can you imagine what they'd say? There'd be a huge stink over this in London. My bosses would get in trouble with Churchill. They'd probably get sacked. I certainly would. So, no, Jonny. No. You don't tell them.'

Her arrogance was beginning to grate. Who the fuck was she to tell him what to do? He felt like hitting her to put her in her place.

'So what the fuck do you suggest I tell them then?'

'You don't tell them anything. They didn't ask for a response. If you go back on the air now, the German intercept operators might pick up the signal and track you down. Just do what you're told. Lie low and watch the frequencies at the scheduled times. If they come back up and ask about the couple chased off the Obersalzberg, say you don't know what they're talking about; your recce went fine. You were alone. You weren't detected. The couple were probably just kids trying to get a look at Hitler.'

That 'I know best' attitude was irritating. The trouble was, she was probably right. London couldn't know for sure that it was him that had been spotted up there. He just needed to make sure he'd thought everything through next time. It would be nice to bring her down a peg or two, but not yet. He still needed her. There might come a time when he didn't but it wasn't now. For now, he needed to keep her happy, keep her on board.

'Thank God you were up on the mountain, Kate. If you hadn't have been there, God alone knows how I would have got away.'

Kate smiled at him, her head cocked to one side, half laughing; no rancour now.

'Nonsense. You'd have got away. You'd have just done it differently.' A warm smile this time. Gently teasing. Inviting. She shook her head. Her hair swaying enticingly. 'You underrate your ability, Jonny. You really do. There was nothing wrong with your plan at all. It was the priest that made the difference and he wouldn't have done it for you. You shouldn't blame yourself for that.'

She looked directly into his eyes. Slowly moving her lips towards his. His movements were deliberate. Almost regimented. He brushed her hair back with a hand. Kissed her. Forced her back down onto the bed. Every move thought out beforehand. Painstakingly methodical. A simple soldier going through a drill. There was no urgency to his lovemaking. No passion. No passion at all. He knew now what he had to do.

* * *

Messel handed Ritter the pathologist's report on the Drexler murder without a word.

'At last. Getting information out of Viktor is like pulling teeth, but he's exceeded even his reputation for tardiness with this one. Does he tell us anything we don't already know?'

'Nothing much. A bit about the knife. But otherwise it's impossible to see why he had to be so laggardly.'

'Laggardly? I wouldn't use that word with Viktor if I were you. He did say there'd be nothing new. I'd better read it through though. Just to make sure.'

While Ritter concentrated on Kozlowski's report, Messel looked around the room at the files still stacked against the walls. 'I see the new filing cabinets haven't been delivered.'

'There's a war on, Messel. I'm sure my new filing cabinets come pretty far down the list of essential items.'

Messel picked up one of the case files and read the title.

'Maria Schilling.'

Ritter looked up from the report and began reciting the bare details of Schilling's case, as if by rote.

'Farmer's wife. Investigated for "improper use of a prisoner" following complaints from a neighbouring farmer.'

Messel opened it. He looked up, surprised that Ritter could remember the detail of such a minor case.

'That's right. Why's it not solved?'

Ritter had resumed reading the report into Drexler's death. He didn't look up this time.

'Not enough evidence. That's what it says there, doesn't it? Can you put it back, please?'

'There's a note here that says the POW admitted it.'

Ritter sighed but continued to read Kozlowski's report.

'Yes, so did she. But in her statement, she denied it.' Did they really have to discuss this nothing case now? Didn't they have more important things to worry about? 'Look, Messel. It's very simple. Her husband was killed at the start of the war. In Poland. She'd been running the farm on her own for eighteen months and the French prisoner of war she'd been allocated had been a great help with the harvest. I didn't see why it was any business of mine or the state's if he'd also been a comfort to her.'

'That's what "improper use of a prisoner" means?'

'Apparently so. Yes.'

'But if you know she did it, surely it isn't a "not solved" file.'

Ritter stopped reading Kozlowski's report and looked at his trainee, then at the stack of files. His face held no expression at all.

'Yes it is, Messel. So far as I'm concerned, it's like all the rest of those investigations. It's not going anywhere until the new filing cabinets arrive, and when they do it will be filed away and never see the light of day again. It's unsolved.'

Messel placed the Schilling case back on the pile. Ritter resumed his reading of Kozlowski's account of Drexler's death.

'Christ almighty. It says here he lost an estimated eight litres of blood. I thought human beings only had seven litres in them.'

'He was a big man, boss. He probably had upwards of nine.'

Ritter paused in his reading and smiled.

'Yet who would have thought the old man to have had so much blood in him?'

'Lady Macbeth?'

'Very good, Messel. I'm impressed. His blood type's AB. The rarest group. It's the same as mine.'

'I wouldn't have imagined the same blood ran in the two of you, boss.'

Messel teasing him. Their relationship seemed to be improving with every day. The phone rang. Ritter looked at it suspiciously, as if it were an intruder interrupting his studies. It was Kurt Naumann on the front desk. There was a woman there demanding to speak to Ritter.

'It's a Frau Gundelach, housekeeper of the priest in Söllhuben. "Urgent police business," she says. She wants to report a crime but she'll only talk to you.'

'All right. I'll be up in a minute.'

Ritter put the phone down and paused, wondering why Gundelach had chosen to come to him now when she'd spent so much time trying to avoid talking to him only a few days earlier.

'Messel. Can you find something else to do? Steiner's housekeeper wants to talk to me. I don't think she'll talk while you're around.'

'I can't imagine why, boss. It's not as if I'd be able to understand anything she said.'

Ritter smiled. Two jokes in the space of a minute. The boy had found a sense of humour.

'Oh, and Messel. Before you go. Did you phone the chemical company about that truck?'

Messel grimaced and shook his head apologetically.

'I did try, boss. I couldn't get through. I'll make another call.'

* * *

Frau Adaleiz Gundelach was short and slim. If she'd been thirty years younger she might have been described as petite. But she didn't show any sign of wanting to make the most of her appearance. Ritter glimpsed a grey pinafore dress under a well-worn, dull green Loden coat; a knitted woollen hat, also dull green; Lisle stockings; and heavy laced boots. She looked precisely what she was, the elderly housekeeper of a priest.

'Inspector. Thank you for seeing me.'

'Thank you for coming to see us, Frau Gundelach. Please, come through here.'

Ritter led her into a small, cold interview room. It was sparsely furnished and unwelcoming. Just one table, bare apart from a blotting pad and a few sheets of paper, with a chair on either side, no other furniture. The only natural light came from a single, heavily barred window high up on one of the walls. Ritter pulled out a chair for her and sat on the other. He took a pen from his inside pocket and lined the paper up in front of him.

'So, Frau Gundelach. How can I help you?'

'I want to report a crime, Inspector. A sex crime.'

Ritter's face betrayed his surprise. He'd expected suspicions and gossip about Schultz and her so-called brother. He hadn't expected Gundelach, of all women, to have been the victim of such an attack. He stood up.

'I should get a female officer, Frau Gundelach. I'm sure you'll feel much more at ease with a woman here.'

'Not me, you idiot.'

She said it so loudly that a *Schupo* officer outside the door opened it to check that everything was all right. Ritter waved him away and sat back down, leaning slightly across the table to encourage Gundelach to say more.

'It's not me, Inspector. It's Father Josef's niece and nephew, Johann and Inge Schultz.'

Ritter looked puzzled.

'They're brother and sister.'

Gundelach nodded knowingly.

'Exactly. Incest.' She paused to let the word sink in. 'He'd left the door of his room open. I saw them together.'

Ritter must have looked sceptical.

'On the bed,' she insisted. 'Close together. Much too close together. She saw me and shut the door very quickly. Gave me a hard look as if to say, 'mind your business.' But it was too late.' Gundelach was almost smirking. 'I'd seen enough. She thinks I'm an old maid. What would I know? But I know what I saw.'

'And have you mentioned this to Father Josef?'

'No, of course not. He'd be distraught if he knew what they were up to. His own flesh and blood. Father Josef must never know.' Gundelach lifted a finger towards him. 'Promise me that.' She waited until Ritter nodded his assent before continuing. 'I want you to have a word with them. Frighten them off. It's illegal, isn't it, incest? Not to mention that they're abusing holy ground.'

Her heavy accent made the *Alpenbayerisch* even more difficult to understand.

'Holy ground? The presbytery, you mean?'

'Yes, of course, a house of God. Not that it would matter to you, I'm sure. But incest's a crime. That's why I've come to you. If you talk to them, it will shake them up. They won't want to get arrested. They'll leave and stop putting Father Josef at risk.'

'At risk? I don't see … through the incest, you mean?'

'No. The other thing. Whatever it is you've been asking about. I heard Father Josef shouting at her. He said you'd been asking questions, that she and her brother were putting his work with the church at risk. She should never have brought her brother to the presbytery. It would compromise his mission, destroy everything he was doing.'

She nodded her head as she spoke, as though punctuating every word.

'How well do you know the niece and nephew? They must have visited him before.'

'She has. A number of times over the past four or five years. I've never seen him before.'

Over the past four or five years. So Schultz and Steiner had been working together since before the war. Her brother was new.

'Thank you, Frau Gundelach. I think you're right. I should talk to them. Are they at the presbytery now?'

'No. I haven't seen them today. They've been spending a lot of time in Riedering with that whore from Berlin.'

The word whore was spat out. Gundelach didn't attempt to hide the offence she felt.

'Marianne Müller?'

'Yes. Her.'

'Where in Riedering? With the nuns?'

'Yes, the holy sisters from the Fraueninsel. They have a refuge for fallen women there. I don't understand how they could let Johann in. What with him being a man. But they do.'

* * *

Litwak couldn't work out why Kate was so insistent that they had to get out of the safe house. It didn't matter what his people in London had said, they had to leave the presbytery. He wondered whether he should ask London first. But he'd have to explain about Kate, and she was right – they'd go up the wall.

'Father Josef is adamant, Jonny. That *Kripo* inspector. Ritter. He's getting too close. If we're not careful, we'll compromise the safe house and Father Josef 's operations. He's right. We've been here long enough. We must get out.'

'Where will we go? Closer to the Berghof?'

'No. The security checks are too frequent there. We'll stay around here.'

'But the police already think we're the priest's nephew and niece. We've already put him at risk wherever we go. Haven't we?'

Kate was becoming irritated. 'Look. We have to get out.' She softened her voice. 'The problem's the direct link between us and Father Josef. We need to draw attention away from him and the safe house. The nuns will help us.'

Certainly, he'd be happy to get away from the priest. Steiner was a tough man. Independent. He could be dangerous. Kate was different. She not only knew what she was doing, she'd proved herself committed to keeping them both alive. Without her, they would never have got off the mountain. The warning from London worried him. Maybe they were right. Kate had said herself that MI6 didn't want him to succeed. He didn't want to have to kill her, but he had to get rid of Hitler. He owed that to his father, and to all the Jews who would die if he didn't succeed.

The more time Kate and he spent together, the more difficult killing her would be. He still hoped he wouldn't need to, that she was honest about wanting to help him. After all, she could have finished him off up on the mountain. She was good. She knew the territory. Kept a cool head.

Chapter Twenty-Three

Friday 5 February 1943

For as long as Ritter had known Viktor Kozlowski, the pathologist had cultivated a reputation for being miserable. So the morose tone of the telephone call came as no surprise. The only odd thing was that Viktor felt he needed to speak to Ritter so urgently that he was ringing from a public kiosk.

'Ritter. Bad news, I'm afraid. We've got another body.'

'Linked to the others?'

'Well, certainly linked to Schinkel's and, yes, quite possibly to Drexler's as well. You'd better get down here now.'

Typical Viktor. Making things difficult. Getting anything out of him was impossible. Ritter hid his irritation and tried friendly patience.

'Down where, Viktor? Where's the body?'

'Down by the bridge over the Inn.'

'What? Like Schinkel's?'

'No. Not exactly.' Viktor really was piling on the misery, drawing the whole thing out. 'It was in the river where all those dead fish have collected. That's why it wasn't spotted earlier.'

The stench of rotting fish. It had been getting worse recently, infiltrating every corner of the old town. Ritter wasn't looking forward to going back down to the bridge. Typical of Messel that he wasn't around when he needed him. A third murder, and by the sound of it the first real link between the Schinkel and Drexler killings.

For no immediately discernible reason, Ritter felt concern. A sinking feeling in his stomach. 'Who is it, Viktor? Do we have an identity?'

'You'd better get down here, Ritter. The sooner, the better.'

It was no longer just Viktor keeping things back because he was Viktor. The adrenaline was pumping through Ritter, tensing his throat, cramping his stomach. He grabbed his coat and the keys to the car and rushed up the stairs, his heart thumping so hard he could almost hear it. The car took three turns of the key before it started. He reversed, the BMW's tyres searching for grip on the frozen snow, and drove at speed down the Adolf-Hitler-Strasse towards the bridge.

They'd hauled Messel out onto the bank. Viktor met Ritter as he got out of the car, holding up his hands to the detective's chest to try to block his path to the body.

'I'm sorry, Ritter. The *Schupo* thought it was a drunk at first. That's why they rang me. It wasn't until I turned him over… that's when I phoned.'

'Who did this, Viktor? Is there any sign of who it might have been?'

'The top of his head's gone. It looks like he blew his brains out.'

'Why the fuck would he do that?'

Ritter realized he needed to restrain himself. No point in swearing at Viktor. That would get him nowhere. He had to treat this like any other murder. That was the only way to get through it.

'How did his body get into the river?'

'He was kneeling beside it when he fired the pistol. Sometime last night. He fell in among the dead fish so he wasn't noticed until this afternoon. It definitely happened here. There are bits of blood on the bank, and his pistol.'

Viktor looked at Ritter's face.

'Maybe we should get one of the other detectives?'

Ritter pushed him aside.

'I have seen this sort of thing before, Viktor.'

He walked over to the body. What was left of Messel's blond hair was discoloured by blood and littered with muck from the river. Scales from rotting fish clung to his clothes. Viktor was right. From the marks in the snow, it looked as if Messel had knelt on the bank, stuck the pistol in his mouth, and pulled the trigger. The boy had been so proud of his Walther PPK. A modern police weapon. Much more effective than Ritter's old-fashioned Sauer. God, how right the boy had been. But Messel had no reason to kill himself – none that Ritter could think of – and how could he have toppled into the river if he was kneeling like that? The power of the PPK would surely have forced him backward, not forward. The boy was smartly dressed. A suit and tie. Why dress up to commit suicide?

For a brief moment Ritter wondered whether Viktor was right. Should they get someone else to do this? Then he noticed the pale pink residue on the boy's shirt. Blood. Washed out and muddied by the river but nevertheless still there. He crouched down beside the body and opened the front of the jacket to get a clearer look.

'Viktor.'

'What's wrong?'

Not the usual Viktor, obstreperous, refusing to back down. This Viktor seemed strangely desperate to do anything to help.

'If Messel put his pistol in his mouth and blew his brains out, why is there so much blood on the front of his shirt?'

'Some of it might have got on there as he fell.'

'Really? This much? Have you seen it? Look at it. It's right across his shirt underneath his jacket. It's on his tie. But there's virtually no blood on the outside of the jacket at all.'

The pathologist bent down and pulled the jacket back.

'You're right, Ritter. It's difficult to see how he could have got that much blood on his shirt shooting the top of his head off. There are no other wounds it could have come from.'

Ritter and Kozlowski looked at each other. Both thinking the same thing: Was there another corpse out there? Ritter looked back down at Messel's body.

Yet who would have thought. So much blood?

Had that really been their final conversation?

'What? What are you talking about, Ritter?'

'Nothing that matters now.'

So whose blood was it if it wasn't Messel's? Had someone else been shot, and why? Messel was wearing a suit and tie. Who was he trying to impress? A girl? The telex operator, Juliana Kraus. She was sweet on him. The boy had told her that only he and she knew about the British spy. Where was she?

Ritter looked up. Kurt Naumann was supervising the *Schupo* operation to prevent any members of the public getting close to the scene.

'Kurt.'

Naumann turned around. Ritter walked over to him.

'You know that new telex operator, Juliana Kraus?'

Naumann nodded. There were unlikely to be many men working in the *Mittertor* who hadn't noticed her.

'She and Messel were close. We have to find her. Send someone back now to make sure she's all right. If she's not on shift, they should go to her home and check on her.'

'No problem. I've finished here. I'm going back. I'll do it myself.'

'Thanks, Kurt.'

Viktor looked at Ritter suspiciously.

'Where does the little teleprinter girl fit into all this, Ritter?'

Ritter wondered. Should he confide in Viktor? Maybe. But not here. Not right now.

'I'll tell you later, Viktor. How long does the boy have to lie here? Surely, you've got all you need? I'm going back. I'll have to inform his parents.'

'His parents? You don't know. I thought…'

'You thought what, Viktor?'

'His parents are dead.'

What? Messel had never said anything about this. He was his boss. He ought at least to have known something about the boy's background. Certainly that his parents were dead.

'How?'

'I'm not sure. It happened some time before he joined up. A traffic accident, I think. A drunk. That's why he became a policeman. He was the only child. Surely you knew. He always seemed so close to you.'

'Close? To me?'

'Yes. He barely spoke to anyone else at work, and even when he did, it was always "the Inspector this." or "the Inspector that."'

There was a hammering sensation behind Ritter's forehead. He shook his head, trying to dull the pain, and turned back towards the car. He walked with his hands clenched in his pockets, elbows tight against his side, huddled into his coat against the cold, against everything.

'I'll move him now, Ritter. But when I get back to the station, we should talk.'

Ritter turned back towards Viktor. Puzzled. Talk about what?

'The link to Kraus? You said you'd explain.'

Ritter gave a slight nod of acknowledgment and turned his back on the river, on the stench of rotting fish, and on the boy who'd wanted more from him than he knew how to give.

* * *

Juliana Kraus was young, in her mid-twenties. Vivacious, always smiling, long dark hair, full of curls. Definitely not the archetypal blonde German girl. Too slim. Her face too finely detailed. There were some who even suspected her of being Jewish. But she was of good Aryan stock, of that you could have no doubt. She was also very beautiful. Even in death.

Her apartment was small. A bed-sitting room with a tiny kitchen area and a separate lavatory. It was tidy – no sign of a struggle. Crockery carefully stacked. No washing-up in the sink. Everything else neatly in its place. Photos of family, posing in their Sunday best. Pride of place for a picture of a pretty young woman. She looked like Kraus but must have been her mother. She had her arms around two young girls. They were all smiling for the camera.

There were a few ornaments: a china dog with chipped paint, an egg timer attached to a blue china windmill, a little Dutch boy in blue overalls, clogs, and top hat. On a bedside table lay a doll with a pallid china face. There was blood on the bed. Quite a bit of blood. But only a few traces elsewhere, leading from the bed to the sink and out to the door.

Nagel had called Ritter into his office before he'd left for the girl's apartment. The *Kripo* boss had been worried. Very worried.

'For God's sake. Couldn't you have kept him under control? It's bad enough having a serial killer on the loose without it being one of my own men. The mayor's frantic. God alone knows what Munich and Berlin will do. And now you say Kozlowski thinks Messel might have killed Drexler as well?'

'I didn't say that, Ernst. All Kozlowski said on the radio was that Kraus had been stabbed repeatedly like Drexler. He doesn't think it's the same killer and nor do I. Messel's found something out about the murder of the Jew and he's been bumped off to shut him up.'

Nagel was back on the nicotine and, by the look of his ashtray, chain-smoking. How much should Ritter tell him? He'd need some pretty good evidence before he started accusing Kleidorfer of murder. And right now, the bloodstain on Messel's shirt made the boy the prime suspect in the girl's killing. It was precisely what Nagel needed.

'So Messel didn't kill Drexler. Only the girl. Good. It was probably a sex thing. Nothing to do with the two other killings. Messel topped himself as a result of guilt and remorse. That's good. An open-and-shut case. We've already got the murderer and he's even saved the courts a job. Go to the girl's flat. Speak to Kozlowski, and make sure you come back with an explanation I can sell to both the mayor and Munich. God. Who knew we had such a maniac in our ranks?'

Nagel at his worst, cherry-picking the facts and inventing a few of his own to make the case go away.

Ritter was absolutely certain that Messel hadn't killed Kraus and he didn't believe the boy had committed suicide. But despite the flaws in his boss's assessment, its central thrust was correct. All the evidence pointed to Messel being the killer and nothing here, in the girl's apartment, suggested anything different.

Viktor had placed a sheet over the girl, covering her nakedness and the gaping wounds in her body, and was waiting for the van from the morgue to collect her. The sheet had soaked up some of the blood in a series of interlocking circles.

'There's a fair amount of blood here, Ritter. Not as much as with Drexler. But certainly enough.'

'No signs of a sexual attack?'

'No. None at all.'

'Was it like Drexler? The stab wounds, I mean?'

Viktor lifted up the sheet so Ritter could see the naked body beneath. There were a dozen or so wounds on the breasts and down the belly. But it was nowhere near as bloody as Drexler's. The girl's head was bent back. She had the look of a tragic Hollywood heroine, her black eyeliner smudged by tears.

'She was stabbed and slashed with a very sharp knife, Ritter. Was it similar to the one used on Drexler? Certainly. But if you're asking me to say it was the same person. No, I wouldn't say it was. There's none of the passion we saw with Drexler.'

'What about the white rose?'

'There's no sign of one.'

'So not Drexler's killer?'

'Definitely not. But that's clear from the wounds. I'm sorry, Ritter. You said it yourself. That blood couldn't have been Messel's. He murders Kraus, some sort of argument between lovers, and kills himself out of remorse.'

The pathologist had walked over to the stove to light his pipe. It was long and narrow with a cherrywood bowl carved in the shape of a stag's head and a tiny pewter cap, like a tankard. A treasured possession. Viktor always spent an inordinate amount of time lighting it, as if it were this that gave him the most pleasure. Satisfied it was lit, he drew on it several times and then stood looking at the girl's body from a distance. Almost as if he was a wholly disinterested spectator. Ritter waited for him to take the pipe from his mouth.

'No. I don't buy it, Viktor. It's too easy. Too pat. Too much of a coincidence.'

'What do you mean a coincidence?'

Ritter looked around. The photographer had gone and the one *Schupo* officer left was outside the door of the girl's apartment stopping anyone coming in. He had to share this with someone, in case he was next, and Viktor was the only person he could even half trust with what he knew.

'Messel had uncovered a link between Kleidorfer and a British spy. There was a telex from Berlin. Kraus was the operator who processed the telex. Messel swore her to secrecy.'

'You can't be serious. You're looking to pin this on Kleidorfer? The new head of the city Gestapo? The man who's screwing your wife?'

Ritter winced. How many people knew? The entire station? He didn't have time to think about it now. It was more important to prove that the boy didn't kill Kraus.

'I'm sorry, Ritter. I shouldn't have said it,' Viktor was muttering. 'Bar-room gossip. They're idiots. What would they know? I really shouldn't have repeated it. I'm sorry.'

'So you said, Viktor. I'm more concerned with trying to work out what happened here. Messel was obviously in the apartment when Kraus was murdered. That's how he got all that blood on him. But I don't believe he killed her. And I don't believe he killed himself.'

Viktor was distracted. Deep in thought.

'The telex about the British spy does put a different complexion on it, I have to say. I'd already begun to ask myself whether suicide was the correct conclusion.'

Really? Then why hadn't he said so earlier? He'd been willing to dump it all on the boy a few minutes ago. Now he was reversing faster than an Italian tank.

'There are signs of a struggle on Messel's hands and a few bits of skin under his nails. Kraus didn't struggle much so far as I can see. There's no sign of damage to her nails and hands, so she couldn't have caused the scratches on Messel's hands.'

The pathologist's enthusiasm for his new theory was increasing with every word.

'And if he did kneel down on the bank to shoot himself, I don't see him falling into the river. More likely he was pushed. In which case, it probably wasn't him that pulled the trigger.'

Viktor had done a complete about-turn. It was out of character for him to rethink his conclusions simply because Ritter – or indeed anyone else – disagreed with them. But it wouldn't convince Nagel.

'Speculation isn't enough, Viktor. I need evidence that someone else was involved. Nagel is only interested in one conclusion: Messel kills Kraus; Messel kills himself. All neat and tidy. No loose ends. The case can be closed and forgot about. That's all he wants right now. No fallout from this landing on his head. There's no way he'd sanction any further investigation, and certainly not of Kleidorfer.'

'You could smash Kleidorfer's head against the wall again. Maybe do a better job this time?'

'I didn't do anything to him last time, Viktor. He slipped.'

'If you say so. But you're right about Nagel. He certainly isn't going to take Kleidorfer on.'

Viktor wasn't ready to accuse the Gestapo officer of murder either. But he did at least seem to accept that there might be more to Messel's death than met the eye.

'The best thing you can do, Ritter, is play along for now. Give Nagel what he wants. You and I can keep looking at it, and if we get any evidence that Messel was murdered, we can take it back to him together. If we both say it wasn't Messel, he'll have to agree to a fresh investigation.'

It sounded like wishful thinking. Largely because that's what it was. Ritter knew Nagel. His boss would never agree to reopen the case once it was closed. If he'd told Berlin, Munich, and the mayor that Messel murdered Kraus and then committed suicide, that there was no link at all to Drexler's death, he wouldn't want to go back and admit he'd got it wrong. He certainly wouldn't want to start accusing a senior Gestapo officer of committing murder to cover up his involvement with a British spy. Ritter knew he had no choice but to write the case up the way Nagel wanted. But he owed it to Messel not to leave it there. To make Kleidorfer pay the price for what he'd done and to clear the boy's name. He was the closest Messel had to anyone who cared.

'There's nothing you can do for him now, Peter. Bide your time. You'll clear his name. It's what you're good at. Hopeless cases. He's just another one to stack up against the wall.'

'So what happened to all that stuff about moral choices, old man?'

'The last time I heard anyone mention them, you were lecturing the boy. The dead can wait. Nothing you can do will bring Messel back. You need to sort out the living.'

'Like who?'

'Like Müller. And what were that British spy and her so-called brother doing up on the mountain?'

'I haven't the faintest idea. The priest says they weren't up on the mountain.'

'And you believe him?'

'He's a priest.'

'That's right, he's a priest. He spends his life telling people a Jewish rebel was strung up and left to die on a Friday and came back to life on a Sunday.'

'Of course, I don't believe him, but I can hardly call in the Gestapo. If I did that, I'd be the one strung up and left to die. At the end of a length of piano wire.'

'And what would two British spies be doing only a couple of kilometres from the Führer's mountain retreat?'

'Spying; what else?'

'Really? What do you suppose they'd learn lying out there in the snow?'

'How well he's protected?'

'Which they'd need to know because.?'

'Because they wanted to kill him?'

'Well done. You got there in the end. Who would have thought that a couple of British spies could want precisely the same thing as any decent German?'

'Careful, old man. That's treason.'

'So what are they going to do? Kill me?'

Chapter Twenty-Four

Monday 8 February 1943

The old Augustine abbey on the Ettstrasse that served as the *Kripo*'s Munich headquarters had been sliced open by the bombing raids a few days earlier. The entire wall of someone's office, from the size of it someone important, was open to the elements like a doll's house. Chains of plaster connected by strips of wallpaper swung precariously from the sides of the gap and snow was beginning to build in small drifts along the open front. Ritter paid off the taxi, turned up his collar, and hurried into the building.

Ritter showed his warrant disc to one of the uniformed *Schupo* officers behind the front desk.

'Inspector Peter Ritter from Rosenheim. Can you direct me to the Ninth Commissariat, please? I'm here to see Commissar Konrad Barth.'

'If you'll take a seat over there, sir. I'll ring the commissar to let him know you're here.'

The *Schupo* officer nodded towards several rows of benches, all of which appeared to be occupied by assorted members of Munich's criminal fraternity.

'Just sit down. Someone will come to collect you.'

Ritter's 'thank you' was deliberately unconvincing. The officer behind the desk glanced up briefly, raised his hand towards the benches, and turned away to do something more important. There had been a time when he would have known all the *Schupo* officers on the front desk of the Munich police headquarters, when they would have been queueing up to help Inspector Peter Ritter, not telling him to sit and wait like everyone else until someone got around to ringing the Ninth Directorate. But he didn't recognize any of the faces behind the desks. Even the older ones. He turned away, ran his eye over several rows of hustlers and whores, and decided he'd rather stand.

Ritter had first met Konrad Barth at Ludwig Maximilian University. The older man was a guest speaker at the law faculty, filling the real detective slot, full of the importance of collecting evidence and assembling the facts. His talk persuaded Ritter that the *Kriminalpolizei* was the place for him and Barth had been his mentor in the early twenties, when he first started at 'the Abbey.' Back then the older man was the inspector, the stickler for 'good, honest detective work,' and Ritter a young up-and-coming *Kriminalsekretär*. It had been Barth who taught him that trying to force the truth out of witnesses or suspects rarely worked. More subtle methods always got closer to the truth.

Barth had given the arrogant young law graduate a few lessons in life and a good grounding in detective work, while all the time impressing on him that only experience, and how he dealt with it, would turn him into a good detective. He'd been brought out of retirement a few months earlier as a commissar. How he'd managed to keep his principles and operate at that level under the current regime was a mystery. But there was a shortage of good detectives. Maybe it was the heads of Munich *Kripo* Control Centre who were compromising their 'principles,' not Barth.

'Peter. How are you?'

Barth gave Ritter a bear hug and for a moment it felt as if he was twelve again, as if it were his father, holding him that one last time.

'Are you staying the night? You must come to our place, for dinner at least. Letta would love to see you.'

'No. I'm sorry, Konrad. I have to go back today.'

'Well, come on up anyway. We can't talk here.'

Barth took him up to the Ninth Commissariat, the centre's 'technical research' section. He told his secretary to bring in two cups of 'proper coffee' and showed Ritter into his office.

'This is my new empire. This is what they called me back for. Too many senior officers going off to the occupied territories. No one spare to head up a new section that most of them don't understand.'

'I've heard what's been going on with the mass killings of Jews in the East. It would be repulsive whoever did it, but that police officers could…'

Konrad lifted a finger to his lips.

'Be careful. This isn't the old Abbey. Walls have ears, and that isn't an exaggeration in this place. My secretary will be in here at any moment with the coffee. My return was not welcomed by everyone in this building.' Barth turned and winked at him. 'But I try not to interfere too much.'

Ritter laughed.

'It would be good to see what you've got here.'

'I'll show you round once we've had a coffee. We can deal with virtually anything here. Ballistics, fingerprints, palm prints, detailed examination of forged documents. Some of the equipment we've got is a bit of a shock for old-fashioned detectives like me.'

The secretary walked in without knocking, carrying a tray with two cups of black coffee. She set them down on the table and went to leave.

'Thank you, Else. Can you make sure that Inspector Ritter and I are not disturbed, please?'

She nodded and shut the door behind her. Barth took a sip of the coffee, savouring it with closed eyes. Then he looked at Ritter. 'So, I suppose I shouldn't be surprised to see you here. You seem to be having a few problems we might be able to help you solve. What is it? Three murders, one of them the local Gestapo boss?'

'Four.'

'Four?' Barth looked surprised.

'Yes. Four. I suspect the one you're not counting is my probationer, Stefan Messel.'

'Ah, yes. Messel. The boy who committed suicide. But I thought he was the killer, of the girl at least.'

'No. He was shot by the real killer and framed for the girl's murder. The problem is that although I'm certain who did it, I can't prove it. That's why I'm here.'

'If you can't prove it, how can you be certain?'

This was going to be difficult. Barth was never likely to accept that Kleidorfer had killed anyone without evidence. He certainly wasn't going to take part in fitting anyone up, even a Gestapo officer. Ritter knew he could convince his old boss that Messel didn't commit suicide, but proving Kleidorfer did it was another matter.

'I just know.'

Barth sat back in his chair, lit his pipe, and adopted the contemplative pose Ritter knew so well from his early career. A return to the mentoring years. Odd that Messel's death had turned him from tutor back to student.

'All right, let's accept for the moment that you're right. Who did it, and why?'

'Klaus Kleidorfer, the deputy Gestapo chief.'

'Kleidorfer? The name's familiar.'

'He was in my class at Ludwig Maximilian, along with Sophie. You taught him. He was one of Sophie's oldest friends, one of her closest friends, even now. They both went missing on the night that Drexler died. Kleidorfer's taken over as local Gestapo boss.'

'Ah. I see.' Barth frowned and fiddled with his pipe. 'Well, that explains some of the difficulties, but why would he want to murder Messel and the girl?'

Ritter explained the background to the Drexler killing, the discovery that the Gestapo chief's mistress was a British spy, and why Kleidorfer needed to cover it up. Barth sat listening to Ritter's account of the discrepancies over the killings of Messel and the girl.

'So you think Drexler's mistress was a British spy but she was also spying on Drexler for Kleidorfer.' Barth shook his head and laughed. 'You should report this spy to the Gestapo, but you can't because Kleidorfer will kill to stop anyone finding out.'

'Exactly. I need to find a way to…'

Barth held up his hand and shook his head. There were raised voices outside. Barth's secretary was trying to explain to someone, a man, that her boss could not be disturbed. The voice was familiar.

'He will see me, young lady. I'm a Gestapo *Kriminaldirektor*. And you would do well to let me in.'

The door was flung open to reveal a large man in a smart woollen suit filling the doorway. He was older and much fatter, but there was no mistaking who it was. Hubert Riedel.

'Commissar Barth. I do hope you don't mind me interrupting. Ah. Ritter. What a pleasant surprise.'

Pleasant was not the first word Ritter would have used, and he doubted that Riedel was surprised to see him. But the Gestapo officer had made it through the door and was standing in the middle of the office smiling broadly.

Barth stepped in.

'Inspector Ritter and I were just discussing how the Ninth Commissariat might help solve the spate of killings he's dealing with in Rosenheim, *Herr Kriminaldirektor*. You'll be familiar with the murder of Commissar Gerhard Drexler.'

'Yes, of course. The town Gestapo chief…'

'City Gestapo chief.'

'Sorry?' From the look on Riedel's face, he wasn't used to being interrupted these days.

'Rosenheim's a city, not a town.'

'Indeed, with a suitably distinguished detective to investigate its murders.'

Riedel seemed to have taken the correction in a better spirit than it was given.

'I wasn't surprised, of course, that my bosses decided that you should investigate the Drexler murder. I have my hands full right now with these White Rose scum. But if you need my help, you only have to ask.'

Barth intervened again.

'Inspector Ritter was, as I say, seeking my advice.'

'I'm sure he needs it, Commissar.'

Riedel turned to Ritter.

'I hear you have another murder on your hands, committed by

one of your own detectives. Nothing like drumming up business for yourselves.'

'You prick.'

Ritter stepped towards Riedel, his fists clenched, but Barth had anticipated it and was up and pushing him back.

'I'm sure you've misunderstood what *Kriminaldirektor* Riedel meant, Peter.'

Barth turned to Riedel.

'I hope you'll forgive his reaction, *Herr Kriminaldirektor*. He was very close to the boy who died.'

Riedel was smiling.

'Don't worry, Commissar. I know Inspector Ritter couldn't stand the heat here in Munich. But he's a good detective, and his bosses in Rosenheim must be pleased to have him… for now. I'm sure I'll be seeing him again soon.'

Riedel turned to go. Then stopped.

'Oh, one thing.'

The smile had gone, replaced by a dark, menacing scowl.

'This is for your ears only, Ritter. I asked that you look into the couple who were run off the Obersalzberg.'

'I am looking into it, but the two so-called suspects have an alibi.'

'Well they'd better lose that alibi, hadn't they? For your ears only. The Führer is on his way to the Berghof for an important meeting. I want those two arrested and handed over to me. And I don't want any of your fucking excuses.'

With that, Riedel left.

Barth opened a file cabinet and took out a bottle of Asbach and two glasses. He poured two large drinks and handed one to Ritter.

'I'm sorry, Konrad. But the man's an asshole.'

'Yes. Well, if he didn't know you thought that before, he certainly does now. I'm not sure it was very helpful.'

'It wasn't a coincidence that he just happened to stroll over here to see you when I'm in your office.'

'Of course not. But if the Führer is on his way to the Berghof, it's not unreasonable to expect you to arrest anyone who might be a threat. And you heard him. He offered to help with the Drexler investigation. There might be a way to turn that to our advantage.'

'There is no way at all. Riedel can't be trusted. He'd stitch us both up as soon as look at us.'

'Which is why we have to stick to the facts, to place our faith in good detective work and in the evidence it produces.'

Barth's homilies were taking him back to his earliest days in Munich. It was hard to believe that only a few days earlier he'd been saying similar things to Messel.

'Facts, Peter. That's what we need. Facts. Get me evidence linking Kleidorfer to Drexler's murder. That's the only one of your murders they care about. Find the evidence and send it to me for tests. I'll draw Riedel's attention to it. He'll jump at the chance to solve Drexler's murder himself.'

'He's Gestapo. He's not going to back me against Kleidorfer. They'll find a way to stitch me up between them.'

'I'm sorry to spoil your illusions, Peter, but arresting you won't get Riedel what he wants. He'll have his eye on the bigger prize. Catching a Gestapo officer who covered up a British spy will guarantee him the next step up the ladder.'

'No honour amongst thieves.'

'Well, no honour amongst charlatans, certainly. I want to see the pathologist's reports and I want to see some evidence linking Kleidorfer to Drexler's killing. If you can produce that, then I'm sure Riedel will do the rest.'

Chapter Twenty-Five

Thursday 11 February 1943

Viktor Kozlowski had his arm deep inside the chest cavity of a young boy, slicing around the innards with a scalpel. The morgue stank of blood, shit, and formaldehyde. The body of Martin Ruffert, aged twelve, from just across the river in Eitzing, lay on a metal grid above the stainless-steel mortuary table, his chest forced upward by the iron block under his back. Viktor had used heavy shears to cut through the ribs. The front of the ribcage opened like a flap to allow the pathologist access to his organs and intestines.

Martin looked angelic. His blond hair was cut short, but not so short that it lacked curls. A bit more weight on him and he could have been a poster boy for the Hitler Youth. A younger version of Messel. He stared up at the ceiling, oblivious to the indignities that Viktor was inflicting on him. Having satisfied himself that he'd disconnected all of the inner organs, the pathologist grabbed hold of the throat and tugged them out in one gory mass, from the tongue down to the testes, like a monstrous bird plucked and skinned. Ritter looked away in disgust.

'Ah, Ritter. Glad you're here.' Viktor placed the boy's innards on a large metal tray. 'I've done Messel.'

Viktor had 'done Messel.' How easily they dispensed with the dead. He'd said similar things himself a thousand times. You never noticed the callousness of it all until it was one of your own.

'He was killed sometime late on the previous evening. So around

2200 hours on Thursday night.' Viktor pulled off his rubber gloves. 'The body had been lying in the river for about fourteen hours when it was discovered, at 12:17 on Friday afternoon.' He had picked up the report to remind himself of the detail. 'All the evidence suggests suicide. There's powder and burning around what's left of his palate. Messel put his pistol in his mouth and fired at an angle of around twenty grads from the vertical. The bullet blasted through his brain and straight through the skull.'

'Could someone else have been holding Messel's hand around the Walther and fired it?'

'Good question, Ritter. The answer is yes. But I don't have any hard evidence to show that was the case, I'm afraid. The fingerprints on the pistol were Messel's, but that proves nothing. There was damage to the skin on the back of his hands and some skin under his nails, as if he'd been in some sort of struggle with someone. Nagel will obviously say that was with Kraus, but there's no sign of any damage to her skin, other than that caused by the knife, and no sign of anyone else's skin under her nails.'

'Thanks, Viktor.' Ritter turned to go, then paused to look at the boy's body. 'Should this be worrying me?'

'Another good question. Two in one day. That has to be a record. I was just wondering myself whether the *Kripo* shouldn't get involved. Come and look at this.' Viktor pulled the boy's lips back to reveal the gums. 'Do you see those thin, purple-bluish lines along the gums just under the teeth?'

Ritter nodded.

'They're known as Burton lines. Discovered by the English doctor Henry Burton, a century or so ago. It's a classic sign. Lead poisoning.'

Viktor looked at Ritter as if somehow the involvement of an English doctor he'd never heard of should be enough to open a police investigation. Once again, Viktor holding back information. Always making life difficult. As if it weren't difficult enough already.

'Yes, Viktor. But lead poisoning's very common. Kids like this get it from playing with toy soldiers or from paint.'

'Not at levels like this they don't. I've never seen anything like it. There's twenty times the safe level of lead in his blood.'

'Does he fish? Could he have got it playing with lead fishing weights?'

'Not unless he ate them by the kilo. No. Young Martin here ingested the lead while swimming.'

'Swimming? In this weather?' Ritter was incredulous. 'The river's frozen.'

'Yes. That's the point. The young boys try to prove their manhood by jumping into the river, breaking the ice.'

Ritter was struggling to believe that anyone would be so stupid. If you jumped through the ice you'd almost certainly get trapped underneath it and drown.

'This wasn't in the Inn. It was in the Sims. Just south of Eitzing. You know where I mean?' Ritter nodded. 'Well, it's less than a couple of metres deep there. Still not entirely safe. They could easily get trapped under the ice. But the risk is probably part of the thrill. I went down there and tested the water. Someone's been dumping waste from the production of tetra-ethyl lead into the river. He must have tipped it through the holes in the ice where the kids were jumping. Probably didn't even realize the kids had caused the holes. The ice stopped anyone seeing the pollution. The gendarmes have put up signs to stop people swimming – though from what I can gather it was only Martin who wanted to do it – and they're watching for anyone dumping waste there. The water supply comes from the Mangfall, so none of the chemicals could have got into the drinking water. But we need to find out who's been dumping them. They're responsible for this boy's death. This is manslaughter.'

Dangerous chemicals? The truck driver with the chemical drums. The one he'd forced Gertrud Heissig and those idiot women to let through. He'd been dumping chemicals illegally. The driver was lucky only one kid had died. So far. Had Stefan rung the chemical company? God, that was their last conversation. It wasn't about Macbeth. The boy had forgot to make the call to the chemical company. He'd gone off to do it while Ritter spoke to the priest's housekeeper. What did the company say? It scarcely mattered now. He'd soon find out. He'd have to follow it up himself. He'd also need to find that truck driver before he came back to Rosenheim. If the reason for the boy's death got out, there'd be a lynch mob looking for him, with Gertrud Heissig urging them on.

'Children are far more susceptible than adults,' Viktor was in his element, reeling off the science. 'Their bodies absorb the lead quicker. They lose weight, which is why this one's so skinny. They also rapidly lose brainpower. Martin here was acting like the village idiot shortly before he died.'

'He couldn't have had that much brainpower to start with if he thought jumping into an icy river would prove his manhood. What's this tetra…?'

'Tetra-ethyl lead. It's what they put in petrol and aviation fuel to increase power. It's vital to the war effort.'

'Yes. That's what the driver said. This tetra-whatever-it-is would kill fish as well, presumably?'

'Tetra-ethyl lead. And yes, it definitely explains the dead fish. If whoever killed Messel…'

'Stefan.'

'What?'

'Stefan. His name was Stefan.'

Ritter spoke slowly, stressing both syllables. He couldn't treat the boy as if he was just another victim. He owed him that, at least. Viktor looked at him. Not in reproach. In sympathy.

'Yes. Well. If whoever killed Stefan had pushed him into the Sims rather than the Inn, they wouldn't have needed to shoot him. That stuff would have killed him anyway.'

Was Viktor playing a game, or did he really believe Messel was murdered?

'I thought you said he killed himself.'

'No. I said all the evidence suggests he killed himself. It doesn't necessarily mean he did. I told you, I'm a pathologist, not a psychic.'

* * *

With Messel's death safely filed away as suicide resulting from guilt over the murder of the girl, Nagel was in a much more buoyant mood. The ashtray was empty. But his abstinence might not last long. While Munich were pleased to find that there wasn't a sex-killer on the loose, they were still demanding answers on the couple who had been run off the Obersalzberg, and on Drexler's murder. Probably best not to mention that the main suspects were British spies. Nagel might have a heart attack.

'I don't understand why everyone in the Gestapo seems to think the Drexler murder is something you should sort out. They spend most of their time telling me the old detectives like you aren't reliable. Now you're the only police officer in Bavaria who can solve a murder.'

'No one in Munich wants to touch it. They want someone who'll dig up the dirt on Drexler, make him look corrupt and make them look clean. Someone prepared to stick a knife into the back of a dead man so they don't have to.'

At first Nagel seemed unsure what to say. He took a deep breath and gestured to the door.

'Well, you'd better go and stick a knife in his back, then, hadn't you?'

Nagel returned to his paperwork, but as Ritter was leaving he remembered something. 'Wait. What's this about a dead boy and lead dumped in the river?'

'It's chemicals from the production of fuel additives. They were dumped in the Sims south of Eitzing. A boy went swimming there and died of lead poisoning. It's not as bad as it sounds. The drinking water comes from the Mangfall, so it isn't affected, and no one sensible is going to be swimming in the river at this time of year. But we need to be careful. If word gets out that this truck driver dumped the chemicals that killed the boy, he'll be lynched.'

'What about the chemical company?'

'It's not clear if they knew. I've been in touch with them to trace the driver. His name's Martin Wehner. They say he was supposed to take it up north to a disposal site. They don't have any idea why he would be dumping it in the Sims. But it was probably to save time. He lives in Stefanskirchen, so maybe he just dumped it on his doorstep and went home. I've asked the gendarmerie to bring him in.'

'Do they know why we want to see him?'

'No.'

'Good. I don't care about the lynch mob, but we have to avoid a panic at all costs. What are you going to do about Drexler?'

'Marianne Müller's the most obvious suspect, but she's got a couple of friends who might also be involved.'

'Where are they?'

'They're staying locally.' Ritter didn't bother mentioning the priest. 'As for Müller, I don't know. She may be with the nuns in Riedering.'

'With the nuns? A prostitute?'

'They help fallen women. I think Müller's holed up in their refuge in Riedering. Either she murdered Drexler or she knows who did. She's hiding from someone. It's just as likely to be the real killer as us.'

'Well, you'd better bring her in quick. I don't want to have to tell the mayor we've got another corpse on our hands.'

* * *

The reception from Frau Gundelach was in complete contrast to the one she'd given Ritter on his previous visit to the presbytery. She bestowed a conspiratorial smile on him as she ushered him into the hallway. A pair of Langlauf skis and poles in one corner explained the priest's fitness and complexion. Gundelach showed Ritter into Steiner's study unannounced. It was dimly lit and full of dark, dowdy furniture. A large wooden crucifix hung in one corner, leaning forward so that Christ could look down on anyone in the room. There was a popular Friedrich Wilhelm Doppelmayr lithograph of the Söllhuben church and presbytery on one of the walls, and a dozen or so paintings on glass and wood of Christ or the Virgin Mary scattered in no obvious order on the other walls. Steiner was sat at a bureau, writing. He put his pen down when he saw Ritter but there was no attempt to hide anything.

'Inspector. How pleasant to see you again.'

Every meeting seemed to be 'pleasant' as far as Steiner was concerned. The priest stood up and reached out to shake Ritter's hand.

'May I offer you a cup of peppermint tea, or perhaps water? I have no beer, I'm afraid.'

There was no offer of a chair. The two men stood for a brief moment smiling at each other. Meaningless smiles. Masks behind which each speculated on the other's intentions. It was Ritter who broke the silence.

'Thank you, no, Father. I've come to see your niece and nephew.'

'Ah. Then I'm afraid you've had a wasted journey.'

'Really?'

'Yes. I'm sorry to say they've gone. Such a shame. I so rarely see them. I fear I had too little time to spend with them. Johann is off to the front at the end of next week. One never knows when one will see one's loved ones again these days.'

At the end of next week? Was that significant? Would they have carried out their mission by then? It was unlikely. He was probably trying to read too much into it. How could they know when the Führer would be at the Berghof? Though no doubt there were other British spies in Berlin.

'Sadly, we never know if we'll ever see anyone again, Father. I'm afraid that's the way with wars. What about the woman Müller?'

'Marianne? I haven't seen her, I'm afraid. I barely know her. She's not really the sort of person I have much to do with. She's Inge's friend, and as I say, Inge and Johann have gone.'

'Gone where?'

The priest shook his head. 'I don't know. Home, I suppose, to Berlin. I imagine Johann will need to prepare his kit and make his farewells.'

Ritter smiled again, scarcely troubling to hide his disbelief.

'I'm sure. Well, once again I've taken up too much of your time. I'll let you get back to your writing. A sermon?'

'What?' The priest appeared puzzled. He turned to look at the sheet of paper on his bureau. 'Oh. I see. No. Not a sermon. A schedule of things that need to be done next week.'

The second suggestion that something was due to happen next week.

'But I must let you go, Inspector. I hear you have yet more deaths to deal with. One of them, sadly, a suicide.' The priest dipped his head in unsought sympathy. 'I'm told it was the young man who was with you in the Gasthof Hirzinger?'

'I don't think so.'

'It wasn't him?'

'It wasn't suicide.'

'Ah. I'm glad of that at least. Though I'm sorry, of course, for the loss of the boy. I imagine you'll want to get on with finding the killer.'

The priest called his maid back in. Gundelach graced Ritter with another smile as she ushered him to the door.

'Thank you so much for what you did, Inspector. With the priest's niece and nephew, I mean.'

'Sorry, Frau Gundelach. That was no thanks to me. They left of their own accord. For Berlin.'

It was the housekeeper's turn to look puzzled.

'Berlin? I don't think so. They've gone to the Fraueninsel, with that woman Müller. apparently, she wants to become a nun. You see, Inspector,' Gundelach paused to cross herself, 'there truly is redemption of the flesh.'

Chapter Twenty-Six

Friday 12 February 1943

Kate watched across the hedge of the herb garden as Jonny hacked at the frozen ground with the hoe. Despite his middle-class, bookish background, his time at Arisaig had left him fit and strong. He'd cleared most of the snow from around the herbs, but he was having to work hard to break up the soil. Kate wasn't alone in watching attentively.

'Careful what you're doing with that hoe, young man.'

The herbs were important ingredients in the secret recipe for the *Klosterlikor* the nuns produced to supplement their income. Sister Gabriella, the plump, middle-aged nun in charge of the abbey gardens, was taking a somewhat less appreciative view of Jonny's efforts than Kate was.

'That borage patch flourished throughout the Thirty Years' War and assorted wars of succession. It won't have a hope of getting through this one if you keep hacking away at it like that. Has no one ever taught you how to use a hoe?'

Jonny looked at Sister Gabriella as if she was speaking a foreign language. She closed her eyes, shook her head, and gave in.

'Go on. Give it to me and get off with you. I haven't the time to list the various things you're doing that you shouldn't be doing, or indeed the things you aren't doing that you should be. These herbs and vegetables might mean nothing to a boy from the city but they're our livelihood, the provision of God's hand.' She waved her own hand out towards Kate. 'Your friend's waiting for you. Perhaps she can teach you to be more careful.'

Sister Gabriella raised her eyes towards her as if in despair, albeit with the slightest of smiles. Kate clearly wasn't the only one to see something in Jonny.

'You be back at seven tomorrow morning, immediately after morning prayers. And don't be late.'

Kate smiled at the rebuke. She was all too aware of Jonny's flaws. He hadn't done badly in training, but he hadn't excelled, and while he was fit, his suitability for the mission rested on his being a native German, able to move around without drawing attention to himself, and on his skill as a sniper.

They'd had no choice but to leave Söllhuben. Steiner had made his opinion of the mission very clear to her on the night that Jonny parachuted in. The priest's concerns over the potential compromise of his work, smuggling agents into and out of Germany, had been exacerbated by the fallout from the failed reconnaissance and the questions of the detective from Rosenheim.

Kate could see Steiner's point. She'd told him her orders were to protect the Söllhuben safe house and the courier route down to Switzerland at all costs, and she was determined to do it. She'd spent a good deal of time and trouble before the war putting the whole thing together. It had been difficult to persuade Steiner to take part, but once committed to running the Hunter Network he'd proved far more adept at skulduggery than one might expect of a priest, a hangover from his time as a communist activist in the wake of the Great War. Kate had no intention of putting the Hunter Network at risk for a madcap SOE mission, which was why she was helping Jonny, making sure he didn't cause any damage.

It was Marianne who'd suggested they hide out on the Fraueninsel. The Chiemsee was the second largest of the Bavarian lakes, covering more than eighty square kilometres. The islands were isolated and the abbey had a tradition of giving refuge to the victims of war that dated back to the Swedish and French rampages of the early seventeenth century.

The holy sisters asked no questions. The Nazis had forced them to turn part of their abbey into a reform school and made them work as nurses in local military hospitals. They had no reason to help such bullies and were more than happy to help Steiner. On his recommendation they'd given Jonny work as an odd-job man and Kate a room in the Father Confessor House, a retreat inside the abbey grounds for women who wanted to spend time in contemplation and reflection. It was a near-permanent home to women displaced by the war. Kate and Jonny would be safe on the Fraueninsel until confirmation came through that the Führer was on his way to the Berghof.

Mother Benedicta had had no idea Kate was British when she authorized her stay. After those years in Berlin, Kate's German was as good as Marianne's or Jonny's. Better than that of some of the nuns. But the abbess knew Steiner was working in some secret way to end the war and she had happily placed her nuns at his disposal on a number of occasions. Whatever Kate and her friend were doing, Steiner's backing was more than enough to ensure them sanctuary on the Fraueninsel.

'I need to discuss the operation with you, Jonny. I've got new intelligence. Let's go up to the old lime tree. We'll be able to talk up there.'

'Why can't I come to your room and discuss it? It'll be safer there.'

One thing on his mind. A nice idea. A very tempting idea, anywhere else, and at any other time. But thoroughly unprofessional now, with the mission only days away. At any event, it would be impossible with all those other women in the Father Confessor House. If she took a man in there it would only draw attention to her, perhaps spark jealousy, or worse, lead someone to complain.

'It's a matter of respect, Jonny. The abbess gave you a job and let me spend time here. It's consecrated ground. We can't abuse that. She would be right to ask us to leave if we did. We should be perfectly safe up there. We'll be able to see anyone coming.'

There were no clouds. The sky was a cornflower blue, deceptively suggestive of a warm summer's day. The Tassilo lime tree had grown on the hill by the old cemetery, the highest point of the island, for near on a thousand years. From where it stood they could look out over the foothills of the Alps, towards the Hochfelln and the Hochgern, 1,750 metres above sea level, their forested lower slopes a mix of white and dark green that highlighted their pure white summits. Further east, and even higher, lay the Hochstaufen, obscuring the Obersalzberg from their view.

Jonny laid his coat on the icy bench in front of the tree. He sat down next to her, leaned across, and kissed her. Just one brief, chaste touch of the lips, nothing more. But enough to reawaken all those suppressed feelings. Kate placed a hand on his cheek.

'It's time to move, Jonny. Marianne's had a message from the priest confirming that Hitler will arrive next Friday, a week today, and Mussolini on Saturday morning. They're expected to take the walk to the *Teehaus* together on Saturday afternoon.'

'How does the priest know that? My orders are to wait for London to give me the go-ahead.'

'Hitler's movements are top secret, Jonny. Most of the time no one knows he's coming. But the priest has a very good source. You're just going to have to trust him.'

Jonny didn't look convinced, but Kate continued. He'd come around eventually.

'We have to act now, Jonny. It's not clear how long Hitler's going to be there. With what's going on in the East, he could leave at any moment. We might not get a second chance.'

'But I've orders to wait for London…'

'I'm sorry, Jonny. But we can't wait for London. The priest is their main source anyway. We've just got the intelligence before them. You've got to act on your own initiative. You'll be proven right in the end.'

Kate spread the map of the Obersalzberg out in front of them and began to talk him through her plan for the assassination of Hitler.

There had been far too many flaws in the original plan worked out by Jonny's bosses in London. Apart from anything else, it was based on the idea that Hitler walked to the *Teehaus* in the morning. Yet all the intelligence suggested he didn't even get up until lunchtime. The walk to the *Teehaus* was always in the afternoon.

The reconnaissance had been a near disaster. Without the snowstorm they would never have made it to Steiner's car. They would have been caught, and would almost certainly have been dead by now. They would need to be much more careful this time. Go in overnight and lie in wait. For as long as it took.

'It's the only safe way. We'll have to remain in position for a long time, perfectly still. We can't use that observation point you picked out last time. It's too obvious. The patrols are always going to be looking at that strip of wood, imagining we're still there. We need to find somewhere else.'

Jonny nodded. Their mistake during the reconnaissance had been in trying to get too close. Humans might not have picked up any noise. But a dog's senses were far more acute. Animals were more attuned to that natural instinct, the surge of adrenaline that told them something was wrong. She and Jonny had to get as far away from the path, and the Alsatians, as possible.

'What's the range of your sniper rifle, Jonny?'

'Good enough. The Holland & Holland modifications to the Lee Enfield and the telescopic sight give it a killing range of as much as two thousand metres. From the results I had at Arisaig, I'd be confident of a kill at a thousand.'

'Good. We need to use that range to ensure the dogs don't sense we're there. A thousand metres means we can get behind cover on the western side of the Mooslahnerkopf and still be reasonably certain of picking him off.'

They would travel down to the Obersalzberg on Thursday, the day before Hitler was due to arrive. A member of the network who lived just south of Kilian, at the foot of the mountain, on the road north out of Berchtesgaden, would drive them to his home. They would stay there until around three on Saturday morning, and then begin working their way up through the forests that covered the Untersalzberg, the lower reaches of the mountain. They would be heading for an old foresters' track, one of many that criss-crossed the side of the mountain. Kate traced their route on the map with a finger.

'There's an old track up to Spornhof that passes around the western edge of the Mooslahnerkopf a few hundred metres below the *Teehaus*. We need to come up through the forest on the Untersalzberg to that track, coming out here at Mausbichl. At that point, we'll be well inside the security zone, past all the checkpoints. There's no one living in this area anymore. So no chance of being compromised. There's an abandoned forester's cabin here. If we head west from this point on the track into the woods, it's only a couple of hundred metres to where we need to be. Here. Just back from the edge of the woods looking out across the southern slopes of the Mooslahnerkopf to a stretch of Hitler's walk to the *Teehaus* – see, here?'

Looking at the map, Kate couldn't understand why Jonny's bosses had ignored the idea of going in from the west. The track was the only point in their climb up to the observation point where they wouldn't have the cover of the woods. It was far safer. Perhaps they didn't believe Jonny was a good enough shot to pick Hitler off from that far away. But he seemed confident enough. Best not to ask too many questions about what his bosses in London thought. All that mattered at this stage was that her route was sensible, that Jonny understood why, and that he was prepared to follow her without question.

'It's uphill, Jonny. But not as steep as it was to the observation point we used on the recce. It's extremely good cover. So as long as we're sensible, keep down, and move slowly, staying back from the western edge of the woods, the chances of being spotted at that time of night are minimal.'

The edge of the woods on the western side of the Mooslahnerkopf was about eight hundred metres across the hill from the path. Well inside the range for a guaranteed kill. But it would only provide a perfect view of the path for about three minutes.

Jonny began to feel more confident now that they were at the heart of the mission, dealing with issues that he must have gone through time and time again, confident enough to point out what he thought were flaws in her plan. 'It sounds sensible up to a point. But we tried coming in from the west during the Arisaig practice runs. There are two problems. Firstly, there's another path he could take to the *Teehaus*, which runs along that western side of the mountain. We had some intelligence that he uses it on his way back to the Berghof.'

'We're not going to be there when he goes back. With any luck, he won't be going back, not alive, in any event.'

Hitler never walked back. He was always driven. Maybe Menzies had been holding back on the intelligence he passed to the SOE. Jonny's thinking still relied too much on the idiots in London who'd left him without a properly thought-out backup plan.

'You said there were two problems. What's the other one?'

'He usually takes some of his cronies with him to the *Teehaus*. Any one of them might block the line of fire. If one of them or even Mussolini is between me and Hitler, it will cause major problems. My orders are to take Hitler down first, so he goes down without warning. If I have to take out Mussolini first, the guards will surround Hitler and we'll lose him.'

'Then you're going to have to be ready to take your chance the moment it comes, Jonny. Because after we messed up the recce, we lost any hope of getting in that close again.'

Jonny didn't respond. He didn't need to be told of the flaws in the SOE plan, she was sure of that. But she needed him to accept that there was no other way to do this, and he still seemed determined to question everything she said.

'How are we going to get away? Will the driver be waiting for us at the forester's cabin?'

'No. The first thing they'll do is put roadblocks across any route into or out of the Obersalzberg. A car would be too vulnerable on the mountain – too easy to spot, too easy a target. But this plan gives us time. There's bound to be a panic at first before they start putting up roadblocks and searching the forest. It will take them a while to work out where the shot came from. It's not the obvious place, and so long as we're sensible and pull back quickly, but carefully, down to the track, they won't be sure where we are. We'll be below the track and hidden in the woods before they start doing anything. That will give us the head start we need. If all goes well we'll be in the car before the dogs pick up our scent.'

'So where will the car be?'

'About two kilometres north of the driver's place. Here.' Kate's finger stopped on the small black rectangle that was the driver's home. 'We can't leave a trail that will take the dogs direct to his home. We'll go into the river, here, to confuse the dogs. It's very shallow at this point. Then up here onto the bridge. That's where the car will be waiting.' She traced the planned route on the map. 'We'll have a head start. They won't know where we are. Won't be able to see us. The forest will give us the same protection the snowstorm did on the day of the recce, and since there's less snow inside the forest, we'll be able to get down the mountain a lot faster than we did then.'

'Wouldn't it be safer to use the priest? How do we know we can trust this driver?'

Kate shook her head emphatically. 'After last time, it would be too risky for the priest to be involved. If he was stopped again it would be far too much of a coincidence.'

She'd told Steiner to make sure he had an alibi for the entire time they were on the Obersalzberg. Something so nailed down it would be clear he wasn't involved.

'No. It will be the same driver who brought us in. He'll take us straight up to the Salzburg-Munich autobahn and then west. With luck, we'll be on the road north before they even start putting out roadblocks. We'll change quickly in the car and get rid of the rifle and our clothes. There'll be checkpoints at some point.

Everything we took up the mountain needs to be dumped before we hit the first one. We'll need to change out of our gear and put on some smart Sunday clothes. Shoes. No boots. By the time we stop at the first checkpoint, we need to look as if we could never have been anywhere near a mountain.'

Jonny was nodding. He seemed impressed. The plan felt like it could work. Dansey wouldn't like her working with Jonny. But Dansey wouldn't like anything she did, on principle. Her father would know

she'd done the best she could, thinking on her feet in difficult circumstances. Whether he'd ever believe her best was good enough was
another matter altogether.

Chapter Twenty-Seven

Friday 12 February 1943

'I'm very happy with the new arrangements, thank you, Inspector.'

Anja Vogel was the perfect secretary for a Gestapo boss. Loyal to the regime and very discreet, a wise move on her part.

'The commissar was a good boss. I miss him. But *Obersturmführer* Kleidorfer is very efficient. He doesn't waste my time.'

Ritter wasn't really interested in Anja Vogel's views on efficiency. He'd hoped to draw more out of her on Drexler's last visit to the Schweizerhof than the nonsense about meeting an informant she'd peddled to Messel. She wasn't playing ball. Kleidorfer came out of his office with a document in his hand.

'Frau Vogel. File this in special surveillance, please. Oh. Hello, Ritter.'

There was hesitancy to Kleidorfer's greeting. Had he regained his memory of the incident with the wall? He needed to find a way to link the Gestapo officer to Drexler's murder. Maybe it was time to up the ante.

'*Obersturmführer*. How are you?'

'I'm fine, thank you, Inspector. Just a slight bump on the head and a few stitches. Nothing to worry about. But I hope I didn't spill too much blood on your case files.'

Ritter couldn't resist a smile at the thought of Kleidorfer's blood running down the wall.

'Not too much.'

'Good. Is there anything I can help you with?'

'Yes, there is. But…'

Ritter raised his eyes, suggesting it was something he wasn't prepared to discuss in front of Vogel, however discreet she might be. Kleidorfer looked across at his secretary and motioned Ritter into his office.

Kleidorfer hadn't changed a thing in Drexler's old office. The desk looked a lot busier, but that was hardly a surprise. Kleidorfer was more industrious than his predecessor. More puritan, in everything bar his willingness to play around with other people's wives, so by extension more dangerous than Drexler. The only surprise was that he hadn't had the plush carpet removed.

'So what can I do to help you, Ritter? I was sorry to hear about Messel. I suspect you didn't think much of him, although for what it's worth I always thought he might turn out to be a competent detective.'

Ritter found it difficult to talk to anyone about the boy's death without emotion, let alone Kleidorfer.

'I'm not here about Messel. I need to speak to you about one of your informants. More of a warning, really.'

'A warning about what?'

'Marianne Müller.'

'What about her?' Kleidorfer was uncharacteristically wary. The skin around his eyes was creased with tension. He was probably trying to work out what it was that Ritter knew. Trying to distance himself from the prostitute. 'She was Drexler's informant originally, Ritter.'

'Yes. Originally. She's also the most likely suspect for his murder.'

Ritter sensed the tension drain away from Kleidorfer's face. Perhaps a sign of relief that Ritter seemed not to know she was a spy?

'That's absolute nonsense. Why in heaven's name would Müller want to kill Drexler? She knew he was as good as dead anyway.'

'What do you mean, "as good as dead"?'

Kleidorfer relaxed. He smiled. Almost friendly. The acting Gestapo boss leaned back in his chair and rested his hands on the desk, leaving the backs of his hands showing. They were covered in scratches.

'We'd been watching him for a while. He'd been taking bribes from traitors to keep them out of jail, to keep them alive. But he got careless. Started confiding in Müller, bragging about his power. That was his mistake.'

Ritter was barely listening. He was looking at the deep scratches gouged in the backs of Kleidorfer's hands. Imagining those last moments by the river. Messel desperately trying to stop the Gestapo officer from pulling the trigger of the Walther. He only caught the last few words of what Kleidorfer had said: "that was his mistake".'

'Whose mistake?'

Kleidorfer realized Ritter was looking at his hands and took them off the desk, rubbing the backs of each one in turn as if trying to smooth out the scratches.

'I had a problem with my car. I made the mistake of trying to fix it myself. My hands got ripped to pieces in the process. It's nothing.'

There was an uncharacteristic nervousness in Kleidorfer's eyes. His attempt to make an excuse was revealing in itself. Ritter no longer had any doubt. Somehow Kleidorfer had found out about the telex from Berlin. He'd killed Kraus and Messel to cover up his own involvement with the British spy. Kraus must have said something. She'd probably said too much to one of the other girls. Signed her own death warrant, and Messel's as well.

'Whose mistake?'

'Drexler's mistake. Taking bribes. He told Albrecht Stolz that in return for cash he could get him off charges of conspiring with the enemy and stop him being arrested.'

So poor, pathetic little Georg Bauer had lost his big catch after all.

'Drexler was right not to have Stolz arrested. He'd done nothing wrong.'

'Listening to Radio Moscow is treason, Ritter. It's that simple. I really wouldn't advise you to defend anyone who backs the commies. Not with things like they are in the East.'

There'd been a complete turnaround in the tone of Kleidorfer's voice. The odious mix of threat and disdain had returned. The same arrogance he'd shown down by the river the night they found Schinkel. But he'd given Ritter a chance to defend the bookseller.

'Albrecht Stolz wasn't listening to Radio Moscow. His wife just made that up so she could move her latest boyfriend into their apartment. Drexler's mistake wasn't keeping Stolz out of the courts; it was getting involved with Müller in the first place.'

Ritter had no reason to defend Drexler, particularly if he'd been blackmailing Stolz. But at least he'd kept the bookseller alive. Though if Kleidorfer managed to persuade Munich of his version of events, Stolz wouldn't remain alive for long. Kleidorfer was keen to depict Müller as a nobody and Drexler as a man whose death was the result of his own corruption. That's why he'd been so happy to let Ritter see the surveillance file.

'Müller's just a whore. Drexler didn't know she was reporting to me. But that scarcely matters given that someone killed him before we could arrest him.'

'It does matter.' Ritter wasn't going to let Kleidorfer off the hook. 'It matters to me. Because whatever Drexler might have done, Munich will want his killer brought to book. They can't let someone kill a Gestapo officer and get away with it, and all the evidence suggests your informant Müller was the murderer.'

He had to keep the pressure on Kleidorfer over Müller – that was where the acting Gestapo boss was vulnerable. But he couldn't use the fact that she was a spy. Kleidorfer had already killed Messel and Kraus to prevent that getting out. The Gestapo officer wouldn't hesitate to kill him. Final revenge for their rivalry at Ludwig Maximilian.

'Don't be ridiculous, Ritter. Marianne couldn't have killed Drexler. He was too big and heavy. She isn't strong enough. Anyway, why would she want to kill him?'

What was his evidence that Müller had murdered Drexler? She was a spy. He knew that. So the theory that Drexler found out, leaving her with no choice but to kill him, was convincing. But it was pure supposition. Take that away and what was left? Just the premise that it was a crime of passion.

'Viktor Kozlowski says whoever killed Drexler got some sort of release from it.'

'Kozlowski. That old drunk. The killer "got some sort of release."
Don't they all? It's scarcely enough evidence to convict anyone. If you
go to Munich with that, they'll just laugh at you. No. If I were you,
I'd go back to your museum. It's where old men like you belong.'

* * *

'Who gives a shit if Kleidorfer doesn't buy the idea that the killer
got some sort of release? Where did he do his doctorate in forensic
medicine? What does he know?'

'Well, he said you were an old drunk, Viktor. He got that bit right.'

'You sure he didn't mean you?'

'It was definitely you he was talking about. Though no doubt he
thinks the same of me.'

'So here we are, Ritter. Two old drunks sitting in a bar.'

'I think you've told me that one before.'

Their laughter was muted. They were alone in Viktor's local, the
Fischkuche. Sitting at the *Stammtisch*, as was the pathologist's right.
Drinking Bierbichler's Weissbier, the cloudy wheat beer the Bierbichler
family brewed out the back.

'So what makes you so sure it was Müller who killed Drexler?'

'You said it was a crime of passion.'

Viktor raised his eyebrows in the same way old man Kuster used
to do whenever he regarded Ritter's conclusions as lacking in "intellectual precision."

'I said the killer got some sort of release. That's not the same thing.'

'No. We discussed it the other day. In your office. You said it was
"possibly fuelled by passion." Whoever did it "hated Drexler with a
vengeance." Your words.'

Viktor might have been drunk when he said it, but he had definitely
said it. He certainly wasn't happy to have his own words thrown back
at him.

'The key word there is "possibly," Ritter. Is that your only reason
for deciding it was Müller?'

'No. One of the prints we found in the Schweizerhof after Schinkel was murdered belonged to the British spy.'

'Messel's spy?'

Ritter nodded.

'And Müller was this British spy?'

'Yes.'

'Shit.'

Viktor's attention turned back to his beer.

'We didn't know she was working for Kleidorfer when we got the telex from Berlin. We didn't even know it was Müller. All they said was that the prints belonged to a female British spy. They couldn't put a name to her. They'd lost her file. I used the presence of a British spy inside the hotel to force Drexler to let me reopen the Schinkel case. I promised him that when I found out who the spy was, I'd hand her over to him. So we'd both get something out of it. I'd solve the murder and he'd be a hero for trapping a spy.'

'So Kleidorfer's working with a British spy.'

'Yes. Berlin found the missing file. They faxed over a photograph. They have her under a different name, but it's definitely Müller. Drexler didn't know that, of course. He must have told her there was a British spy in the hotel. A woman. But from that point onwards, Müller had no choice but to kill him.'

Viktor had lit his stag's head pipe. He drew on it several times while he thought through the Müller connection. He seemed unconvinced.

'I'm not sure. Müller couldn't have done it on her own. She wouldn't have been strong enough to hold that pillow over his face.'

'She was probably helped by her friend Schultz. They're a double act.'

Ritter thought back to the interview at the Riedering refuge.

'Who are we talking about here, Ritter? The woman with the birthmark on her neck and the multiple personalities?'

'Yes.'

'And if Müller's a British spy and Schultz is helping her, Schultz must also be a British spy.'

'Exactly.'

Ritter decided not to tell Viktor about the brother or the priest. Two British spies were quite enough for one day.

'And Kleidorfer kills Kraus and Messel, because they both know Müller's a spy.'

'Yes. He had no choice. She was one of his informants. He was effectively running a British spy. Munich wouldn't have taken too kindly to that. He could tell them for as long as he liked that he didn't know she was a spy. They wouldn't believe him. Even if they weren't sure, they'd kill him just in case. Messel told Kraus about Müller because she'd seen the telex from Berlin, to keep her quiet. He told her he was keeping it from me. It's probably the only reason I'm still alive.'

'So if Kleidorfer finds out that Messel did tell you Müller was a spy, you're a dead man.'

'Yes, but I won't be alone, will I, Viktor? Because now you know too. So Kleidorfer will have to kill us both.'

'Only if you tell him.'

'Well, there's an idea.'

'Yes. Thank you, Ritter. Such loyalty to your friends. Very reassuring.'

Ritter grinned and took another swig of the beer. Viktor drew on his pipe.

'So what about Schinkel? He's the one who started it all. Who killed him?'

'I don't know. There are definite links between the Schinkel and Drexler killings. The use of suffocation to disable the victim, and the white rose.'

'You don't think it is the White Rose people?'

'No. I suspect the suffocation and the white rose mean it was the same double act: Schultz and Müller, trying to make it look like it was the opposition.'

'But Müller's with Drexler when Schinkel's murdered. She couldn't have done it.'

'Exactly. That's the problem.'

They sat there silently drinking their beer, both deep in thought,

Ritter trying to work out why Müller and Schultz used the knife on Drexler but not on Schinkel.

'That's it, Viktor. Müller was with Drexler.'

'I think that's what I said.'

'Yes, but she was with Drexler, keeping him out of the way. Making sure he got the body moved, to draw attention away from the murderer, Martyl Scharf, the young Swiss woman, or Inge Schultz. Whatever she's called. To protect her fellow spy.'

'So you have a pair of serial murderers?'

'Yes. That's why there's no blood in the Schinkel case. They're trying to stop us working out where he was killed and Müller doesn't actually take part in that murder. She just orchestrates the cover-up, persuades Drexler he needs to get rid of the body. Whereas with Drexler's murder, she gets her release.'

Viktor nodded sagely and stared ahead, taking the occasional swig of beer.

By the time Ritter set off for home, they'd drunk several litres of Bierbichler's. It didn't take more than a couple of glasses of Asbach for him to doze off in the professor's leather chair.

'So what are you going to do about it, Peter?'

'About what?'

'This Schultz woman and her plan to kill Hitler.'

'I'm going to talk to her.'

'And say what?'

'That I want to help her.'

'You're mad. Kleidorfer's watching you. Just waiting for you to put a foot wrong. You've worked out what's going on. How long do you think it will take him to do the same?'

'It's a gamble, Professor. But it's worth it. Remember what you said about Schultz and her brother only trying to do what any decent German would do?'

'Yes, but I didn't expect you to be that decent German. If you get this wrong it won't be just you they come for. It'll be Sophie as

well. But maybe you don't care about her anymore.'

'She'll be fine, old man. Don't you worry about your cherished daughter. She's a Party member now. And Kleidorfer will protect her.'

'Like I said, Peter. You're mad.'

'Maybe. Or maybe I'm just the only sane one left.'

Chapter Twenty-Eight

Saturday 13 February 1943

'Haven't you got a boat that'll cut through the ice?'

Willi Keil shook his head. He'd been the town gendarme for Gstadt for more than a decade and claimed never to have seen the Chiemsee frozen solid for so long. There was about half a metre of snow on top of the ice.

'It's too thick to get through. Langlauf is the easiest way by far.'

Ritter was far from certain he agreed. 'Are you sure it will support my weight?'

'Yes, Inspector. I'm sure.' Keil grinned and patted his belly. 'If it can support my weight, it can certainly support yours. Do you want to go to the Fraueninsel or not?'

Ritter nodded and put on the skis. He hadn't been cross-country skiing since he was a boy and was worried he'd make a fool of himself in front of Keil. The gendarmerie out in the countryside were a welcome throwback to a different, more basic kind of policing, much closer to the community they served. Less influenced by the idiots in Berlin and Munich. But they were unlikely to miss the chance to make a townie detective look a fool.

'It's barely a kilometre away, Inspector. It's the shortest route to the island. You'll be perfectly safe.'

It was already too late. He was destined to be ridiculed as the detective too scared to cross the ice to the Fraueninsel. But after a few moments he was surprised to find that his childhood familiarity with the skis came back to him.

The Abbey Frauenworth was hidden from view by a demure veil of mist and trees from which protruded the white onion dome of an old watchtower. Originally built to provide a warning against tenth-century marauders from the east, the thick-walled octagonal tower remained on guard against any intruder. The reeds on the banks of the island formed an outer cordon, standing frozen and erect, like silver daggers. There was a gap where the snow had drifted down to the edge of the lake. It had formed a gentle slope onto the ice that allowed Ritter to ski easily up onto the island. He was happy to get across the lake without incident, without the sound of ice cracking beneath him, relieved to remove his skis. Though not looking forward to the return journey.

'So where's this Schultz woman work, Inspector?'

'I don't know. Who's your contact here?'

Keil shrugged.

'No one in particular. I usually ring the bell and speak to whoever comes to the gate.'

As they walked up the path to the ancient stone gatehouse and the church, a group of nuns came down the slope towards them. Most wore long black habits over white wimples, their heads covered in black veils. But one was wearing a plain black dress, her hair tied back under a headscarf. Marianne Müller looked away as Ritter passed, but he recognized her immediately. He stopped and watched the nuns as they walked down towards the water.

'Willi. That woman. Why isn't she wearing a habit?'

'She's probably new. A postulant. She'll not get a habit until she commits herself to the life of a nun. Then she'll become a novice – the ones with the white veils.'

'How long does it usually take them to make up their mind?'

'Usually it's anything between six months and a year. But quite a few of the sisters have been sent to work in military hospitals, so they're pushing new recruits through quickly.'

Did Müller really intend to take vows? Surely not. It was just an easy way of keeping out of sight of the Gestapo. Out of reach of Kleidorfer.

Now that the Gestapo boss knew she was a spy, she was as much at risk as Messel and Kraus had been.

The Abbey Frauenworth covered the entire southern end of the island. Its accommodation and education blocks took Ritter back to his military training during the last war. They had the stark discipline of an army barracks. They were four stories high and surrounded by a thick two-metre brick wall. Both the outer wall and the convent buildings themselves were coated in whitewashed stucco. To the west and north, the buildings formed an enclosed square around an area of lawn, paths, and statues. To the south and east, the wall followed the curve of the island's coastal path. Ritter peered through the black wrought-iron gates of the abbey. The centrepiece of the ironwork was a shield on which stood the lamb of God alongside a banner emblazoned with the single word 'Salvation.'

Keil pressed an electric bell several times. After a few minutes, one of the nuns walked across from the main building.

'May I help you, gentlemen?'

'Yes, Sister. Thank you. The inspector here is from Rosenheim. He's looking for a woman called Inge Schultz. He thinks she's staying at the abbey. He needs to ask her a few questions, that's all. She's not done anything wrong. She isn't going to be arrested.'

Keil was exceeding his brief, suggesting limits to Ritter's intentions that didn't exist. But he let it go. The sister showed no sign of concern. She simply nodded to Ritter.

'I'll ask her to come to the gate, Inspector. I can do no more.'

'Thank you, Sister.'

The nun went to find Schultz. Ritter told Keil he wouldn't need him for the interview.

'It'll put her off talking openly about the things I need to know.'

'I understand, Inspector. I can easily find somewhere else to go.'

'No, stay here. I'll take her to the church. It'll be quiet in there.'

It only took a few minutes for Schultz to come to the gate. She didn't seem worried by Ritter's arrival. Just slightly bemused.

'What an interesting surprise, Inspector. What can I do for you?'

Despite her apparent lack of concern, Ritter got the distinct impression that she was less than happy to see him. Who could blame her?

'Just a few questions, Frau Schultz. Perhaps we should speak in the church? It will be more private there.'

Schultz said nothing. She let herself out of the gate and followed Ritter into the graveyard and through the heavy wooden doors of the church, further protection from the outside world. Ritter stood in the central passageway of the nave looking down towards the high altar, above which was an oil painting of Christ appearing to his mother, Mary, after the resurrection. Ritter was overawed by the beauty and size of the painting. An old master? Maybe Italian. It was several metres high, framed by an over-elaborate blue-and-gold wood carving. Above him, the gilt edges of the gothic vaulted ceiling created a line of stars leading to the altar; the plasterwork between them was decorated with delicately painted floral designs. Something buried deep inside him was telling him to kneel and cross himself, perhaps to protect himself from the dangers that lay ahead. But he stood firm, staring silently at the image of Christ, naked apart from a flowing red cloth that covered the lower part of his body. Blood red. The sign of the sinner? Or the martyr?

Ritter was avoiding the issue, hesitating before committing himself to help the British spies to kill the Führer. Schultz had stayed a few metres back, waiting more patiently than he'd imagined she might. After a couple of minutes he felt a light touch on his shoulder and turned towards her. She motioned him into the dark silence of the pews under the organ at the back of the church.

Even after they'd sat down, Ritter remained mesmerized by the painting, his left elbow resting on the shelf at the back of the pew in front of him, his hand wrapped around his chin, silently absorbed by its magnificence.

Schultz broke the silence.

'It's an Amigoni. There's a more primitive painting of Saint Irmengard, the first abbess, on the back of that. Like the one in the refuge in Riedering. She was Charlemagne's granddaughter. Her bones are in the altar behind that glass panel. They turn the paintings round to mark her saint's day, so she's standing above her own remains.'

Ritter looked across at Schultz. She was hunched forward with her hands clasped on her knees, as if ready to pray. She was young enough to be his daughter. What to say to her? He could scarcely ask if she was about to murder Hitler. Oh, and if you were, I'd be perfectly happy to help. But there was little point in coming all this way, forcing himself to cross the ice, only to say nothing.

'Why are you here, Inspector?'

'I'm concerned that you're about to commit a crime.'

'A crime?'

'Yes, a crime. And one that will be highly dangerous without specialist assistance.'

There was no response. The silence seemed to last forever. He had to find a way of drawing her out. He needed at least some sign that she was open to his offer.

'I saw your friend Marianne Müller on the island. Is she planning to become a nun?'

'She's considering it. Yes. She feels called to serve God.'

It was a laughable concept. But now was probably not the time to dismiss Müller's intentions. There was no point expecting honesty from Schultz on that front.

'It was Marianne who persuaded the abbess to allow me to come here. If this is about Drexler, you've already questioned her. There's nothing more she can say.'

Ritter was trying to dance with a woman who wouldn't move a centimetre. He had no option but to be more candid. It was the only way forward. He kept his voice low, almost a whisper.

'Frau Schultz. It's my belief that you and Müller murdered Commissar Drexler together.'

'You have a vivid imagination, Inspector.'

She was impassive. Unmoved. But he'd expected nothing different, and he pressed on.

'The image we have of what happened in that room is certainly vivid.

You both held him down. One of you, probably you, pressed a pillow over his face until he passed out and then Müller stabbed him repeatedly.' Despite the measured softness of Ritter's voice, he spoke firmly, determined to stay in control. 'It was a very brutal crime. An extremely sharp knife. There was a lot of anger in the crime. The pathologist believes the killer got some sort of emotional release out of the stabbing.'

'I thought you told the sister that I'd done nothing wrong? That I wouldn't be arrested?'

'I didn't say that at all. That was the gendarme, and I certainly didn't suggest he say it. But it's true that I'm not going to arrest you. Not now, in any event. I don't have enough evidence to bring charges against you. In fact, the new Gestapo boss, *Obersturmführer* Kleidorfer, insists that Müller couldn't possibly have murdered Drexler.'

Schultz smiled for the first time. 'So it would be safe for her to leave the island?'

'I wouldn't advise it.'

'Why? If Kleidorfer says she couldn't possibly have done it, she's safe.'

'Not quite. He's told me she couldn't possibly have murdered Drexler. What he didn't say is that he knows something about her that makes her even more vulnerable. Something that might make *Obersturmführer* Kleidorfer feel he has no choice but to get rid of her.'

'So what precisely is it that he knows, Inspector?'

'He knows she's a spy.'

'I'm sorry, Inspector – now Marianne's a murderer and a spy? You've been watching too many films. If Marianne or I have done something wrong, all you have to do is arrest us. We both know the police no longer need any real evidence to take people away.'

'I don't want to arrest you. Nor do I want to stop you from doing what you're planning to do. I know precisely what you were really doing near Berchtesgaden, with the priest, when you were stopped by the roadblock.'

Schultz was obviously an accomplished liar. It was easy to see why the young reservist Schäffer had been fooled into believing the story she and the priest had concocted to justify their presence so close to the Berghof.

'My brother and I were with Uncle Josef, visiting an old friend of his. Nothing more than that. Your suspicions are misplaced, Inspector.'

'I don't actually have any suspicions, Frau Schultz. I don't suspect. I know.' He edged closer to her, looking her directly in the face. She was pretty behind that hard exterior. 'Look, I just think I might be able to help.'

It was more than a hint. As far as he could go without any acknowledgment on her part. He placed his hand on her arm, trying to reassure her. She seemed to freeze at his touch. He took his hand away. Too quickly, perhaps, a little out of guilt. Still Schultz didn't respond to his offer. She looked him in the eyes. Saying nothing. Waiting for him to make the next move. He could hardly blame her. Why should she commit herself to anything? She didn't know what he was offering, and for all she knew it was a trap. Even he didn't really know how far he might go to help. But he could certainly lead the SS off the track after the event, disrupting the hunt for the killers. He was prepared at least to do that.

How far could he afford to push it to make Schultz realize he was genuine? If she went to Kleidorfer he could deny the conversation ever took place. But the Gestapo boss wasn't stupid, and who knows what Messel might have told him to try to stave off his own death.

'Look, Inspector. It's very flattering that you see Marianne and me as femmes fatales, but you're on the wrong track. We were with Uncle Josef and my brother playing cards on the night Drexler died. We told you. There really is nothing more to say. If you have some sort of evidence, arrest me. Otherwise, I'm sure we both have better things to do.'

It had been foolish to expect her to discuss it. Why would she? There was too much at risk. So much that she might even try to get rid of him. He felt in his pocket for the reassurance of his Sauer. There was nothing he could do. No way either of them could crawl out on a limb to trust the other. He had no choice but to sit and wait. Let it run, and hope the British spies were better at their job than Hitler's SS guards.

Chapter Twenty-Nine

Monday 15 February 1943

Kate was already waiting on the bench by the old lime tree when he arrived. She was reading but must have sensed his approach.

'Jonny, are you all right?'

'Yes. I'm fine.'

His response was brusque, deliberately allowing some of his irritation over the timing of the meeting to come across. But if Kate noticed, she ignored it. She was business-like. As if whatever he thought was irrelevant.

'Marianne's had another message from the priest confirming that the targets are both due to arrive in two days' time.'

Kate paused. She was looking over his shoulder. He turned to follow her gaze. Marianne Müller was walking up the hill. She was wearing the black tunic and white veil of a novice.

'What the fuck's she doing wearing their uniform? I thought they had to wait a while.'

'It's not a uniform. It's a habit. She has waited. She's been receiving instruction from the nuns for months now, at the refuge at Riedering.'

'She was still whoring when she was at Riedering. What about that Gestapo goon? She must have been screwing him back then?'

'What do you think made her decide to become a nun?'

'They let a whore become a nun?'

'Don't be naive. Lots of nuns have past lives they regret. Mary Magdalene was a prostitute. Marianne took her vows yesterday. The priest recommended her.'

He'd thought better of the priest than to go along with this stupidity. He'd never been happy about the involvement of the whore. He could see the usefulness of the priest. What would he have done without the safe house and the priest to bring him in? But Müller's relationship with the Gestapo put the entire operation at risk. Müller came up next to them. If she'd heard their conversation, she hid it well. She got straight to the point.

'You have to act now. We know they're coming but there's no guarantee they'll be here long. I've spoken to Liesl. She's agreed to let you stay at the hotel for a couple of nights.'

'How can we be sure they're there? Who is this source you claim the priest has inside the Berghof? London hasn't said a thing. We have to wait for them to give us the go-ahead.'

Müller turned on him. Perhaps she had heard him after all.

'We know he's coming, Jonny. You just have to accept it. It's not down to me or Father Josef. Kate set this network up before the war. There's a girl in Berchtesgaden who has regular contacts with the SS guards. She's completely reliable.'

Completely reliable? Another whore? He was about to protest when Kate intervened.

'It's a good network. Trust me. If the priest's people say they're on their way, then they are. I told you. London's waiting for the same source. We've just got the intelligence before they have. When it comes to what the SS are doing down there, our girl's on top of it.'

No doubt. Quite literally, probably. Litwak turned away. Let them get on with it. They weren't interested in anything he had to say. He stared out to the south towards the Bavarian Alps. Somewhere over to the left was the Obersalzberg, hidden from view.

He could trust Kate, he was sure of that, and he could probably trust the priest. He was a professional. But the Müller woman was a liability. To make matters worse, some detective was sniffing around. He'd made Kate some sort of offer of help. Müller was relaying the priest's reaction.

'Father Josef thinks we can use your detective friend. But we need some sort of insurance. We need to give him something that keeps him happy but leaves him exposed if he tries to double-cross us.'

'So the priest thinks we should do the deal.'

'You're in charge, Kate. It's your choice. But yes. He thinks having a cop on the books will be useful. Our man inside the mayor's office says Ritter's genuinely anti-Nazi. Anyway, Father Josef knows him, believes he'll want to help. How much he'll be willing or able to help is another matter. But Father Josef thinks we should push it as far as we can.'

Litwak grimaced. They were taking too many risks. The detective's offer could be a trap. Security was too lax. Talking about the mission, the priest, the network, out here in the open – and Müller kept calling Kate by her real name. They were breaking all the rules.

'Father Josef suggested you meet Ritter again, Kate. Make a gesture of good faith. We need to draw him in.'

'What sort of gesture?'

Müller pulled a tightly wound piece of white cloth out from the sleeve of her habit.

'He says Ritter's under pressure to find Drexler's killer. So give him this.'

Kate unrolled a pillow case. There were bloodstains on it. Inside was a long knife.

'The priest's source says the *Kripo* have got a single print for one of us. They have it down as the print of a female spy.'

'They can't have. We wiped the room for prints, and we both wore gloves.'

'Yes. But it was under a toilet seat in the bathroom. I didn't think to wipe under the seat. You never went in there. It has to be mine. It's going to be fine. So far as the abbey's concerned, Marianne no longer exists. The priest's sorted all that out.'

'The knife doesn't have your prints on it. You wiped it on the pillowcase.'

Müller gripped the handle of the knife.

'It didn't. But it does now. Don't worry. I'll be safe here. If he tries to come for me, the sisters will protect me. They're used to hiding people. He'll never find me.'

Kate still seemed concerned, and Litwak could see why. She was looking at Müller as if she was trying to get something straight in her own mind. But eventually she nodded.

'You're probably right, Marianne. I'm pretty sure he's genuine. He must have guessed why we're here. He could have arrested us both when he came here. He didn't.'

'I'm sure it'll be fine. We're giving him something big. It's a real test. If he goes along with it, he's trapped, and if he doesn't, we'll know we can't trust him.'

'All right. Tell Liesl to get him to the hotel. I'll do the rest. At least we'll know. Father Josef's right. Having someone that high up inside the police will be very useful one way or another.'

'Exactly. All Ritter's got to do is match the fingerprints on the knife with the set he got from the hotel bathroom. Tell him to say he can't find me. I've disappeared. He'll have a killer. That's all he needs. They can put out a warrant for my arrest. They won't find me. Marianne Müller no longer exists. From now on, I'm Sister Odilia.'

Litwak wasn't convinced. He didn't trust Müller or the detective. But Kate was no fool. She and the priest had got him out of trouble on the mountain, and her plan was better than the one drawn up in London. So long as they followed the plan, so long as she got him close enough to Hitler and Mussolini, he'd be able to follow his orders. He was certain of that. But if he had any more trouble from Kate or the whore, he would have to get rid of them both. Nothing was more important than the mission.

Chapter Thirty

Tuesday 16 February 1943

Ritter was dozing in the old man's leather chair when Liesl rang. Sophie was in the kitchen preparing dinner. It was rare that they should sit down to eat together. An attempt on both their parts to find a way of living together in some semblance of harmony.

'Peter. You've got to come now. The Scharf woman is back, the young one. She's with a man. Her brother. Only she's got German papers. You have to come and talk to her, Peter. I don't want any more murders in the hotel.'

'Are you sure it's the same woman? What's the name on her papers?'

'Schultz. Her papers say her name's Inge Schultz. Her brother's called Johann.'

'All right, Liesl. I'll come straight away. Try to keep them there.'

Ritter went to the sideboard and took his Sauer out of the drawer, checking that it was loaded, making sure the safety catch was on. He put on his coat, slipped the Sauer into his pocket, and stood in the kitchen door.

'I've got to go out. Liesl's got a problem.'

'Liesl?' Sophie hated her as much as he despised Kleidorfer. She always had. Even though Ritter hadn't shown any interest in Liesl since he had come back to Rosenheim.

'She needs help. It's connected to the killings. I've got to go.'

Sophie threw the saucepan she was holding into the sink in disgust. Ritter turned away. He'd no idea what he was going to do when he got to the Schweizerhof.

Liesl was at the reception desk waiting for him when he arrived at the hotel.

'Thank God you're here, Peter. I didn't know what to do. I'm sure it's her, the daughter of the Swiss woman, but she has German papers.'

'Don't worry, Liesl. What room's she in? I'll go up and speak to her.'

'Seventeen.'

Ritter looked at her as if she was mad. The same room Drexler was murdered in. She shrugged.

'Well, what am I to do? No one wants to sleep in that room. She didn't seem to care.'

Ritter nodded. 'It's all right, Liesl. I'll sort it out.'

Liesl went to pick up the phone. But Ritter put his hand over hers, forcing the receiver back down.

'No. I don't want her prepared.'

Ritter wasn't at all sure what he'd find when he got up to the room. There was no one in the corridor. He knocked on the door and Schultz opened it immediately. As if she'd been waiting for him. Had Liesl rung ahead? No. He'd have heard the phone. He went in and looked around, unsure what he was looking for. The last time he'd seen this room, it was covered in Drexler's blood. There was still a large stain on the carpet by the side of the bed. Schultz motioned him into a chair and sat down on the bed.

'Frau Schultz. What are you doing here? I thought you were on the Fraueninsel, praying with the nuns.'

'I was, but the game is about to begin, and before it does, you and I have something we need to discuss.'

'Really?'

'Yes. Your offer of help. I've talked it through with my colleagues. We're prepared to accept.'

Now that the moment had come, Ritter was suddenly having doubts. Was he making the right decision? They hadn't really discussed any detail in the church, hadn't discussed anything. 'Your offer of help' seemed much more than he'd intended. What was he committing himself to? What precisely was 'the game'?

'What is it you think I can do?'

'What was it you thought you could do, Inspector? You need to be ready. Things could happen very quickly now. When they do, we will need someone to remove any trace of our existence, to help us disappear. But the most important thing is that, whatever happens, you protect the priest at all costs.'

The priest seemed perfectly capable of protecting himself. Assuming they aimed to kill Hitler, helping her and her friends evade capture was probably as much as Ritter realistically could do, as much as he wanted to do. Anything more would be too dangerous. But he held back. Their roles had completely reversed since their meeting on the Fraueninsel. Now Schultz wanted his help, and he was trying to get as much information out of her as possible.

'Why should I trust you? What assurances can you give me?'

'It was you who approached us, Inspector. Not the other way round. But as a sign of good faith, I'm going to provide you with the evidence you need to solve the murder of Commissar Drexler.' She placed her hand on top of a suitcase that was beside her on the bed.

'Provide me with what? Whatever it is, I don't need it. I know who killed Drexler – you and Müller.'

'I'm going to give you the evidence you need to prove that Marianne did it. It has her fingerprints on it. You can show your bosses that you've solved the case. But in return you have to promise not to arrest Marianne.'

It didn't seem likely that, given physical evidence that Müller had murdered Drexler, Ritter could avoid arresting her. He said nothing. Trying to make Schultz sweat. Let her worry it might be a trap. Or that he wasn't prepared to make a deal. Force her to do the talking.

'Don't even think of arresting Marianne, Inspector. She'll simply disappear and the Gestapo will find out about our arrangement. Do we understand each other?'

That question again. He might have had to take it from Kleidorfer or Drexler in the past. He had no intention of taking it from Schultz. He stood up and hauled her off the bed by her collar, furious at the crass attempt at blackmail.

'Who the fuck do you think you're talking to? You don't make the rules here.' Ritter released his grip, letting her slump back onto the bed. 'You've got nothing to bargain with. You were here in the hotel when two murders took place. You've got forged papers. I could have you measured up for a piano-wire necklace right now. No one would listen to your lies.'

For a moment, Schultz looked shocked. But she recovered quickly.

'Inspector. I'm sorry. Believe me, I'm not trying to insult you, or blackmail you. But you must understand, I have to be careful.'

'We all have to be careful.'

'I know, Inspector. That's all I…'

'Let me make this absolutely clear. Any help I give you is strictly limited. I'm not at your beck and call. I'm not doing this for you. I'm doing it because what you call your "game" could help Germany get out of the mess that idiot's created. The real Germany. The one that used to exist and will again, one day, whatever you and your friends do. That's the only reason I'm even considering helping you. The only reason you're not already in jail. Just give me whatever it is you think will help me and I'll go.'

Schultz moved towards him, her head cocked slightly to one side. Leaning in. Looking directly into his eyes. It was far too obvious. Like the performance in Riedering.

'I'm sorry. I didn't mean it to be like this.'

She let her hand rest lightly on his arm, the same way she had done with Müller in the nuns' refuge.

'It's just that back in the church…'

She shook her head, letting the memory of that previous meeting hang in the air, and turned to unlock her suitcase. Her underwear lay on the top of her clothes. She waited a moment before moving it to one side and took out a roll of white linen. The missing pillowcase.

'Here's the evidence.'

She unrolled it on the bed to reveal a double-edged knife. It was about twenty centimetres long. Both edges looked very sharp. There was no serration. It matched Kozlowski's assessment of the weapon used to kill Drexler. Ritter thought for a moment.

'I don't want it.'

'Why not? It's got Marianne's fingerprints on it. It will let you solve the case.'

It would let him do a good deal more than that. His mind was racing over the possibilities; he needed to buy time, to work out a plan.

'I don't want it. Where am I supposed to have got it from? I want you to wipe your friend's prints off of it and put it somewhere it can be found. I'll let you know where that is when we talk about your so-called "game."'

'As you wish. But we have to sort out your role by tomorrow evening. I'll be gone by Thursday.'

Ritter nodded.

'There's a Gasthof on a fork in the road just over a kilometre out of the city as you drive north towards Ebersberg. The Hofbrau-Keller. I'll see you in the back room at one o'clock tomorrow afternoon.'

He left her sitting on the bed. Out in the corridor, Heinrich was standing on a ladder, fiddling with a light fitting. He grinned down at Ritter, that same lopsided grin.

* * *

'You've got some tough questions to answer, Ritter.'

It hadn't taken long. Ritter was just about to leave for the night when Kleidorfer barged in.

'Questions about what?'

Kleidorfer's face was dark, his voice threatening. All pretence at friendly cooperation, that curious feature of their recent conversations, had gone.

'The woman Inge Schultz you were talking to earlier. In the Schweizerhof. Who is she?'

'You don't know? There's a surprise. You seem to know what I'm doing at any minute of the day. Every little detail of my life. She's the woman in the SS report about the suspect couple up on the Obersalzberg. The woman who was in the car with the priest.'

'She's a spy.'

'A spy?' Ritter laughed. 'You're letting your imagination run away with you. I told you she's the niece of Father Josef Steiner, the priest at Söllhuben. I've spoken to Steiner and I've interviewed the army officer in charge of the roadblock. They've both confirmed she's the priest's niece. You and Riedel wanted me to talk to her, so I have.'

Kleidorfer didn't have an answer to that. But he remained suspicious. Heinrich had passed his report to Kleidorfer already. But he'd only had half the story. Overheard a fragment of what his mother had said to Ritter. Did Heinrich know that Inge Schultz was the same woman who had checked into the hotel two months ago as Martyl Scharf? Had he recognized her? Had Liesl told him? If Heinrich did know, or if he'd overheard Ritter's conversation with Schultz, Kleidorfer might be able to pin something on him. But if not, all he'd been doing was his job.

'She isn't a spy. She's the woman the SS wanted me to look into. You said yourself that I should talk to her. I promised I would. I was only doing what you told me to do. Her papers are in order. If you don't believe she's the priest's niece, go and check them yourself.'

'Don't worry. I will, and if I find out she's a spy, I'm bringing her in, and you with her. And not before time. I'm not the only person who thinks you need to be brought to heel.'

'Brought to heel? It will all look pretty transparent if you arrest me. Do you think people don't know you're sleeping with my wife?'

'I told you that's nonsense, and more importantly, it's an irrelevance. Munich are concerned about you. There are people there who haven't forgot you. If they find out you're linked to a spy you're done for.'

Ritter was desperate to find that one piece of evidence that would convince Barth that Kleidorfer was a killer. Time to play the final card.

'But it's not me that's linked to a spy, is it? We both know that, and we both know who the spy is. Marianne Müller. Your informant.'

It stopped Kleidorfer in his tracks. He'd been fooled by Messel's claim that Ritter didn't know Müller was the British spy. But he recovered quickly, laughing to cover his surprise.

'Oh. Müller's a spy. I see. Five minutes ago, she was Drexler's killer. Now she's a spy. I'm not the one whose imagination's running away with him. You're not well, Ritter. Sophie thinks you're paranoid. She's too close to you to see it. You're not paranoid. You're completely insane.'

'There's nothing wrong with me. I'm just doing my job. Looking for the woman who killed your boss. All the evidence suggests your informant, Marianne Müller, murdered Drexler.'

'You've lost it. All this stupidity over Sophie has sent you over the edge. If this Schultz woman's a spy, she'll be executed, and you with her.' Kleidorfer turned to walk out, but stopped and turned back. 'Oh. I nearly forgot. My memory seems to be coming back. You'd better make sure you're doing your job, or I might have that word with my friends in Munich after all.'

* * *

'Drexler's mistress was a British spy? Brilliant, Ritter. Brilliant.'

Ernst Nagel couldn't hide his relief that Ritter seemed to have solved the Drexler killing. The news that the killer was a British spy, making the case the responsibility of the Gestapo, was just the icing on the cake.

'Berlin told you it was an old fingerprint? But you wouldn't give up? You're like an Alsatian. Once you've got your teeth into someone's ankle, you never let go. I've always said that. Well done, Peter. Yes. Very well done.'

Nagel couldn't stop grinning at his sudden change of fortune. Life was treating him well. The Messel case solved and now the Drexler case. Not a cigarette in sight.

'Have you picked Müller up yet?'

'No. She's disappeared. No one's seen her for more than a week.'

Nagel wasn't going to let that ruin his good mood.

'No problem. It's on Kleidorfer's desk now, not mine. Well done, Peter. This should shut those Gestapo idiots in Munich up. Excellent. Another murder off our books!'

Ritter wasn't so easily satisfied. There was still one more killing left to solve and he'd no intention of letting it go.

'That's good, Ernst. It just leaves the Schinkel case.'

'Schinkel. For Christ's sake. Are you still going on about that? Look, he was just a fucking Jew. Whoever killed him saved us a job. Forget Schinkel. The murders that matter have been cleared up. At least we know there isn't some madman on the rampage.'

Chapter Thirty-One

Wednesday 17 February 1943

The Fenks had run the Hofbrau-Keller for as long as anyone could remember. The beautiful view across the fields of Rosenheim with its backdrop of the Alps made its *Biergarten* a popular resting spot for hikers. Ritter's father had brought him up here before the first war. Sunday afternoons – first the long walk, then the beer in the Hofbrau. The *Biergarten* was always packed back then, with Anna Fenk, the landlady, patrolling the tables, chatting to everyone.

Old Anna was dead. Her daughter Rosa had taken over and while the number of visitors was nothing compared with what it had been before the war, during the summer months the view still brought in enough money to keep her going. There were far fewer customers in winter, a few local farmworkers, the habitual occupants of the *Stammtisch*, and at lunchtime most of those were still out in the fields. It was the ideal place to meet. No one here was going to bother a *Kripo* inspector. They'd keep their distance, avoiding trouble. There were no Gestapo informants among the regulars of the Hofbrau.

There was an old black Opel 4 parked outside. Was that hers? Rosa looked knowingly at Ritter as he walked in, nodding her head towards the back room. So Schultz was already there. It must be her car. He found her sitting on a bench against the rear wall reading the previous week's *Anzeiger*. She looked up and smiled at him, folding the newspaper and putting it down on the table.

'Inspector. You're here. So we have a deal.'

'Yes.'

'What is it you want me to do in return for your help?'

Ritter took a piece of paper out of his coat pocket and put it in front of her.

'The evidence you offered me?'

'Yes.'

'You need to hide it in the boot of this car.' Ritter underlined a registration number and an address in the city that were written on the paper. 'This is where you'll find it overnight.'

Schultz glanced at the note and put it in her pocket. Ritter looked into her eyes, making sure she understood.

'It has to be done by tomorrow night.'

'Don't worry. It will be. I'll be gone by tomorrow night.'

Again, the slight cock of the head, the smile, and her hand reaching out to touch his. Was it all theatre? There was something he wanted to ask but he wasn't sure how.

'In the church, on the Fraueninsel…'

She pulled her hand back, shook her head slightly, and smiled.

'Inspector. I'm sorry. I don't have time for reminiscing. I have to go.'

'Hold on. You haven't told me what you want me to do.'

She slid the newspaper across the table towards him.

'All you need to know is in there. Do what you can to make sure our car gets away, but the most important thing is the priest.' She looked straight into his eyes. 'You have to protect the priest.'

'Your car? The Opel parked outside?'

'Yes.'

'What's the number?'

She was already halfway through the door. She turned to look back at him. That smile again.

'I told you. It's all in there.'

He watched her leave, taking in her body and the way she walked. It was a while before he picked up the newspaper. He'd expected it to contain some hidden note. There was nothing. Then on the last inside page was an announcement of a football match between a local reservist unit and the police. The beginning and end of the last sentence had been crossed out in pencil, leaving the words: The game will begin on Saturday. That was it. Nothing more.

On the back page, someone had circled an advertisement for a black 1924 Opel 4. Alongside it, written in pencil in a very neat hand, was a registration number. Ritter folded the newspaper up and put it into his coat pocket. He nodded to Rosa as he left, politely rejecting her offer of a beer, and went over to the BMW. He opened the door and then stopped, as if he'd forgot something. He went back into the bar and told Rosa he'd changed his mind. He would have that beer after all.

He watched her pour it and comb off the head with that same fascination he'd had as a child watching Old Anna do it. Then he took it over to his father's favourite table in the *Biergarten* underneath the largest chestnut tree. He sat on the same wooden bench on which he'd perched alongside his father and took in the view of Rosenheim framed by the foothills of the Alps. The two towers of the Cathedral of Saint Nikolaus and the Church of the Holy Ghost dominating the city's skyline with the sixteen-hundred-metre-high Hochsalwand behind them standing guard. Over to the left, the pyramidlike Heuberg. Famous names ingrained in him since childhood. Would this be the last time he saw this view, savoured its beauty, felt at peace with the world and the city he loved?

* * *

Ritter had long since grown used to the idea that his world could be turned upside down in an instant. But over the years he'd become so immune to the prospect that when it finally happened he was caught completely off guard. After leaving the Hofbrau, he'd gone back to the office to take another look at the files on Drexler, searching for that vital piece of evidence. So it was late – well past ten o'clock – by the time he turned into Kufsteiner Strasse.

The Mercedes was parked outside his house. He could see Kleidorfer standing on the doorstep talking to Sophie. She put her hand up to Gestapo officer's cheek and kissed him on the lips. He smiled at her and turned to walk down the path. As he did so, Ritter put his foot down and accelerated in front of the Mercedes, the tyres on the BMW screeching in protest. He parked across the road, angled into the curb, blocking Kleidorfer's escape. But the Gestapo officer had moved fast and was already in his car, frantically trying to start it. Ritter was out and tugging on the door of the Mercedes when its engine finally fired. Kleidorfer reversed back down the street, so fast that the car slewed from side to side. Ritter took his pistol from his coat pocket and stood in the middle of the road, the little Sauer 6.35 gripped in both hands, tracking the dark shadow of Kleidorfer's head in the driver's side of the car. As the Mercedes reached the corner with Brixstrasse, the Gestapo officer wrenched the steering wheel around to the right. The sharp turn stalled the Mercedes and Kleidorfer tried to restart the engine. He glanced back towards Ritter. The reflection from the headlights caught the Gestapo officer's face and for a brief moment their eyes met. Kleidorfer looked terrified. Ritter steadied himself and aimed the pistol at the Gestapo officer's head. His finger squeezed the trigger until it met resistance. But as he was about to fire, the engine on the Mercedes burst into life. Kleidorfer put his foot to the floor and drove off.

Ritter slowly lowered the Sauer. It was probably for the best. There was still time to sort out the evidence that would convince Barth. Killing Kleidorfer while there was a chance of fitting him up for the Drexler murder would have been foolish. He slid the safety catch on, slipped the Sauer into the pocket of his coat, and turned back towards the house. There was a movement in a next-door upstairs window. Gertrud Heissig in black widow's weeds clutching the edge of her bedroom curtain. As he looked up, she dragged it back across. No chance of keeping his confrontation with Kleidorfer, or the reason, quiet now. Half the street must have heard the noise, and seen Sophie very much alive. She was still standing at the door, looking terrified. Ritter hissed at her between clenched teeth.

'Get in the fucking house.'

She pressed her back against the wall, swaying slightly as he pushed past her. Ritter caught a whiff of brandy on her breath. He grabbed hold of her wrist, pulled her inside, and slammed the door, dragging her down the hall, determined get the truth out of her.

'What are you going to do now? Slam my head against the wall too? You bastard. Who the hell do you think you are to interrogate Klaus about me?'

So Kleidorfer's memory had returned. Or perhaps he'd never lost it in the first place. Then why the pretence? Was he scared of the loss of face? Or maybe he'd been biding his time rather than take on both Ritter and Kurt Naumann. But he wouldn't have left it there. Not Kleidorfer. He'd been talking to Munich. Who was it there who'd been so 'concerned' about him? Riedel? Ritter knew that rattlesnake of old. Whatever Konrad might think, Riedel could no more be trusted than Kleidorfer.

Sophie was leaning against the stairs. She was drunk. He'd never seen her drunk before. A little tipsy on occasion, but never drunk. She'd obviously worked herself up into a fury.

'I simply asked him what you and he was doing. You're my wife. I'm your husband. Or had you forgot?'

'Me? Had I forgot? I'm not the one who spends all his time working. And when he does deign to come home is usually stone drunk.'

'Do you blame me? My wife's screwing a member of the fucking Gestapo.'

Sophie turned her back and stormed off into the kitchen. He followed her. Kleidorfer had left his gloves on the kitchen table. Ritter stood in the doorway staring at them, as if they somehow gave their owner a continuing presence in his home. He was incandescent at Kleidorfer's incursion and Sophie's refusal even to deny the affair.

'So it's true, then?'

'What's true?'

'You and Kleidorfer. It's all over the station. Most of Rosenheim seems to know. Not that I'm surprised. I saw you kissing in the Munchener Strasse. Now you invite him inside our home. What the fuck did you think you were you doing? As if it wasn't obvious from that little cameo on the doorstep just now.'

'You've been watching me? And Klaus?' She was beginning to slur her speech. 'Watching us? Like a snoop?'

'That's a bit rich. You do know what that bastard does for a living, don't you?'

Sophie sat down at the table and picked up her glass. It was empty. She pulled the cork out of the bottle of Asbach she'd been drinking and poured herself another one.

'You're the bastard, not Klaus.'

Sophie stood up, shaking her head, close to tears. She grabbed the bottle of Asbach and threw it at him. He ducked, but as it hit the doorframe, it smashed, spilling the contents over him. A piece of glass hit his forehead, slicing it open. Sophie hurled herself at him, pummelling her fists into his chest before running off up the stairs, weeping and screaming abuse. Ritter staggered into the kitchen with his hand rammed against the gash above his right eye to try to stop the blood. He picked up the half-full glass and took a long swig of the brandy. He stood, exhausted, watching as the blood dripped slowly onto Kleidorfer's gloves.

Ritter rummaged in a drawer for a clean cloth and pressed it against the wound. He felt his way into the front room and sat in old man Kuster's chair. Doing nothing. Looking for no one. There would be no consolation in any conversation he and the professor might have right now.

He didn't hear her come back down the stairs. Didn't know she was there until she leaned over behind him and kissed the top of his brow. She looked at the wound, took the cloth from his hand, and pressed it firmly against his forehead, staunching the flow of blood. Then she kissed him again on his cheek before moving her lips down towards his. He reached out to her, more desperate for some sign of affection than he could remember being at any time in their marriage.

'I'm truly sorry for the accident.'

'You're sorry? I'm the one who threw the bottle, Peter. Why should you be sorry?'

'No. The loss of the child. I'm so sorry I put you through that.'

'Oh.' He felt her pull back, caught the confusion in her eyes. 'It wasn't your fault. I shouldn't have blamed you for that. You've worried over it all this time? I had no idea.'

'You don't blame me?'

'No. No.' She shook her head. 'There was nothing you could have done. Anyway, I was distraught when it happened. But look at where we are now, our marriage, the war. What a world we would have brought him into. Could you have lived with that?'

The answer was yes. Of course he could have lived with it. But he didn't say. He just held her arm against his neck until she bent down and kissed her again on the lips. That night they had sex for the first time in more than five years. For a while afterward, lying beside her, it felt like a relief. As if the storm had broken. As if somehow their shattered relationship had been repaired. Or had it just been the last rites, the final throes of something they were both too scared to abandon?

Chapter Thirty-Two

Thursday 18 February 1943

'What the fuck did you think you were doing?'

There were several half-smoked cigarettes in the ashtray. Two days ago, Ritter could do no wrong and Nagel was relaxed. Now the paranoia was back. He'd left a message for the inspector to come and see him the minute he got in. No ifs, no buts. None of that Ritter bullshit about some case he was working on. He was to go to Nagel the minute he came in. It wasn't difficult to work out why.

'I've had the mayor's office on the phone three times this morning already. They say you were drunk, waving your pistol around last night in the street, frightening decent Party members. And what on earth did you do to your face?'

'I slipped on some ice. It's nothing.'

'It looks a mess. Go home. Take a week off.'

'I can't. I've got too much to do.'

'You don't have a choice. You're suspended. On the orders of the mayor.'

'What?'

'What did you expect, Peter? You pulled a pistol on the local Gestapo chief.' Nagel shook his head and held up his hands. 'Look, I know. The thing with Sophie. Who would blame you? But he's Gestapo. You just can't mess around with these guys.'

Kleidorfer wouldn't have complained. Not to the mayor. The 'decent Party member' had to be Gertrud.

'Ernst. I know Gertrud Heissig saw me. But she's got it wrong. I thought it was a burglar.'

Even Nagel was never going to believe that.

'You thought Kleidorfer was a burglar? Do you think the mayor's stupid? Do you think Gertrud Heissig didn't give him a full report?'

Of course she had. No doubt every detail, from Kleidorfer's arrival to his departure, precise times and circumstances of greetings exchanged between the various parties carefully noted down, including the kiss – especially the kiss.

'I need your warrant disc and your gun.'

Ritter put the warrant disc on the desk.

'I haven't got my gun with me.'

Nagel raised his eyebrows but didn't make a fuss. He was as anxious as ever to make any nastiness go away.

'Look, Peter. Go home, take a rest. It's just for a week. I've calmed the mayor down. I told him it was only because you insisted Messel was innocent that we finally found out he was murdered. Like Kraus.'

'What?'

It was difficult to believe that Kleidorfer had finally been caught out. Had Viktor discovered something new? No, he would surely have told him.

'Yes. We've got the real killer. Good news, eh? Poor Messel. A really clever kid. I told you when he arrived that he'd be going places. That's why Munich gave him to you to train up. What a waste. And that girlfriend of his, too. Dreadful. Poor girl.'

'It was Kleidorfer.'

'No. It was you, Peter. Kleidorfer worked out who did it. But he wouldn't have got there without you. That's what I told the mayor. A stroke of genius on your part, that's what it was.'

'Kleidorfer worked out who did it?'

'Yes, Peter. He doesn't have your natural instincts to help him, but he got there in the end.'

Maybe it was the knock on his head, or the loss of blood, and the amount of alcohol he'd drunk the previous night. But Ritter's head was reeling. He couldn't understand what Nagel was talking about.

'Kleidorfer and Eckart had a look at the Messel/Kraus murders. Apparently, there was something about the whole thing that tied in with one of their cases. The bookseller Albrecht Stolz. Remember him? Used to have a shop in the Max-Josefs-Platz. He wasn't fit to fight so they sent him up to Munich to supervise French prisoners of war cleaning up after the bombing. He comes home and finds his wife in bed with some SS guy. Goes mad. Runs off and forces his way into the girl's flat. Apparently, she used to work in his shop. He rapes her and then stabs her to death. But Messel's got a date with her. He turns up at the apartment. Stolz ties him up, keeps him prisoner until the early hours, and then takes him out and stages that supposed suicide. It's as much a relief to me as it must be to you. That suicide idea always seemed a bit unlikely to me.'

'Ernst, I'm sorry, but that's rubbish. It doesn't fit with any of the evidence. Talk to Viktor. There was no sexual assault of any kind, and how would Stolz have got Messel down to the river?'

'At gunpoint. He had Messel's Walther PPK. The one the kid kept flashing around. He's a clever man, that Stolz. Bookseller, see? Had me fooled. I really did think Messel had done it for a while.'

'Ernst. Talk to Viktor. I'm certain Messel was innocent. But Stolz definitely wasn't the killer.'

'You're just too loyal to these people. These intellectuals you used to hang around with. There's no doubt at all. Stolz had blood all over him. Kleidorfer and Eckart extracted a full confession. Stolz has written it all down in his own hand. Very articulate, apparently.'

Jesus Christ. They'd 'extracted a full confession' from Albrecht. What did 'extracted' involve? What did they do to the poor sod? Kleidorfer must have realized that the scratches on his hands had given him away. Hopefully Albrecht 'confessed' quickly. The blood all over him was probably his own. It would have been better for him if Drexler had never intervened. If the bookseller had been arrested in Munich and pushed through the Special Court, he'd have suffered far less than he must have done at the hands of that thug Eckart.

'Ernst, you really do have to talk to Viktor about this. Nothing Kleidorfer says matches the evidence.'

'Listen, Peter. I've got nothing against Kozlowski. I know you're old friends and he's got a lot of experience. He's a really good guy. Truly. But he has his limitations. I'm not averse to a drink myself. And I really don't hold that against Kozlowski. But a guy like that… he can make mistakes.' Nagel shook his head, as if he was reluctant to criticize Viktor. 'Don't misunderstand me. Most of the time, he's right. I'd go to Munich and insist they listen to him. Really, I would. But this is one of his mistakes. It happens.'

'So you've told Munich?'

'Yes, of course. Well, Klaus had to tell them. Obviously.'

Klaus. Obviously. Nagel was already bowing and scraping to that prick.

'I can see what you're thinking, Peter. And I understand why. Of course I do. But he's like you. He doesn't take the easy way out. He got Messel off the hook. You have to give him credit for that.'

If Kleidorfer had got Messel off the hook it was only to get himself off the hook. He knew Ritter was never going to accept Messel as the fall guy for the Kraus killing, so he had to find another one. Stolz just happened to be easily to hand. Not that Nagel would ever believe that.

'Apparently, it goes back to Drexler and his shoddy way of doing things.' The *Kripo* boss was in full flow. He held one hand up, rubbing the thumb and fingers together to indicate a bribe. 'He knew Stolz was suspect but he took some cash to keep quiet.'

'What did Munich say?'

'About Messel? Well, they're pleased, obviously. It's never nice to think one of your own might have done something like that.'

'No. It isn't.'

Everything Nagel said was laced with unintentional irony.

'The mayor's pleased too. Not about you and Kleidorfer, obviously. He's just pleased that we don't have a serial killer on the loose. That's why he agreed to keep the suspension to a week.'

'What about the original killing? The Schinkel case?'

'That's a good question. It's exactly what the mayor said. Did you ever find out why Drexler wanted you to start investigating that again?'

'Well, to be honest, Ernst, I persuaded him it was in his best interests.'

'I knew it. I said so at the time. You denied it, didn't you? But I knew. I knew you'd pulled a fast one. I didn't believe that fat pig Drexler would get worked up over the death of a Jew. Not for one moment.'

Nagel was laughing. Drexler's downfall had made him relaxed about Ritter's deception, and the mayor had asked about Schinkel. So now Nagel would want that case reopened as soon as possible. That's why the suspension was for just one week. Drexler's involvement would give Nagel the excuse he needed to reopen it.

'I couldn't tell you at the time, Ernst. It would have been too difficult going up against Drexler. But he was definitely involved in the cover-up. He was in the Schweizerhof that night with Müller. He had Schinkel's body dumped down by the bridge to make sure no one found out what he was doing.'

Nagel was nodding furiously.

'Well, you see, this is why Munich wanted you on the Drexler case.' The *Kripo* boss jabbed his finger at Ritter enthusiastically. 'You spot these things. They pass other people by. But not you. I trust your judgment on this. Take the week off, just to keep the mayor happy, and when you get back have another go at the Schinkel killing. But any more dirt you get on Drexler, you pass it on to me. You know, you really could have told me at the time. I would have backed you. I really would have done. You do know that, don't you?'

Chapter Thirty-Three

Friday 19 February 1943

There was something very familiar about the way the body was lying on the bed. Completely naked. The head bent back at an awkward angle. Like Juliana Kraus, but without any of the blood. Ritter looked around the room. There was no sign of a struggle. Viktor had pulled back the covers on the bed. The sheet was crumpled. There was some bruising around the neck. Similar to Schinkel. But with one crucial difference. Even dead, Schinkel seemed far too tough to have let anyone strangle him. This one looked to have given up the ghost at the first sign of trouble.

Ritter was used to Liesl ringing him up at home whenever she had a problem. The ever-reliable Peter Ritter. There whenever she needed him. But today she'd chosen to phone the *Mittertor* to talk to the duty *Wachtmeister*. It was Nagel who rang him. In the circumstances, the mayor was reinstating him. They had very little choice.

By the time Ritter arrived at the Schweizerhof, Liesl was incandescent.

'What kind of a detective are you, anyway? How many people have to die here before you find the killer?'

Ritter had been under no illusions when he spoke to Inge Schultz that he was making a pact with the devil. He'd known there were risks. That one or even all of those involved in the process would end up dead, hopefully without implicating him. But in his mind at least that could be justified. With Hitler dead, Germany could be saved.

Viktor was digging around inside the victim's mouth looking for something. Another fragment of cloth from a pillowcase? He was singing to himself. '*Komm zurück*,' the hit Rudi Schuricke song. It seemed inappropriate to be so cheerful. But then, Viktor didn't know the dead man had been supposed to assassinate Hitler.

Maybe Inge Schultz had realized that her so-called brother wasn't up to the job and had decided to get rid of him, to do the job herself. Maybe he'd carried out his mission already, before he was murdered. Would the news have got out yet? They couldn't just announce it. What would that do to morale? There was bound to be a delay before they admitted the Führer was dead.

The game will begin on Saturday.

It hadn't happened. It was never going to happen. Ritter had just wanted it too much. Played the role of dupe to perfection. Inge Schultz hadn't had to work too hard to draw him in. He'd offered himself up, laid himself bare, and she'd used him. Hitler hadn't been killed. If he had, the entire area would have been swarming with Gestapo officers and SS troops by now. Kleidorfer would have been everywhere, throwing his weight around, making himself look busy. The Gestapo boss was nowhere to be seen. Nor, come to that, was Sophie. He suddenly realized that he wasn't sure if she'd come home the previous night. Not that it seemed to matter anymore.

'So what's happened here, Viktor?'

'The killer of your man Schinkel has been kind enough to leave us a little more evidence.'

'This is the same killer?'

The pathologist didn't look up. He just nodded.

'You're sure?' Ritter wanted to be absolutely certain. 'You're sure it's not a copycat?'

'Absolutely certain. The same small hands, the same positioning around the neck.' The pathologist held his own hands as if they were about to strangle the victim. 'And that's not the only link to the Schinkel case. This man was circumcised at an early age.'

'He's Jewish?'

'Was Jewish. Almost certainly, yes. The only difference between the two murders is that nobody bundled this one out of the back door and down to the river.'

'But you thought the Schinkel murderer was a woman, Viktor. The small hands. Possibly a woman. That's what you said.'

'Exactly. I said "possibly." I can't say for sure one way or the other. Yes, they're definitely small hands. So more likely a woman than a man. I might be more certain once I've had a chance to examine the body.'

'But right now. What's your best guess?'

'I don't do guesses, Ritter.' Viktor at his most difficult. He saw the expression on Ritter's face and relented. 'What I can tell you is the victim was relaxed to make him easy to kill. Alcohol? Drugs? Sex? I can't be sure. But there's what looks like it might be semen on the sheet. Once I get the body and the sheet back to the lab, I'll be able to tell you for certain.'

Viktor picked up the pillow and showed Ritter a stain of some sort on the pillowcase. Dry. Not blood. Saliva? A bit of bile?

'You want a guess? It was a woman. She had sex with him. Smothered him with this pillow to knock him out, hence that stain on the pillow-case. Then she strangled him to make sure. As I say, just like Schinkel.'

'Thanks, Viktor. Liesl says he registered as Johann Schultz. He's supposedly the brother of Inge Schultz, aka Martyl Scharf. She's the only person bar Liesl and Heinrich Jr. who was in the Schweizerhof both last night and on the night that Schinkel was killed, and she's gone.'

Liesl was adamant that Müller hadn't been near the hotel in weeks. She'd become a nun, which made all that nonsense Ritter had been spouting about Marianne bringing men back to the hotel look foolish. He ought to be ashamed of himself impugning the reputation of a devout servant of God. Ritter ignored her. He was sure that, having found sanctuary in the abbey, Müller wouldn't have taken the risk of re-emerging for this. In any event, she couldn't have murdered Schinkel. She'd spent that particular night screwing Drexler. Viktor seemed to agree that Inge Schultz was the most likely suspect.

'It fits with her helping Müller to kill Drexler. He was smothered first too. It's only the stabbing that makes his killing different. So you did have a serial killer on your hands after all. The Schultz woman.'

The woman Ritter had made a deal with, a deal that had probably ensured she got away with all three murders. Had she even fulfilled her part of the bargain?

'When did this one die, Viktor?'

'Hard to say. The body's stone cold. Probably sometime yesterday afternoon or evening.'

So after his meeting with Inge Schultz.

'Any sign of a motive?'

'Good question. The motive for Drexler you know. You tell him about the spy. He tells Müller. Doesn't realize she's the spy. Why Schultz kills her brother or Schinkel, I've no idea. But I'm not the detective.'

'No, you're not. But it's never stopped you offering an opinion before. Anything else?'

'Oh. I nearly forgot.' Viktor picked up an evidence bag. 'Nothing particularly interesting about the clothes. All German. Cheap. Could have been picked up in any department store. But this was in his buttonhole.' He handed Ritter a tiny, fragile white rose.

'Why did she bother, Viktor?' She knew Ritter had worked out that she was behind the Schinkel and Drexler murders. He was scarcely going to be fooled into thinking the White Rose were responsible for this one.

'No idea, Ritter. Perhaps she was sending you a message. Shouldn't you be out looking for her?'

'I doubt she's hung around. If this happened yesterday, she'll be long gone.' What was it she'd said? I'll be gone by tomorrow night. It seemed to have an altogether different meaning now.

Liesl's mood hadn't changed as Ritter left. She scurried out from behind the reception desk to confront him.

'So. Have you worked out who the killer is?'

'I'm sorry, Liesl. You'll have to be patient.'

'Patient? That's the third murder in my hotel in as many months. People are too scared to stay here. It's destroying my business, and what about Heinrich and me? This is just like the last war. Everyone else ends up in the shit and Peter Ritter comes out of it all the hero.'

'Not this time, Liesl. Not this time.'

Ritter stepped around her. He didn't look back. Liesl had to have been complicit in some way. Müller must have set it up with her for Inge Schultz to use the room and Liesl had got him to the hotel so that Schultz could offer him the knife and seal the deal. She was in no position to criticize.

* * *

Ritter realized something was wrong the minute he walked into the *Mittertor*. Kurt Naumann was stood at the front desk looking worried. Very worried.

'Ritter.' Naumann came out from behind the counter and took Ritter by the arm, steering him away from the other *Schupo* officers. He leaned forward to whisper in Ritter's ear. 'Gestapo. Three of them. From Munich. One of them a *Kriminaldirektor*. They're downstairs. They demanded I let them into your office. I really had no choice.'

Ritter grasped Naumann by the arm and smiled. As if it were he that needed moral support. 'Don't worry, Kurt. You did absolutely the right thing.'

Naumann half-smiled in return. A mix of sympathy and regret.

'I suppose you must have known it would come eventually?'

Ritter nodded.

'I did.' He sighed. 'I did know. Yes.'

Ritter turned and went downstairs. Better to face them now than later. Kurt was right. He'd been expecting it. He was determined to stay calm. He wouldn't let them rile him. That would only give them the upper hand.

All three were in civilian clothes, still wearing their coats. One was half seated on the desk. Resting a briefcase on his knees, smiling sardonically at Ritter. A second was leaning against a wall. Flicking through one of the 'not solved' files. It looked like the same one that Messel had picked up. Riedel was sitting behind Ritter's desk.

'Ritter. We've been waiting for you, haven't we, boys?'

They both looked at Ritter and smiled. The one leaning against the wall held up the file he was reading.

'This French prisoner of war admitted he'd slept with the woman Schilling and yet it says the case is 'not solved.' Don't you arrest people for improper use of a prisoner in this town? Or have you got something going with her too?'

'It's a city.'

'It's a what?'

He was sneering. Threatening. A warning to Ritter not to contradict him again. He had to remain calm.

'Rosenheim's not a town, it's a city. Has been since 1864. And Maria Schilling is small fry. There's nothing to be gained from jailing a woman who's producing food for the troops.'

'He's got a point, Heller.'

Riedel was obviously getting bored.

'This woman's just small fry. We're here for… um, a slightly bigger fish?'

Slightly bigger. Riedel enjoyed his joke. But Ritter was determined not to show any sign of nerves. Bullies like Riedel thrived on fear.

'I did wonder what brought you here. I assumed you must have run out of dangerous students to track down.'

'As it happens, Ritter, we have. For the moment. When are those three White Rose idiots we arrested yesterday being executed, Gippert?'

The Gestapo officer sitting on Ritter's desk looked directly at Ritter as he answered.

'They go before the People's Court on the twenty-second of February, sir.'

'That's Monday to you and me, Ritter. Don't mind young Gippert here. He's a stickler for the rules. Go before the court. Executed. What's the difference? You and I know that. But he's young. An idealist.'

Really? Messel had been an idealist. Gippert and Heller seemed more like sadists. Just like their boss. Cats playing with a mouse before they killed it. They'd probably had fun when they were kids pulling the wings off dragonflies.

Riedel stood up and placed his hat firmly on his head.

'All right. Let's go. Now, careful with Inspector Ritter, boys. By all accounts, he's not very fond of Gestapo officers, forever smashing their heads against the wall or pulling his gun on them. Which reminds me, Ritter.'

Riedel held out his hand. Ritter took out his Sauer and gave it to the Gestapo officer.

'Thank you, Ritter. Now let's go. I've no intention of spending any longer in this boring little town than I have to.'

Gippert grinned. A sly, stupid grin that reminded Ritter of Heinrich Jr.

'It's a city, boss. Inspector Ritter said.'

'Oh, yes. So he did. Did you hear that, Heller? It's a city, and Inspector Ritter here is going to give us a guided tour. Where are we going first, Ritter? Tell you what, why don't we go and take a look at the local Gestapo headquarters? Let's go and talk to our friend *Obersturmführer* Kleidorfer.'

Riedel let Ritter lead them out. There was complete silence at the front desk. Naumann and the two *Schupo* officers were almost standing at attention. As if paying their respects to a dead man.

The walk across the Ludwigsplatz seemed to take far longer than it ever had before. Ritter noticed for the first time the subtle shading in a painting of the Holy Mother above the doorway of one of the shops, and took a long look at the beautiful church of Saint Nikolaus.

Once they got to the Gestapo offices, Riedel led the way. He doffed his hat to Anja Vogel. She seemed to have been expecting them. As did Kleidorfer, who smiled and stood up to shake Riedel's hand.

'*Herr Kriminaldirektor*. It's good to see you. And the prisoner. I'm glad to have been able to help, although the credit goes entirely to you, of course. I assume you have all the evidence you need.'

So Riedel and Schultz between them had sold him up the river. This was it. Well, the way things were with Sophie and the job, maybe it was just his time.

'Indeed, we do have all the evidence we need, *Obersturmführer* Kleidorfer.' Riedel turned back to Gippert. 'Come on, man. Where is it?'

Gippert opened the briefcase and handed him a large brown paper evidence bag. Riedel took a rolled-up piece of linen out of the bag and placed it on Kleidorfer's desk. He took hold of one end and, like a conjurer pulling a tablecloth out from under a set of china, tugged hard. The knife that Ritter had refused to take from Schultz clattered onto the desk.

'Do you know what that is, *Obersturmführer* Kleidorfer?'

Kleidorfer looked confused. Riedel had stopped smiling. Stopped making jokes.

'It's the knife that killed your boss, Commissar Gerhard Drexler. The cloth is a pillowcase that was missing from the room in which he was murdered. And see that blood on the pillowcase? It's apparently the same rare blood type as Drexler's.'

'I don't understand, *Herr Kriminaldirektor.*'

'That's unfortunate. Because nor do I. I don't understand how it came to be in the boot of your car.'

So Schultz had kept to her part of the bargain after all.

Kleidorfer was beginning to panic.

'I don't know how it got there. I didn't put it there.'

'Really? Where's that other item we found, Gippert?'

Gippert produced another brown paper evidence bag from the briefcase. Riedel took out a pair of gloves.

'Do you know what these are?'

Kleidorfer shrank into his chair.

'No? Well, I'll tell you what they are. They're a pair of gloves. And you see that blood on them there? That's also precisely the same rare blood type as Drexler's. Do you know where we found them?'

Kleidorfer shook his head.

'No. No. I don't…I didn't.'

He was close to gibbering. He looked anxiously around the room, as if hoping for a friendly face. He settled on Ritter.

'I shouldn't bother looking at Inspector Ritter. He wouldn't know. He couldn't solve the case. That's why we're here. We found them with the knife and the pillowcase in the boot of your car.'

You had to admire Riedel. He hadn't found the gloves. Ritter had sent them to Barth for 'testing' and the old man had passed them on to Riedel. Barth was right. Ritter didn't need to stitch Kleidorfer up – Riedel was perfectly happy to do it for him.

'They're not mine.'

'Really? Then what were they doing in the boot of your car?'

'I don't know. But they're not mine.'

'Well, they're issue gloves. So if these aren't yours, where are your issue gloves?'

'I've lost them.'

'Did you hear that, boys? He's lost them. Well, don't worry, *Obersturmführer*. I think we've found them for you.'

'Fitting Kleidorfer up for a murder he didn't commit? What happened to all those moral principles of yours, Peter?'

'Give the moral principles stuff a rest, old man. Kleidorfer murdered Messel and the girl and then set up Albrecht Stolz to take the blame. Having him executed for Drexler's murder is called justice.'

'Really? Would you have fitted Kleidorfer up if Messel hadn't been one of his victims, or if he hadn't been screwing your wife?'

'That's irrelevant. He murdered two people; he deserves what's coming to him.'

'You do like dispensing judgment, don't you, Peter? So what happened with Hitler?'

'It's not going to happen. Johann Schultz was supposed to do it and his sister killed him.'

'Why?'

'How should I know?'

'Maybe the British decided they didn't want Hitler dead after all, Peter.'

'Why wouldn't they want Hitler dead? It would help them win the war.'

'Really? You said it yourself. He's got us stuck between Russia on

one side and America on the other. He seems to be helping them far more alive than he would do dead.'

'But if they don't want him dead, why send someone in to kill him?'

'Maybe they couldn't agree. One group wanted to kill him and the other group thought they'd be better off keeping him alive.'

'That's madness. You need to work together to win a war.'

'What, you mean like you and the Gestapo?'

Chapter Thirty-Four

Saturday 20 February 1943

The border-control point on the lakeside road from Bregenz to the Swiss town of Rorschach was a simple affair. A long metal pole reached out across the road, balanced at one end by a large block of concrete, making it easy for one border guard to lift by hand. The red-and-white German flag with the black swastika drooped from a five-metre flagpole next to the barrier. There was a small single-story wooden hut with a covered veranda. The German border guards spent most of their time inside, warming themselves against the stove that sent a stream of grey smoke out of a pipe protruding from the roof. To the south, behind the border post, lay the high, snow-covered peaks of the Alps. To the north, the gently lapping waters of the Bodensee stretched out for more than sixty kilometres towards Bavaria.

It was a bright sunny morning and several of the guards had left the comfort of the stove to check the papers of some Swiss farmers who were on their way to market in Bregenz. They were wheeling a handcart carrying various baskets of farm produce and several squabbling chickens. One farmer was driving a couple of cows in front of them. The guards knew they'd be able to get some butter and eggs, maybe if they were lucky a ham, in exchange for an easy passage into the Ostmark and back. They sat around on the veranda waiting for the farmers, relaxing in the sun, drinking ersatz coffee and smoking illicit cigarettes. The farmers handed over some eggs, butter, and bread and, after a few friendly words, the barrier was lifted to let them through.

As they ambled on towards Bregenz, an elderly black Opel trundled past them, heading for Switzerland. It eventually made it to the barrier and a stout middle-aged woman got out, beating the dust from the skirt of her dark black coat with her hands and primly rearranging a straw hat from which fluttered a long red ribbon. One of the guards turned to his colleagues.

'Leave her to me, lads. I'll sort her out. She looks like Heini's mother… really easy.'

There was laughter from all but one of the other men. The old woman offered the border guard her passport. He looked inside the car, recoiling at the stink of the chicken shit, and made a cursory examination of her passport. Bettina Grob. Swiss citizen. Fifty-six years old. Divorced. From Zurich. The guard handed the passport back to the woman, who turned and struggled back into the car. The guard looked at his colleagues, grinning behind him, and put both his hands out in front of him as if to ease Grob back into the car by her backside. As she shut the car door, he clicked his heels together and gave a Nazi salute. She frowned at him as if unsure what he expected her to do and drove off. The guard turned back to his colleagues, who were laughing and grinning. An officer came out, barked some orders, and the border guards hurriedly smartened themselves up and filed back into the hut.

Kate drove on at the same leisurely pace. No point in putting her foot down. She was in Switzerland. Safe now. No reason to give the German border guards any reason to doubt she was the plump, aging Swiss woman Bettina Grob. The same plump, aging Frau Grob who'd passed that way a couple of months back, a few days after Hans Schinkel died. She wasn't planning to use the identity again, not now, although you could never be sure. Hopefully the idiots from Baker Street wouldn't send in someone else to assassinate Hitler. If they did, she'd argue against using the priest or the safe house again. They couldn't allow the Hunter Network to be put at any further risk.

It hadn't gone entirely to plan. But she'd managed to carry out her mission. Jonny had been relatively simple to handle. Once his initial anxieties had been soothed, he was easily convinced she was on his side. The threat to Marianne had forced her to act earlier than planned. She'd had no choice but to terminate the mission, and Jonny with it. But he had been dispatched as painlessly and humanely as possible. She'd exceeded her brief by killing him, but Menzies would understand. She'd had no real choice, and with the detective protecting the priest, and Marianne hidden away on the Fraueninsel, the Hunter Network would be safe.

The mission had given Dansey the evidence he'd demanded of her ability to be more brutal. You couldn't have got more brutal than the stabbing of Gerhard Drexler, and although it was Marianne who'd wielded the knife, London would never get to know that. Whether it would make any difference to Dansey's opinion of her, she had no idea, and cared even less.

The important thing had been to do the job, and to prove to her father that she could do it as well as any man.

Or maybe it was simply to prove it to herself.

* * *

The phone rang. Ritter watched it, counting the number of rings. There were three. Then it rang off. He silently counted out the thirty seconds before dialling the Munich number.

'Barth.'

'Konrad. It's Ritter. How are you?'

'I'm very good, Peter. And you?'

'Fine. Just about. I think.'

'It went well?'

'Yes. It was touch and go. Riedel had me worried for a moment. Playing his games. But yes, I suppose it did go well, all things considered. How about your end?'

'Very well. Riedel's been over in person to thank me for the tipoff and the gloves. He can't stop grinning. He seems to think the best thing about it all is that he solved a case you couldn't crack. Made you look a fool. I was almost tempted.'

'Don't even be tempted. I'm more than happy to let Riedel have the glory on this one.' They both laughed. 'I'll try to get down to Munich to see you soon, Konrad. I owe you a beer.'

'Yes, and bring Sophie. Letta would love to see you both.'

There was a pause. A moment while Ritter tried to acknowledge the truth, to voice something that until now he hadn't been able to put into words, hadn't even said to Sophie.

'I don't know. Maybe.'

'Ah. I'm sorry, Peter.' Another pause, as Ritter struggled to respond. It was Barth who broke the silence. Someone had to say something. 'Perhaps if you give it a bit of time.'

'Perhaps. Yes, perhaps you're right.'

Wednesday's lovemaking had seemed more of an end than a new beginning. But perhaps time would heal the wounds. With Kleidorfer gone, there must be hope things could return to the way they once were.

* * *

Nagel was nervous. He'd been thrown by the way in which Riedel and his men swooped down from Munich to arrest Kleidorfer. But he was relieved to hear that the Schultz murder replicated the Schinkel case, right down to the victim's circumcision.

'Another Jew. There's an idiot out there taking the law into his own hands.'

'We don't know for sure Johann Schultz was a Jew, Ernst. He was circumcised at birth and was using false papers. That's all we know. It doesn't necessarily mean he was Jewish.'

The look on Nagel's face made it clear he didn't agree. So far as he was concerned there was absolutely no doubt that the dead man was Jewish and solely responsible for his own demise.

'The mayor will be relieved that it's only Jews. Though we need to find the killer, of course. If we can. I don't understand why these people don't realize they'd be much better off in the camps. It would do them and everyone else a favour. It's not called protective custody for nothing.'

'For Christ's sake, Ernst. You can't really believe that. You certainly can't be surprised that they don't believe it. How many Jewish families are there left in Rosenheim? What happened to them all? Half the shops in Rosenheim were run by Jews before Kristallnacht.'

Nagel looked as if he was about to have a heart attack. He pressed his hands repeatedly downward, trying to stop Ritter shouting. 'Calm down. They'll be able to hear you all the way down the Adolf-Hitler-Strasse. Do you want to be the next one carted off to Dachau? You know I never got involved in all that anti-Jewish stuff. I'm like you. I think it's all wrong. Always have. But what can one do?'

He trailed off. Not quite sure what to say. Probably trying to work out what it was safe for him to say.

'I thought you said you had evidence that Müller killed Drexler.'

'I thought I did, Ernst. But I saw the evidence Riedel had on Kleidorfer. There wasn't much doubt.'

Nagel nodded soberly. He was still badly shaken. Then he remembered something and smiled.

'Berlin have been on the line. About the truck driver. The one dumping chemicals. The Führer's very keen on the Nature Protection Law. Thinks there haven't been enough prosecutions. They want to make your driver a show case.'

Wonderful. First Albrecht Stolz and now the truck driver Martin Wehner. Kleidorfer deserved to die. But Stolz and Wehner? The truck driver was certainly culpable for the boy's death, but it wasn't premeditated. He couldn't have expected anyone to be so stupid as to jump into a frozen river. And Stolz was completely innocent. Both now faced the guillotine. Along with Kleidorfer. At least the Gestapo boss deserved it. Thank God for Konrad coming out of retirement. There was no way he could have laid a finger on Kleidorfer without his old boss pulling the strings in Munich. But Müller and Schultz had got away with murder. Meanwhile, Nagel hadn't the faintest idea of what had really been going on.

'Look, Peter. I understand why you get worked up over these killings. You're right. Murder is murder. Even when it's Jews. The killer might easily move on to real Germans.'

Listen to Nagel. Real Germans. He used to be a good detective. A good friend. Someone you could trust. But underneath, this is what he really was. Just another survivor. Kept alive by his own desperation to do whatever it took. Keeping the mayor happy. Keeping Munich happy. Keeping Berlin happy. There was no arse in the Reich too big for Nagel to lick.

'To be honest, Peter, one dead Jew I could have lived with. Two? You'd better at least try to track down the killer.'

That was typical of Nagel. Reluctant to investigate it properly until it was too late. Ritter didn't need to track down the killer. He knew who'd killed both Schinkel and Schultz, but he couldn't do anything about it. It was just another file to be stacked against the wall.

'Peter. I know how you feel.' Nagel spread out his hands in the classic gesture of bureaucratic helplessness. 'Berlin. Munich. I know. All idiots. But one day they'll be gone. You and me. We'll still be here solving crimes.'

Nagel had a point. But when this lot did finally go, they'd only be replaced by another bunch of idiots, with no more idea of how to do the job properly than their predecessors.

As for Inge Schultz, the professor was probably right. She'd never wanted to kill Hitler at all. Her job was to kill the real assassins. First Schinkel, and then her so-called brother. At least Schinkel had looked capable of murder. Johann Schultz hadn't looked capable of killing anyone. Inge Schultz and Marianne Müller, on the other hand, had proven themselves capable of anything.

Messel had been right. The women were the key to all this. There was something about a female killer that always surprised people. Ritter had never understood why. When it came to ruthlessness, Schultz and Müller could have shown even Kleidorfer a trick or two. Ritter had spent more than twenty years as a detective and arrested quite a few killers in his time. It was only the men who ever regretted it. Never the women.

For a brief moment, he'd believed that Schultz – Scharf – whoever she really was – might end the madness. He'd fooled himself into thinking that somehow he and she might be on the same side. The stupid thing was, he'd thought he was the one being cynical. When in reality, he was simply being naive. He should have known better. But maybe that was the human condition. Somehow, hope never dies.

Author's Note

The British Special Operations Executive did create a plan to assassinate Hitler. Operation Foxley, as it was known, offered a number of options, which did include persuading one of the Frenchwomen who cleaned the Führer's personal train to poison the water supply, but focused largely on a lone sniper picking Hitler off during his daily walk to the *Teehaus*. The plan was opposed by MI6 on the basis that Hitler was a poor general whose decisions helped the allies, so his replacement would almost certainly be more of a threat, and that killing him would create a heroic martyr, making the Germans more determined to continue the fight. Operation Foxley never took place, so the events in this book, although not the backdrop, are entirely fictional.

Please turn over to start the second
adventure starring Peter Ritter,
A Most Unlikely Spy...

A MOST UNLIKELY SPY

Chapter One

Inspector Peter Ritter had always regarded Jens Schemm as an unlikely recruit for the SS. The deputy head of Rosenheim's Gestapo post had only been based in the city a few months, but up until now he'd always been scrupulously polite. Whenever Schemm asked Ritter or any of the other Kripo detectives to help him out on an investigation he always said please, and he said it as if he meant it. He also used his proper Gestapo rank of Inspector rather than the more intimidating SS ranks favoured by most of the thugs down on the Adolf-Hitler-Strasse. Ritter didn't normally find much to like about the Gestapo, but Schemm was a decent enough sort. He was honest. He didn't beat up suspects, even when they were clearly guilty, and his smile was friendly and genuine. But he wasn't smiling now.

He was lying naked on the bed, a look of helplessness frozen on his face, his head half off the pillow, bent back in an unnatural pose, but with his arms lying straight down either side of his body, as if someone had deliberately straightened them out. The blankets were pulled back, the sheets crumpled beneath him. He wasn't very old. Ritter couldn't remember his precise age. Somewhere in his thirties? Schemm had told him once, over a beer. The Gestapo officer still had a very boyish face. Some would say a very girlish face. There'd been a bit of gossip that he didn't have much interest in women, and the evidence here in his flat seemed to confirm that view. He clearly hadn't been alone when he died.

There was no-one else on the bed but slumped beside it was the body of a second dead male. Another pretty boy. Also naked. Ritter recognized him from somewhere but couldn't think why. There were five empty bottles of *Schnapps* lying on the floor. The amount of alcohol seemed excessive, even to Ritter. Schemm wasn't a hard drinker and the kid could scarcely have managed more than a few glasses. Nor was that all. Ritter stepped across the younger man's body. There was a hand mirror lying on the bedside table, the remnants of a line of white powder running across it at an oblique angle. Given the circumstances, Ritter resisted the temptation to test it on his tongue.

He moved back to the door to survey the room, looking for anything he'd missed. It had a strangely decadent feel to it. He'd seen this sort of thing before in Munich, back in the twenties and early thirties. But it seemed distinctly out of place here. Rosenheim might be a city in name but in real terms it was just a small town, with small town values, still struggling to come to terms with the contradictions between the deeply held Catholic beliefs of most of its inhabitants and their near unanimous faith in the Führer.

Maybe it was just what it looked like. Schemm seduced the kid and somehow it went wrong. Something in the cocaine perhaps? But it all seemed a bit too easy. Ritter turned his head towards Naumann.

'Who's the kid?'

Wachtmeister Kurt Naumann was one of the more efficient members of Rosenheim's municipal police force. If you ever turned out on a job where he was leading the uniform team, you knew things would be organized properly. He wouldn't put up with any of those shoddy practices that had crept in as the more enthusiastic officers were sent off to the eastern front.

'His name's Franz Renteln. Eighteen. Member of the Hitler Youth. He was shadowing Schemm, learning how the Gestapo worked ahead of joining as a probationer.'

Ritter nodded. He knew now where he'd seen him before.

'Is he local?'

'His mother lives on Aventinstrasse. Just round the corner.' Naumann consulted his notebook. 'Aventinstrasse 21, apartment 6. His Dad's dead. She's someone important in the party.' Ritter looked across at Naumann.

'Someone important? Really?'

'Just locally. She's a friend of the mayor's apparently.'

Ritter nodded again. So he had to find a solution to the case that would please both the Gestapo and the mayor. Nothing was ever easy any more.

'We haven't broken the news to her yet.'

'Don't worry. I'll do it. After I've spoken to Schemm's parents.'

'Schemm's father's dead as well.'

Ritter nodded in acknowledgement, still surveying the scene, imagining what had happened. Was Schemm really the sort to take advantage of a boy in his charge? It seemed unlikely.

'Has Diemer been told?'

Kriminalkommissar Ludwig Diemer. Head of the Rosenheim Gestapo. A sadistic toad of a man, as different from Schemm as it was possible to get.

'I haven't spoken to Diemer but it was the Gestapo who got the call. The local block warden found them and reported it in. Hans Loferer. He's in the kitchen. I haven't bothered asking him anything. I thought it better to let you deal with him.'

There was a look of distaste on Naumann's face. Ritter nodded. Few people got on with the block wardens. It was understandable. They weren't a likeable lot. But they were obliged to spy for the Gestapo. It wasn't a matter of choice.

This one was short and bald, in his late fifties, maybe early sixties, and his clothes were a mess. There were several holes in his jumper, his trousers were covered in dark stains, and there was a faint smell of urine.

'This is Inspector Peter Ritter. He's investigating what happened here. Make sure you don't forget to mention anything or I'll forget that I have to protect you from the people you snitch on.'

3

Naumann clearly didn't feel a need to show the block warden any respect.

Loferer had a limp, sweaty handshake and it was obvious from his face that he'd rather be somewhere else.

'I told the Kriminalkommissar. I was just worried because I hadn't seen Inspector Schemm today. He usually collects my reports every morning. I thought maybe it would help if I brought them over to him.'

So Diemer did know. Why wasn't he here?

'You've spoken to Kriminalkommissar Diemer already?'

'Yes. I've told him everything I know. There's nothing else I can tell you.'

Loferer turned as if to go. Naumann reached out, gripped him by the upper arm and yanked him back round so he was facing Ritter.

'The Inspector hasn't finished with you yet, Loferer. You'll go when he says so and not before.'

Loferer didn't resist. It was the right choice. Naumann might be one of the good guys so far as Ritter was concerned but he was just as capable of dishing out a beating to a recalcitrant suspect as any of the Gestapo's thugs.

'It's all right, Wachtmeister. I don't think Herr Loferer meant to cause any offence.'

'No. Of course I didn't.' Loferer looked indignant at the very suggestion. 'I've got nothing to hide.' He glanced at the huge hand wrapped around his arm and looked up at Naumann, as if to suggest the Schupo officer release the pressure. The warden winced as Naumann tightened his grip slightly, making it clear Loferer wasn't going anywhere. Ritter smiled at him, encouraging him to talk.

'Explain to me in detail precisely what happened.'

'I've told you already. The Inspector always drops by my place to collect my reports. I cover five apartment blocks between Am Rossacker and Samerstrasse. I keep my eyes open, report anything I see that doesn't look right and I keep a special watch on the people who were lefties back before the Führer took over. The Kriminalkommissar has commended me several times for my reports. You can trust me.'

It seemed the very last thing that Ritter would want to do. A commendation from someone like Diemer wasn't exactly something to brag about.

'So Inspector Schemm didn't come to collect the reports. Is that unusual? Maybe he was busy?'

'No. He always comes every day, whether or not he's busy. So I rang the Gestapo offices to see where he was.'

'Who did you speak to?'

'The Kriminalkommissar. He picked up the phone personally. He always speaks to me. Like I say …'

'Yes. I know. He's commended you several times. You said. So you told him Inspector Schemm hadn't shown up?'

'That's right. He told me I should go round to the Inspector's apartment and deliver the reports myself. So I did.'

It seemed an odd thing for Diemer to do. Surely, he could leave the collection of reports from a low-level informant to Schemm?

'I thought you said it was your idea to bring the reports here?'

'Yes. I mean … the Kriminalkommissar said it was a good idea as well. So I came down and found this.'

'How did you get in?'

'I have pass keys for all the apartments on my block. But I didn't need a key. The door was open.'

'Was anyone else here?'

'No. It was just like it is now. It was a shock. I hadn't expected depravity like this. I thought the Inspector was a decent man.'

There was a look of disgust on Loferer's face not unlike that on Naumann's. Although the warden's initial impression of Schemm had been right. If it was possible to find a decent man in the Gestapo, it seemed reasonable enough to suggest that Jens Schemm was that man.

'So you rang the Gestapo again?'

'Yes. I spoke to the Kriminalkommissar. He told me to wait here. He'd be down immediately.'

Loferer shuffled his feet nervously. There was a stench of body odour as Naumann tightened his grip on Loferer's shoulder. Ritter had to resist the temptation to draw back.

'And was he?'

'Yes. About five minutes later.'

'He didn't tell you to ring the police?'

'No. He just said to wait for him.'

'How many Gestapo officers were there?'

'It was just the Kriminalkommissar.'

'Was he surprised to see this?'

Ritter gestured towards the bedroom.

'No. He said he'd always known the Inspector was depraved. It was good they'd found out now for sure.'

'He didn't say anything about the kid?'

'No. He just told me to wait here for you guys. He'd be sending you down.'

'Did he? Well, you don't have to wait any more.' Ritter looked at Naumann. 'Get someone to take him back to the office and get a statement from him. Then he can go.'

* * *

Hilde Schemm was a timid, slight woman. She was in her fifties but already bent over by the weight of life. The apartment was freezing cold and in half-light; the curtains still drawn, the furniture old. She showed Ritter into the dining room and offered him a drink.

She spoke haltingly, her voice as worn by time as her body.

'I have mint tea or coffee. The coffee's ersatz, I'm afraid. I prefer mint tea.'

'Frau Schemm. I'm very sorry to …'

'Oh, you mustn't worry about disturbing me. My Jens is in the police too. The Gestapo. He's a good boy. Comes by to check on me every day.'

'It's Jens I'm here to see you about, Frau Schemm.'

Ritter followed her into the kitchen. She was struggling to light the match for the stove. He went over, took the matches from her and lit the ring. She put the kettle on it, looked up at him briefly and gave him a sad smile before turning away to set the cups.

'Thank you, Inspector. His father died in the war. At the first battle of Flanders. Jens has been the man of the house since he was a little boy.'

She knew. Something inside her already knew. How close they must have been, Schemm and this poor, slight widow. Just the two of them for all those years. Ritter took the cups from her and set them on the side.

'Go and sit down, Frau Schemm. I can do this.'

She sat on one of the chairs placed either side of a drop-leaf table set against the wall that had one leaf down. He took the two cups of mint tea over and placed hers on the table beside her. He stood waiting, giving her time to take a drink before he spoke. She looked up at him, the sorrow already spread across her face.

'How did it happen, Inspector?'

'We don't know yet, Frau Schemm. It looks like an accident. There was someone else with him. The pathologist will need to carry out autopsies on both bodies. I'll let you know as soon as I know.'

There was no need to share the detail with her. Not just yet. She nodded and looked down at the cup and saucer resting on her lap.

'Had he shown any signs of worry over anything recently?'

She thought about it for a few seconds, staring at the worn carpet in front of Ritter's feet and then shook her head.

'No. Not that I can think of.'

'He'd said nothing at all? Done nothing that was different, not normal?' She looked up at him. 'Nothing he didn't normally do, I mean? No change in routine?'

'No. I … He hadn't been round. He usually would have been round.' She was looking down again at the carpet.

'You've never known him or any of his friends to use drugs?'

She looked up again.

'No. Was it some kind of overdose?'

'We're not sure. I will let you know.'

There was a knock on the door. She went to get up. He placed a hand lightly on her shoulder.

'It's all right. You sit there. I'll go.'

Diemer was on the landing, looking back down the stairs as if he was expecting someone to follow him up. He turned as Ritter opened the door. From the expression on his face, he wasn't looking forward to speaking to Hilde Schemm. Ritter's presence was an obvious relief.

'Ah, Ritter. We need a word.'

Ritter stepped back and stretched out his arm to invite him in.

'Of course, Kriminalkommissar. Frau Schemm's in here. I'm sure you need to talk to her first.'

Diemer had the good grace to look embarrassed.

'Yes. Yes, of course.'

She didn't look up as Diemer walked in.

'Frau Schemm. My heartfelt commiserations. If there is anything we can do …'

Still she didn't look up.

'We'll organize the funeral of course. A proper funeral …'

Diemer seemed at a loss as to what else to say. She hadn't once looked up at him. Hadn't shown any interest in what her son's boss had to say.

'Is there anything I can do …?'

She shook her head but didn't look up.

'Well, we have to go. Inspector Ritter has to finish his investigation.'

Now, she looked up. But not at Diemer.

'I'm sure the Inspector will investigate it properly.' She let her insistence hang in the air for a moment before ending Diemer's embarrassment. 'I'll see you out.'

Diemer didn't need any encouragement to head for the door. Ritter waited for her to get up and let her lead him out. The Gestapo Chief was already halfway down the stairs. Ritter stepped out onto the landing and turned back to face her.

'Frau Schemm. Thank you. I will let myself …'

'Inspector.'

'Yes?'

'You said there was someone with him.'

'Yes. That's right. There was.'

'A woman?'

Ritter shook his head. But he was only telling her what she already knew.

*A **Most Unlikely Spy*** will be available to buy soon!

www.safehousebooks.co.uk

Printed in Great Britain
by Amazon

23052588R00152